THE
WOLVES
ARE
WAITING

THE WOLVES ARE WAITING

Natasha Friend

LITTLE, BROWN AND COMPANY
New York   Boston

Little, Brown and Company
Hachette Book Group
1290 Avenue of the Americas, New York, NY 10104
Visit us at LBYR.com

First Edition: March 2022

Little, Brown and Company is a division of Hachette Book Group, Inc. The Little, Brown name and logo are trademarks of Hachette Book Group, Inc.

The publisher is not responsible for websites (or their content) that are not owned by the publisher.

Library of Congress Cataloging-in-Publication Data
Names: Friend, Natasha, 1972– author.
Title: The wolves are waiting / Natasha Friend.
Description: First edition. | New York : Little, Brown and Company, 2022. | Audience: Ages 12 & up. | Summary: Fifteen-year-old Nora sparks an investigation into institutional sexism in her small college town after she becomes the target of a fraternity game by athletes.
Identifiers: LCCN 2021004741 | ISBN 9780316045315 (hardcover) | ISBN 9780316045384 (ebook) | ISBN 9780316045179 (ebook other)
Subjects: CYAC: Sexism—Fiction. | Sexual abuse—Fiction. | Universities and colleges—Fiction.
Classification: LCC PZ7.F91535 Wo 2022 | DDC [Fic]—dc23
LC record available at https://lccn.loc.gov/2021004741

ISBNs: 978-0-316-04531-5 (hardcover), 978-0-316-04538-4 (ebook)

Printed in the United States of America

LSC-C

Printing 1, 2022

For Luna
Love, Stella

Show me a hero,

and I will write

you a tragedy.

—F. Scott Fitzgerald

PART
ONE

NORA

SHE WAS LYING ON THE GROUND, SPREAD-EAGLE, breathing in the scent of earth. There was a horrible taste in her mouth, like metal and olives. She turned her head to the side, gagging. Just thinking about olives made her want to hurl.

"I think you got it all out," a voice said.

Who was talking? She tried to look, but light stabbed her eyeballs. She tried to swallow. Her tongue felt thick and furry. Weird. Could a tongue grow fur overnight? She needed water.

Thirsty?

Yeah.

Let me get you a drink.

I don't drink.

Not a drink *drink. A pop... Sprite? Coke?*

A *pop?* Who said pop instead of soda? And what was this fragment of conversation?

"Nor. Open your eyes."

She tried again. More daggers of light. *Better to stay here, in the dark.*

"Nora." A hand on her shoulder, squeezing. "Wake up. You're scaring me."

That's when she recognized the voice. It was her best friend, Cam.

Her thoughts began to crystallize. What was Cam doing here? They were mad at each other. They'd had a fight last night...about...something. There was a boy...in a red shirt. Or had Cam been wearing the red shirt? Now her brain was as furry as her tongue. A furry tongue, for eff's sake. How was that possible? She really needed something to drink.

Mountain Dew? Root beer?

Root beer, please.

Ice or no ice?

Ice, s'il vous plaît.

You're cute.

Merci.

"Nor. Please. Look at me."

Why was root beer called *beer* anyway? It didn't have alcohol. And was it actually made from *roots*?

"*Nora.*" A poke now. An actual poke in the ribs. And another.

She opened her eyes. "Stop that!"

"Good. You're alive."

Everything was so bright. Painfully bright. She had to squint to see Cam's face looming over her. Cam's hair was every which way. Her mascara was smudged.

"Oh, hey, raccoon eyes," Nora murmured.

"Shut up," Cam said. "It's your fault. I've been sitting here all night making sure you weren't dead."

"Huh," Nora said, lifting her chin. There was a dull ache at the base of her skull. "Where am I?"

"You're on the Faber University golf course. Ninth hole."

The Faber University *golf course*? Nora didn't *golf*. And what was this pain? Had someone clubbed her on the head?

"I got a text," Cam said, "from your phone. Saying you needed help. There were these guys—"

"Guys?" Nora sat up. The green grass swam in front of her eyes. "What *guys*?"

"I don't know," Cam said. "Adam Xu doesn't know, either."

"Adam Xu?"

"He's the one who texted me. To say you were in trouble. He said there were these guys—"

"*Adam Xu* texted you."

"Yeah. From your phone. He didn't have my number."

Nora felt her head bob. The motion made her dizzy.

"You need to thank him," Cam said. "He chased the guys away with a baseball bat."

Baseball bat. Adam Xu. Golf course. It was all so confusing.

"Also...I found your underwear hanging from the flagstick."

Nora blinked. "What?"

"The flagstick." Cam pointed. "That yellow thingy poking out of the hole. Your underwear was hanging off it."

"My underwear." Nora felt a little sick. She looked down at herself. Black scoop neck. Jean miniskirt.

"I put it back on you."

"Oh." Nora nodded. Cam had put her underwear back on, like she was a baby or a grandma in a nursing home. She should be embarrassed. She *was* embarrassed.

"Nor," Cam said gently.

"What?"

"Do you remember anything about last night?"

"The frat fair," Nora said without hesitation. She was still wearing her blue wristband, the one that allowed unlimited rides.

"What did you do at the frat fair?"

"Rode the Yo-Yo." That was an easy one, too. She remembered soaring over everyone's heads, the wind in her hair. She remembered squeezing her knees together so no one could see up her skirt.

"What else?" Cam said.

"I ate funnel cake," Nora said. She could picture it: the greasy disk of dough as big as her head, heaped with powdered sugar. "It made me really thirsty. I had to wait in line all over again to get a drink."

Cam put a hand on Nora's arm. Her raccoon eyes were comically wide. "What did you drink? Rum? Vodka? . . . *Tequila?*"

"No, *Camille.*" Nora was annoyed. Cam knew she didn't drink alcohol. Ever since that sleepover at Becca Bomberg's house the last day of ninth grade, when the three of them drank an entire bottle of Manischewitz and Nora projectile-vomited into a potted plant on Becca's porch. "I had a root beer."

"A root beer," Cam repeated.

"Yes." Nora raised her chin triumphantly. "In a red cup. With ice." She remembered this clearly now, holding the drink in her hand, lifting it to her lips. The bubbles had tickled her nose.

Cam was looking at her funny.

"What? You think I'm lying?"

"No," Cam said slowly. "I think you're telling the truth. But…"

But. Nora did not like this *but.*

"When I got here…you were passed out."

"Passed out," Nora repeated.

"Like…comatose."

"Ah," Nora said. As though this explained everything, when, really, it explained nothing. *Ah.*

She turned her head and barfed onto the beautifully manicured grass.

CAM

THERE WERE THREE THINGS CAMILLE AISLING DODD knew for sure:

1) Sometime last night, her best friend passed out on the ninth hole of the Faber University golf course in the presence of three unidentified males, one of whom REMOVED HER STARS-AND-STRIPES UNDERWEAR and hung it on the flagstick.

2) Adam Xu chased the guys away with a baseball bat before texting Cam from Nora's phone to say, **Nora needs you.** (Seriously, Adam Xu. Boy most likely to spend every Friday night of high school playing Dungeons & Dragons in his basement. Tragic. But hello? Fending off villains with a Louisville Slugger? Surprisingly badass.)

3) Nora swore all she drank was root beer—and Cam believed her, because best friends tell the brutal truth—and yet, Nora remembered *nothing* between drinking the root beer and waking up on the putting green. Which meant—holy shit—anything could have happened.

Anything.

It was crazy, because Nora Melchionda was literally the last person in Faber, New York, Cam would expect to find passed out on a golf course, pantyless, beside a puddle of her own puke. Chelsea Machado? Yes. Anna Golden? Definitely. But Nora was the girl in the front row of American lit with her hand in the air, or on the bleachers with her dad on a Saturday afternoon, eating kettle corn and cheering on the Blue Devils. Nora and her dad were insanely close. He would have stroked out if he'd seen her half-naked on the ninth hole, so it was a good thing Nora had told him she was sleeping over at Cam's. Even though she'd never actually slept over. Because Cam and Nora had a fight.

It was stupid. Cam had wanted to go to a party at Kyle Tenhope's house. Nora hadn't. Nora had wanted to go to the frat fair, a fundraiser the Faber fraternities hosted every fall on the town green, to raise money for local charities. Cam thought the frat fair was lame. How many times could you play "smack the rat" before dying of boredom? But Nora insisted. Nora got up on her high-and-mighty give-back-to-the-community horse. Cam called Nora a goody-goody. Nora called Cam a social lemming.

Cam said, "I just want to have *fun*. Have you heard of *fun*?"

And Nora—classic Nora—said, "Riding the Yo-Yo *is* fun."

And Cam said, "Fine, go to the stupid frat fair. I'm going to Kyle Tenhope's rager."

And Nora said fine. Which is why Cam hadn't been there when Nora rode the Yo-Yo and ate funnel cake and drank root beer. Cam had only shown up later, on the ninth hole, after the text from Adam Xu.

Which didn't mean Cam was a bad friend. She wasn't. Cam and Nora had known each other their whole lives, literally. Cam's mom, Imani, and Nora's mom, Diane, had met in pregnancy yoga class back when Cam and Nora were the size of jelly beans. Cam and Nora had been born thirty-six hours apart in the same hospital. Besides the fact that Cam was biracial and Nora was white, they were basically twins. Because Cam didn't have any siblings of her own, Nora was it. Who else was Cam going to fight with? That was just part of the package. But when it came down to it, Cam would do anything for Nora.

She would wipe the puke off her face.

She would rescue her underwear.

She would offer, when Nora finally woke up and made it back to Cam's house, to inspect her best friend's pubic area for bruising or forced entry.

Cam wasn't squeamish about body parts. Her mom was an obstetrician-gynecologist. Imani had taught her, from a young age, to use the proper names for her anatomy. Vulva. Labia. Clitoris. Not "pee pee," or "down there." When Cam was in sixth grade, Imani had gone so far as to bust out a hand mirror, to show Cam which part was which. Yes, Cam knew this was weird. But she was glad she got a hippie feminist ob-gyn for a mother. Imani had taught her everything there was to know about the female body, so whenever Cam needed that information as a reference, she would have it.

And the time, apparently, had come.

ADAM XU

ADAM XU ATTENDED NEITHER KYLE TENHOPE'S PARTY nor the fraternity fair on the town green. He hadn't even heard about the party. He had known about the fraternity fair—a person would have to be living on the moon not to know about the fraternity fair—but he didn't go. He had felt no need to put himself in that position. Wandering the game booths would have been fine. Riding the Ali Baba and chucking candy apples from the top of the Ferris wheel would have been okay, too. But at some point in the night, one of the guys would bring out a bottle—whatever they could find in their parents' liquor cabinets—and pass it around. To avoid drawing attention to himself, Adam would take a few sips. Fifteen minutes later—bam. His face would heat up and start to tingle. His eyes would go bloodshot.

It wouldn't take long before someone would say, "Dude. What's wrong with you?"

Then someone else would yell, "Look at Xu! He's plastered!"

At which point, everyone would turn to stare at his red, pulsing face.

He hated when that happened.

It actually had a name; he'd googled it once. "Asian flush syndrome." Technically it was a genetic condition that affected 36 percent of East Asian people. The reaction in Adam's body was the result of an accumulation of acetaldehyde, a metabolic by-product of the catabolic metabolism of alcohol. Not that he would ever try to explain that to the guys on the baseball team. They had only just started asking him to hang out with them. He didn't want to ruin it.

Adam often wondered if moving to Faber in fourth grade had been part of the problem. If he had started in kindergarten with everyone else , maybe he wouldn't have had to work so hard to fit in. But by the time he arrived, groups had already formed. There was a reigning Adam— Adam Courtmanche—who was tall and blond and captain of every dodgeball game. Adam Xu, small and klutzy, could never be just "Adam." He would forever be "Adam Xu." The Adam on the sidelines. The lesser Adam. It didn't help that 99 percent of the students at Faber Central School were white. Nine times out of ten, Adam Xu would be partnered with Fumi Ikemoto for class projects, even though Fumi was Japanese American, not Chinese American, and they had no more in common than their school and their town and the fact that no one ever invited them to parties.

All that changed freshman year, when Adam Xu shot up six inches, gained some muscle, and made the JV baseball team. Suddenly, people started to see him as someone other than a wimpy, uncoordinated nerd. Now he was an athlete, a role he took seriously. Instead of going to the fraternity fair or to Kyle Tenhope's party, Adam spent Friday night alone, hitting baseballs on the Faber University golf course. Not real baseballs—those were too loud—but the Precision Impact Slugs he'd ordered online. They glowed in the dark. So did his bat. Whenever he made solid contact, the night-vision camcorder he'd jerry-rigged to the top of his bike helmet quivered, but it never fell off. The quality of the videos was decent.

Nobody, not even Adam's parents, knew what he did in the middle of the night. They thought their son was in bed. Adam's mother had been known to check on him at odd hours, opening his door and peering across the room to make sure he was sleeping. He always took the necessary precautions, stuffing his comforter with pillows before climbing out the window, leaving his phone behind.

Adam's mother was obsessed with sleep. She wanted him to get ten uninterrupted hours a night so he could be his optimal self. He had tried once, after reading an article about adolescent brain development, to explain to her that the sleep cycles of teenagers were different from those of adults. He couldn't go to bed early because he *could not shut off his brain*. But his mother wouldn't listen. Sleep deficiency, she said, was linked to an increased risk of heart disease, kidney disease, high blood pressure, diabetes, and stroke. Did he want to have a stroke at age fifteen?

Adam loved his mother. He respected her. But lately, her presence in his life had begun to chafe, like a too-tight necktie.

Hitting balls in the dark was only a minor rebellion, but it helped. With every swing, he felt looser. The Precision Impact Slugs were filled with sand. They didn't make the satisfying *crack* of a baseball sailing through the air. Their sound was a heavy, labored *wump*. But Adam appreciated the *wump*. Because the Slugs traveled only a few feet, they forced him to hit dead center, with the barrel of the bat, to avoid cutting or rolling.

As he hit, he didn't just think about form or bat speed. He thought about fourth-grade gym. Until he moved to Faber, he had never picked up a bat or a glove. Mr. Milner must have smelled it on him, because that first day of the baseball unit, he put Adam Xu last in the order. Which was actually a good thing. Adam got to observe the first twelve batters, so that by the time he came up to the plate, he had a fair handle on what to do: swing the bat, hit the ball, and run. His first two strikes had been embarrassing. He swung and missed in dramatic fashion, spinning in a full circle on the first pitch, falling down on the second. Then, by some miracle, instead of striking out, he connected, hitting a weak dribbler up the third-base line. He ran like hell, cutting left at first base and heading to second because the third baseman bumbled the ball.

That's when it happened. The kid playing first, a floppy-haired loudmouth named Kevin Hamm, yelled, "He didn't touch first! He missed the bag!"

And everyone on Adam's team started yelling, "Go back! Touch the bag! Touch the bag!"

So Adam ran back to first base, squatted down, and touched the bag. With his hand.

If he closed his eyes, he could still hear the laughter. It was the funniest thing they had ever seen. The Chinese kid touched the bag! *Touched* the bag! *Literally*! Hahahahahahahaha!

The feeling of disgrace never left him. Adam tended his shame like a small plant, watering it, pruning it, vowing to himself that he would learn everything there was to know about baseball so that, one day, he could wipe the smirks off everyone's faces. One day, he would earn their respect.

Wump. Last spring, he'd finally done it.

Wump. He'd made JV.

Wump. This year, he would make varsity.

Hahahahahahahaha!

The sound of laughter, deep and low. It took him a moment to realize this wasn't a memory bubbling to the surface of his brain. He was hearing it in real time.

He turned his head. The sky over the golf course was clear, full of stars. The sound would be easy to follow.

Hahahahahahaha!

He walked quickly.

Partyers? he thought.

He remembered the fair. It would be over by now. But the college students were probably just getting started.

He saw figures up ahead, dimly lit by the moon. Three of them...no, four. One was flat on the ground.

The closer he got, the clearer the scene became. One of the figures was holding something in the air. A phone? Another was bent over the body on the ground.

"Dude, she's completely out."

The third was—wait. Was he *taking off his pants*?

"Hey!" Adam shouted. He hadn't planned to. It was pure instinct.

The three figures turned. They were big, way bigger than Adam. For a second, he panicked. But then he remembered the bat in his hand, and something took over—some strange, subterranean part of him.

"Ting xia lai! Huai dan!"

He was yelling in Chinese, words his mother yelled at their dog, Bao Bao, for chewing on the furniture—*Stop it! You bad egg!* Between Adam yelling and the glow-in-the-dark baseball bat slashing Z's through the air like Obi-Wan's lightsaber, he must have freaked them out, because the figures took off running.

Three of them were gone.

One was still lying on the ground.

Adam did not realize, at first, who she was. He saw only that her clothes were half off.

"Hey," he said. "Are you okay?"

No response.

His head spun. Was this a *crime scene*? What was he

supposed to *do*? The girl was so still, so utterly motionless, he was almost afraid to touch her.

But he did. He had to. He knelt down to brush the hair off her neck so he could check her pulse.

And there she was.

Nora Melchionda.

The rhythmic throbbing of her heart against his fingertips.

Nora Melchionda with the golden braids and the triple-pierced ears and the eyes that crinkled into aqua slits when she smiled. No-ra-Mel-chi-on-da. Her name was a water-fall of sounds.

Okay, fine. Yes. Adam had never admitted this to anyone—but it was true: He loved everything about her. Nora Melchionda. No-ra No-ra No-ra-Mel-chi-on-da.

She probably didn't remember, but in fourth grade, the day before winter break, his milk carton exploded when he tripped over a chair and went flying. He had been living in Faber for only a week, and already he was on the floor of the cafeteria, covered in milk. Everyone was staring.

"You okay?"

He had looked up, and there she was, squinting down at him. She was wearing the ugliest sweater he had ever seen, a reindeer head covered in pom-poms and sparkles. He could do nothing but nod.

"Up you go." She reached out a hand and yanked him to his feet.

He nodded again, in thanks. She was four inches taller than he was. Maybe five.

"Here," she said, thrusting a fresh carton of milk into his hand and smiling a dazzling smile full of braces. "Merry Christmas."

This time he managed to say it: "Thank you."

"No prob." She shrugged. "I'm lactose intolerant. I always give away my milk."

That was the first thing Adam learned about Nora Melchionda: She was lactose intolerant; she always gave away her milk.

He discovered other things, too, over the years. Countless details, like how she bit the nails on her left hand but not her right, and how green apple Airheads were her go-to candy, and how she loved classic rock. There was so much to be learned about a person just by paying attention. Not that Adam was a stalker or anything. He wasn't. He was merely an observer, a quiet satellite in Nora Melchionda's extraordinary orbit, gathering information.

It didn't take a genius to see that Camille Dodd was Nora's best friend. They were inseparable. And all Adam had to do was listen when Nora read her personal essay out loud in freshman English to learn that her favorite movie was *The Fighter*, based on the real-life story of boxer "Irish" Micky Ward. As for knowing her astrological sign—Aquarius, the water bearer; intelligent, unyielding, grounded—he just had to watch every year on February 2, when Nora's friends decorated her locker and showered her with gifts and cupcakes from the Blue Bird. Nora always laughed and did a silly birthday dance in the hall, not caring who was watching.

All those things had endeared Nora to Adam and made him want to know her better. He had once gone so far as to read an article entitled "What Attracts an Aquarius Woman," where he discovered that "an Aquarius female loves a good conversationalist." Although he had always felt too shy in front of Nora's many admirers to strike up a conversation with her, if, by some miracle, they ever ended up alone, he would know what to talk about. The final boxing scene from *The Fighter*: "Head-body, head-body!" The ingredients in green apple Airheads: Blue 1, Blue 2, Red 3, Red 40, Yellow 5, and Yellow 6, but *no actual green*. Crazy, right?

Crazy.

But not as crazy as this: kneeling on the grass of the golf course at 1:27 AM, two fingers to Nora Melchionda's neck, the closest he had ever been to her, and he couldn't even prove what a good conversationalist he was. If she could see him on Dungeons & Dragons 3.5 Live, talking about metamagic feats, she would know that he could articulate clear and intelligent thoughts without turning red in the face. But this wasn't D&D Live. Not even close.

"Nora? It's me, Adam Xu...from school...Can you hear me? Nora?"

Nothing.

He straightened her clothes, gently, careful not to

touch any more of her body than he had to. He could have, of course—no one was there to see. But he never would. That was the difference between Adam and the Neander-thals he'd chased off with his baseball bat. Adam had loved Nora Melchionda since she was a scrawny ten-year-old kid, before she had any "body" to speak of—before every guy in Faber started noticing her. Just thinking about those three guys lifting up Nora's shirt, pulling down her underwear, made Adam feel as unhinged as he had ever felt in his life. He wanted to tear through the night with his baseball bat cocked.

But no. He had stay focused.

He removed her phone from her pocket, and he held the screen to her face. Gently, he lifted her eyelids, and when the phone unlocked, he found her best friend's number.

It's Adam Xu. Nora needs you. Faber golf course 9th hole, asap.

NORA

"YOU ARE NOT INSPECTING MY VAJAYJAY," SHE SAID.

She was standing in the middle of Cam's bedroom, on the braided rug where she had stood a million times before. The whorls of purple and blue made her dizzy.

"Vajayjay?" Cam gawked at her.

"I'll call it what I want," Nora said. Her head was still throbbing. She'd chugged three glasses of water in Cam's kitchen, but it hadn't helped. "And you are not getting out that stupid hand mirror."

"How are you going to see your pubic area without a hand mirror?"

"I'll see it fine," Nora said.

This was exactly like that time when they were twelve and Cam insisted on showing her how to put in a tampon—not just provide moral support from the other side of the bathroom stall like a normal friend—*show*. Cam's comfort level with her body, her freakish lack of embarrassment, made Nora feel like a sixteenth-century nun. *Privates are private.* That's what Nora's mom always said. Unlike Cam's mother, Imani, who said things like *Own your pleasure, girls.*

"Take some pictures with your phone," Cam told Nora. "If you see any bruises or scratches, you'll need documentation."

"Okay, CSI Miami."

"This isn't a joke, Nor. You woke up half-naked on a putting green. You don't remember anything. What if you were *gang-raped*?" Cam's voice dropped to a theatrical whisper, and Nora rolled her eyes. Drama queen.

"Nora." Cam's face meant business, like Principal Hicks during assembly that day the seniors toilet-papered freshman hall.

Okay, fine...*could* she have been gang-raped? Three guys in a remote location? Her memory a blank? Yes, she supposed it was possible—if this were New York City, where crazy things happened in the dark. But not in Faber. In Faber, the crime rate was 0.01. No one locked their doors. There were only two traffic lights. A rocking Friday night meant the Red Barn roller rink and two slices of bacon and pineapple at NY Pizzeria. If it weren't for the university, no one outside of Chenango County would even know this place existed.

"Enough stalling," Cam said. "Go look at your body."

Nora did not appreciate Cam's bossy tone, but she didn't have the energy to argue. She shuffled into the bathroom to the left of Cam's bed, flicked on the light, and shut the door behind her. The brightness made her eyeballs ache.

Nora lifted her shirt up over her head, let it drop to the floor. She unhooked her bra, flung it over the shower rod. She stepped out of her skirt and underwear and stood there, in front of the full-length mirror, squinting.

She could see her whole self.

I am a ghost, she thought, pressing her fingertips to the hollow beneath her neck. She could literally see the veins running like blue-green highways under her skin. Over the summer, she'd been a nice toasty color from weeks spent at the lake. In Cam's mirror, she was translucent. How had that happened?

Cam always told her she was lucky, that there were women the world over who would kill to look like Nora, blond and curvy. It was the law of bodies, Nora supposed, that girls always wanted what they didn't have. Whenever she watched Cam run the 200-meter, those long legs pumping, quad muscles gleaming, she felt a spark of envy.

"Your body is amazing," Nora had said once, after a track meet. "You're like the female Usain Bolt."

Cam, being Cam, had bristled at the compliment. She was an athlete in her own right, she'd told Nora.

"Listen to this," Cam said from the other side of the door. "I googled 'What happened last night? I don't remember anything,' and here's what I got. 'The signs of a sex crime may be very obvious or very subtle. You wake up in a strange place. You have bruises or scratches or unusual pain. You feel hungover even when you didn't drink alcohol...'"

Cam's voice was urgent, but Nora was barely listening. She didn't like standing in front of the mirror, everything on display. Her skin was so pasty. Her breasts were so... breasty. They had come out of nowhere. All her life she'd been thin, like her little sister. She'd assumed she would look like that forever. Then, suddenly, Nora's body had gone into hyperdrive, morphing from a string bean into what her friend Becca called a "loaded potato." Everyone, it seemed, had something to say about this new development, even Nora's brother, who'd stood in her doorway a few weeks earlier, looking supremely uncomfortable.

"I have to tell you something," he said. "Guys at school are starting to talk. Seniors."

When Nora asked him to elaborate, Asher said, "They're making comments about your...you know...appearance. Compliments, technically, but still."

At first, Nora had felt a strange rush of pride, like she'd won a contest. *Senior boys have noticed me!*

But then Asher said, "When you wear things that are too tight...or too short...some guys see that as an invitation."

At which point Nora had felt the opposite of proud. She'd felt ashamed. As though she had done something wrong by growing boobs and hips, by not dressing like Laura Ingalls Wilder.

Ugh. She didn't want to think about that. She didn't want to think about her body. She didn't want to think about what happened on the golf course. All she wanted to do was pull on sweatpants, crawl into bed, and sleep.

But no. Cam was still going. "Do you see anything? Bruises? Blood? Hairs that aren't yours?"

Nora stepped closer to the mirror. The front of herself looked normal. She wasn't bruised or bloody or covered in random hairs. She turned slowly to the left, then to the right, glancing over each shoulder at her backside. Nothing.

Wait—there was a strange bluish mark on her upper arm. Maybe one of the guys grabbed her? Nora stepped closer to the mirror.

Ha!

It wasn't a bruise. It was the temporary tattoo Nora's sister, Maeve, had insisted on giving her a few days earlier, after some Potterhead event at the library. The tattoo was a Ravenclaw crest. That's what Nora was, Maeve told her: a Ravenclaw. *Intelligent, witty, wise.*

"Do you need the hand mirror?" Cam asked from outside the door.

"No," Nora said. She most certainly did not need the hand mirror.

"You sure?"

"Yes!"

God, Cam was bossy. If she weren't three feet away, insisting that Nora inspect her privates, Nora wouldn't even bother looking. But there Cam was, right outside, and she wouldn't stop yammering until Nora did it.

So fine.

She took a deep breath, squatted, and bent over. *It's just another body part*, she told herself. *It's perfectly normal to be checking out your own crotch.* She squinted, trying to focus. Okay. This was completely weird. Flipping upside down, poking around at her nether region, checking for signs that some strange guy, or *guys*, had been down there without her knowledge. What was she even *looking for*? Suddenly, Nora was filled with a sick, dizzy feeling. Did she want to know? No. She did not. All she wanted was to pretend the frat fair never happened.

"Well?" Cam said from outside the door.

Nora rolled up slowly so she wouldn't get a head rush. "I'm fine," she said. Not just to Cam, but to her own reflection. To the pale, naked girl standing there with her hands clenched.

I'm fine.

I'm fine.

I'm fine.

CAM

CAM HAD TWO MAIN CONCERNS. THE FIRST WAS HER best friend, who seemed to be in denial. When Nora walked out of Cam's bathroom, she was calm. She hadn't seen anything on her body, she said. No scratches, no bruises, no blood, no hair. She hadn't smelled any strange smells on her skin or clothes. The only pain she felt was her head. Nora was telling the truth—Cam would know if she weren't—but still. If Cam had woken up half-naked on the golf course, and there was a witness who had spotted three guys at the scene, she would be screaming. She would be punching a wall. The fact that Nora was showing zero emotion only made Cam worry more. *How dare anyone hurt her best friend?*

Nora was the most decent, loyal person Cam knew. She had been there for Cam through every hard time in her life. When Cam got her tonsils out, Nora showed up at the hospital with two kinds of ice cream. When Cam's grandfather died, Nora sat in the front pew and held her hand while she cried. When Cam tripped in the final lap of the

4x400 relay, Nora ran out onto the track and helped her up. That's the kind of friend she was: decent and loyal.

Well, it was Cam's turn to be decent and loyal. She would show up for Nora. She would absorb whatever emotions Nora was feeling but could not express. She would be a true friend.

There was just one thing. Cam's second concern: her cell phone, pinging from the back pocket of her jeans. There were three texts already. She had read them while Nora was in the bathroom.

Wow

Still reeling

No regrets

All three texts were from Nora's brother, Asher. Nora's brother, Asher, who Cam had inadvertently made out with in a closet at Kyle Tenhope's party.

She hadn't planned to. Really. She had been just as surprised as anyone when Asher Melchionda rolled up on his bike in front of the Tenhopes' house. Even though Asher was a senior, he didn't go to parties. (As a sophomore, Cam typically wouldn't have gone to an upperclassman party, either, except that Kyle Tenhope was captain of both the cross-country team and the track team, and he had invited her because—not to brag or anything—she'd been a varsity runner since freshman year.) So there Cam was on the Tenhopes' front stoop, holding a beer and scrolling through her phone, when Nora's brother rolled up on his silly bike.

Asher had his driver's license, but he rarely drove. Over the summer, he'd found an old, beat-up beach cruiser at the dump. He'd fixed it himself and painted the frame yellow. He'd named it Odd Duck, which was appropriate because Asher Melchionda was pretty much the opposite of every guy Cam knew in Faber.

For starters, he didn't play sports. He painted huge, splattery canvases and sketched random objects with charcoal. He kept his hair long, sometimes in a ponytail, sometimes in a bandanna. He wore a silver hoop in his left ear, like a pirate. His eyes were brownish-gold. He was taller than Cam, and thin, but his arms and shoulders were as chiseled as an Olympic gymnast's. From painting all the time? Or maybe he lifted weights in the garage. Who knew what he did out there all day? Cam had spent half her life at the Melchiondas' house, but Nora's brother was as much a mystery to her as a senior as he had been back in elementary school, when all he did was juggle and eat butter-and-bacon sandwiches.

Was Asher attractive? Cam supposed he was, in an offbeat, bohemian banjo player sort of way. Nothing like his dad, though. It was kind of funny to admit, but it was true: Mr. M was Cam's first crush. She wasn't alone, either. Everyone loved Mr. M. All Nora's friends, all Nora's friends' mothers. Even the eighty-year-old waitresses at the Blue Bird got a spring in their step when he walked in. Rhett Melchionda was Faber's own force of nature. His hair was thicker, his smile was wider, his personality was bigger than anyone else's. Asher wasn't like that, which was why Cam had never thought of him as crush material. He was just...Asher. Nora's big, weird brother.

So the thing that had happened between them in Mrs. Tenhope's closet—what *was* that? An accident, Cam decided. A party foul.

And yet—her cheeks warmed at the thought—neither of them had been drinking. By the time Asher pulled up to the Tenhopes' front stoop, everyone inside the house had been well on their way, but Cam had only had two sips of warm keg beer. In truth, she had been finding the party boring. She'd thought there would be games. Quarters, beer pong, something for her to compete in, but there was nothing.

"Hey," Asher said when he saw Cam sitting alone on the steps. "What are you doing here?"

Cam shrugged. "Party hearty."

"Huh," Asher said. He was straddling his bike.

Since the last time Cam saw him riding, he'd added a wicker basket to the handlebars. A wicker basket. Like a grandma! She had to admire a guy who wore a pirate earring and rode a grandma bike and didn't give a crap what anyone thought about it.

"What are *you* doing here?" Cam asked.

And Asher said, in all seriousness, "I'm having a paint emergency."

"A paint emergency," she repeated.

"Yup," he said. "Is Mrs. T. home?"

It had taken Cam a moment, but then she remembered that Kyle's mother was not only the high school art teacher but also a professional painter. "She's in Vermont," Cam told Asher. "Hence the party."

"Right." He nodded. "Rats."

Rats, he'd said. Any other guy would have dropped the f-bomb.

"Just how serious is this paint emergency?" Cam asked—joking, of course, because it was a ridiculous question.

But Asher answered, "Life-or-death."

So she said, "Well, then, I'll help you."

And he said, "Your mission, should you choose to accept it, is to find me some Tahiti Blue acrylic paint."

And she said, "As always, should I or any of my force be caught or killed, the secretary will disavow any knowledge of my actions."

Was that where it started, with the two of them quoting *Mission: Impossible* to each other like a couple of dorks? Cam didn't know. All she knew was that she'd made Nora's brother smile, which was something she had never done before. He was always so serious. Seeing the corners of Asher's lips rise gave her a little jolt of pride.

"Come on," she said. "Let's go find Kyle."

Asher parked his bike and followed Cam into the Tenhopes' house. As they wove their way through the bodies—it seemed like half the high school was jammed into the living room—Asher shouted in Cam's ear so she would hear him over Lady Gaga, "How many drunk teenagers does it take to screw in a lightbulb?"

"How many?" Cam shouted back.

"Two! One to hold the bulb steady and another to drink until the room spins!"

She laughed, not because the joke was so funny, but because she and Asher seemed to be the only sober people in the room. Aaron Mischke, the second-best pole vaulter in the state of New York, was wearing a yellow construction hat attached to two beer cans and was drinking through a tube. The Stampler twins had stripped off their shirts and were dancing on a coffee table. Someone was peeing out a window. Cam laughed because what she saw was so comical.

She hadn't known, then, what was happening on the other side of town. She hadn't known about her best friend drinking from a red cup and losing an entire chunk of her night. She hadn't known about the three guys or the ninth hole or Adam Xu or the shitstorm that would follow. She hadn't known how her friendship would be tested. All she knew, in that moment, was that she had a mission: to find Tahiti Blue acrylic paint.

They found Kyle in the far corner of the kitchen, pumping beer from a keg. His hair was freshly buzzed and he was wearing a "Faber Track & Field" tank top.

"Speedy!" he crowed when he saw Cam. He'd given her the nickname the season before, after she'd won the 200-meter at the Sequoia Valley invitational.

"Hey," Cam said.

Kyle grabbed her arm and pulled her into a hug. His skin was warm and damp. His breath smelled beery. "You look hot! Like Zendaya!"

Cam looked nothing, *nothing* like Zendaya. But that's what guys did sometimes. They tried to give compliments by comparing her to some black celebrity. Yara Shahidi. Amandla Stenberg.

"You look drunk," Cam said, pulling away.

Kyle laughed. "Ha!" A steamy blast in her face. "I am!"

"Where does your mom keep her paint?"

"Huh?"

Cam tried again. "Where. Does. Your. Mom. Keep. Her. Paint? Asher. Needs. Some."

"Hey, man," Asher said, stepping forward to shake Kyle's hand.

"Anaconda!" Kyle laughed again, spit flying through the air. "Dude! I thought you didn't party!"

"I don't. I'm working on an art project, and I ran out of paint. Your mom said I could—"

"Dudes!" Kyle yelled across the room. "It's Anaconda!"

Drunken cheers erupted. "Anaconda!"

"What's with the anaconda?" Cam asked Asher when they'd finally communicated to Kyle what they needed, and he had directed them, vaguely and cheerfully, through a back door.

"Melchionda Anaconda," Asher said. "He's called me that since third grade."

"He's big on nicknames," Cam said.

"A real Shakespeare, that one," Asher said. Then: "Careful on the steps. They're steep."

There was a narrow flight of stairs that led up to the second floor. The light in the stairway was dim, and there was no railing.

"Here," Asher said, reaching back. "Just in case."

Cam took his hand. "Thanks."

Surely they'd held hands before, as kids. Playing blob tag. Jumping off the dock at Lake Moraine. But this—Asher's eighteen-year-old fingers, strong and sure, wrapped around her own—made something happen in Cam's throat. A catch of surprise. A rush of warmth. Then she caught herself: This was Nora's *brother*.

As though he'd read her mind, Asher asked, "Is Nora here?"

"No," Cam said. "She's at the frat fair." Instead of stopping there, she expelled breath she hadn't known she was holding and said something she hadn't known she was thinking: "We're starting to want different things."

"Yeah?" Asher said.

"Yeah. Completely."

As soon as she spoke the words, she realized they were true. Cam didn't know how to explain it, the feeling of restlessness that had begun to nibble at her. Nora seemed content to keep doing what the two of them had always done: movie nights and baking nights and game nights. The same old boring traditions: marching in the July Fourth parade, buying matching folders for school, riding the Yo-Yo. Cam used to like those things, too. But the sameness was beginning to wear on her. She had tried to inject some excitement into their lives once, at the end of ninth grade. It had been a boneheaded decision, in retrospect, to drink an entire bottle of Manischewitz from Becca Bomberg's parents' wine cellar—Nora had barfed her guts out—but at least it was something new and different. Novelty! That's what Cam craved. Something unexpected. Something to set her on fire.

She and Asher reached Mrs. Tenhope's bedroom: half sleep space, half art studio. Cream-colored walls, track lighting, easels. Works of art in various stages of completion tacked up everywhere, including a sketch of a nude woman, hanging over the king-size bed. A nude woman! Cam wasn't shocked by the nakedness—or by the reminder that, after Kyle's father died, Kyle's mother had suddenly come out as a lesbian (it had been the talk of Faber for a while)—but walking into Mrs. T's private sanctuary without her permission felt wrong. Cam was a trespasser. A burglar. The thought made her giddy. She and Nora's brother prowled around the room, sliding out drawers, lifting lids.

"Aha!" Asher said finally. He had opened a closet, inside of which was a cabinet full of paint. Rows and rows of paint. Tubes, tubs, bottles. "Help me look," he said.

Cam joined him in the closet. The paint colors had great names. *Juneberry. Aster. Nacho Cheese.*

Who knew how long they searched? Five minutes? Twenty? At some point Asher cried, "Jackpot!" and waved a bottle in the air. "Tahiti Blue, baby!" Then he reached into the pocket of his jeans and pulled out a ten-dollar bill, which he placed on the shelf.

"She would have just given it to me," he said, "but... paint's not cheap."

He looked around until he found a scrap of paper and a stub of charcoal. *Desperate measures, Mrs. T,* he scrawled. *Needed some tahiti blue. Thx. —Asher.* He placed the note on the shelf beside the money. Then he looked at Cam and grinned. Again!

Cam stared at him. He was wearing a mustard-colored T-shirt with a ripped collar. It brought out the gold in his eyes.

"What?" he said.

She shook her head. "Nothing."

"I know this is weird," he said.

"What?"

"Having a paint emergency on a Friday night." He shrugged, tucked a hank of hair behind his ear. "I'm a freak. I admit it."

"No," Cam said. "You're a serious artist. I respect that."

Asher looked at her. Really looked at her with those tiger eyes.

"Thanks," he said. "For saying that. My dad thinks I'm wasting my life."

Cam had spent enough time at the Melchiondas' to know that Mr. M and Asher didn't always get along. But Mr. M wasn't in Mrs. Tenhope's closet, so Cam could speak freely.

"You're not wasting your life," she said.

"You don't think?"

"*No.*"

His face was thoughtful now. He looked so quintessentially *Asher* that Cam was overwhelmed by a sudden desire to hug him. Hug Nora's brother! Her brain gave the order, and her arms obeyed.

It was a little awkward. Her nose rammed into his shoulder. She stepped away almost as quickly as she'd stepped toward him.

But then. Then.

Cam felt something warm on her face. It was... Asher's hand, cupping her cheek. This was *not* a brotherly gesture. Cam was shocked, but she made herself keep breathing.

Innnn. Ouuuut.

Asher Melchionda's hand on her cheek. Cupping it! This was crazy. And yet, it was happening. There, in Mrs. Tenhope's closet full of paint, he bent down and pressed his lips to hers. Cam was 100 percent sober, but Asher's kiss was like three slugs of Manischewitz straight from the bottle. When she came up for air, she felt warm and dizzy.

"Was that okay?" he said.

And she said, "Definitely."

They kissed again. And again.

While they had been kissing, Nora had been passed out on the golf course, clueless to the three guys removing her underwear.

Now, Cam's guilt was a boulder in her gut. She should have gone to the frat fair!

Nora was out of the bathroom and standing on Cam's rug. She was fine, she said. She'd checked her body and hadn't seen anything.

"You sure?" Cam said.

"I'm sure," Nora said.

Cam thought about the phone in her back pocket.

Wow
Still reeling
No regrets

Should she come clean about hooking up with Asher? She and Nora had promised each other, back in sixth grade, always to tell the brutal truth, even if it hurt. They had vowed to share every boy-related detail, which was how Cam knew that Nora had tongue-kissed a Jersey boy named Evan Fendelbaum at Becca Bomberg's bat mitzvah, and Nora knew that Cam had seen Kyle Tenhope's erection through his swim trunks at the track team's end-of-season pool party freshman year. But those things were different. Who cared about Evan Fendelbaum's lizard tongue or Kyle Tenhope's boner? Asher was Nora's *brother*. Cam had to tell her about the kiss, right? Of course she did. And at some point, she definitely would. But not now. Now, Cam decided, was not the right moment.

"We should go to the police," she said. "Or the hospital. They can test your blood or urine or whatever."

Nora looked at her like she had three heads. "Are you insane?"

"No," Cam said. "I'm logical."

"No freaking way."

"Nor," Cam said, as gently as she could. "I'm pretty sure you got roofied. That's why you can't remember."

"So?"

Now it was Cam's turn to look horrified. *"So?"*

"I told you I'm fine," Nora said. "I don't need the whole town knowing I was passed out on the golf course."

There were so many things Cam wanted to say, but Nora was being deaf to reason. "There is one person you need to see," she said, "and that is nonnegotiable."

"Who?" Nora said.

"Adam Xu. He deserves a thank-you."

ADAM XU

THE DOORBELL RANG WHILE HE WAS SITTING AT THE DIN-ing room table, studying for his chemistry test. His mother was in the kitchen. He knew, just from the smell, that she was making his favorite breakfast. Thick slices of warm tomato topped with scrambled eggs and zha cai. Scallion pancakes cooked in oil, perfectly crisp and salty. At school, he ate cheeseburgers in the cafeteria like everyone else, but at home he ate this: the best food in Faber.

The doorbell rang a second time. Bao Bao started barking. His mom started yelling.

Adam sighed and propped his chemistry book open with a pen. He walked to the front hall. Through the glass he saw two heads: one dark, one light. Wait—was that...? No. No possible way. And yet...this wasn't completely unexpected, was it? Nora Melchionda on the golf course, clothes half-off? His cheeks flushed at the memory.

He opened the door.

"Hey, Adam Xu."

It wasn't Nora who spoke; it was her friend Camille.

There had been a time, years ago, when Adam thought that he and Camille Dodd might become friends. That her Blackness and his Asianness would somehow bond them together. But it hadn't worked out that way. Instead, Adam had become friends with Tobias Muenker. The two of them met the summer before sixth grade, in a fantasy-fiction club at the town library, where they were the only members. During the course of their friendship, Tobias had not only dressed in full body armor to help Adam practice baseball, he had also introduced Adam to Dungeons & Dragons, which they played continuously in the Muenkers' basement and sometimes in the school cafeteria. Guys like Kevin Hamm loved to mock them, but being called a "dungeon geek" hadn't bothered Adam then. He and Tobias were a team—at least until last year, when the Muenkers moved to Cleveland and Adam went right back where he started. Playing D&D on FaceTime just wasn't the same.

"Can we come in?" Camille asked.

Could they come in? Adam blanched at the thought. The last time Nora Melchionda and Camille Dodd had set foot in his house was on his tenth birthday, when his mother invited the whole class over to celebrate. The event had been an unmitigated disaster. Unlike the Shuang Wen School back in New York City, where all of Adam's friends from kindergarten through third grade had been just like him, the kids in Faber knew nothing of Chinese traditions. When his mother brought out the longevity noodles for everyone to slurp, Kevin Hamm and Adam Courtmanche had deliberately bitten their noodles in half and joked that everyone in the room would die young.

"Well?" Camille said. She widened her eyes.

"Right," Adam said. "Yeah. Come in."

He stepped backward into the hall and watched as both girls entered his house. This was unprecedented. This was... miraculous. Nora Melchionda was brushing past him, carrying with her the scent of grass and earth.

Was this her natural scent, or the scent of the golf course? He noticed that she'd changed her clothes. Instead of the skirt, she was wearing baggy black sweatpants and a hoodie. Her hair was scraped up in a ponytail.

He couldn't bring himself to look her in the eye. Instead, he concentrated on leading the way into the dining room, where his mother was setting a plate of food on the table, Bao Bao sniffing at her heels.

"Hey, Mrs. Xu," Camille said, smiling like they were old friends. "Cute dog."

Adam's mother did not smile back. Adam's mother thought American girls were "hen suibian de," which was the Chinese equivalent of "easy." She thought they showed too much skin and lived like pigs. She had gotten this impression from her job cleaning Faber University sorority houses. While Adam's father was busy teaching Mandarin and writing academic papers for publication, his mother was vacuuming pulverized Cheetos out of the couches and scraping vomit off the carpets of Kappa Kappa Nu. Adam had tried to convince his mother, on more than one occasion, that not all American girls were party animals with loose morals, but she wouldn't listen.

"We're having a study group," he told her now. "For chemistry." It wasn't exactly a lie. Just because Nora and Camille took basic chem, not honors, that didn't mean they never studied.

"Yes." Camille nodded, playing along. "Thank you for having us over. We could really use your help." She pulled out a chair and sat down. Nora did the same.

Adam's mother huffed. "Do homework," she said.

When she and Bao Bao walked back into the kitchen, Adam was tempted to apologize.

But Camille spoke first: "Nora has something to tell you."

Nora had something to tell *him*.

Adam glanced across the dining room table. Was it really her? Yes, those ocean eyes, impossibly wide and blue. If he looked too deeply, they could swallow him whole. So he focused on her chin.

"Thank you," Nora said, her voice low. "For helping me last night. I really appreciate it."

"Oh…" He forced his gaze upward. His heart rose and thudded at the base of his throat. "You're welcome."

"Did you see what they looked like?" Camille said.

"Hm?"

"The guys. On the golf course. Did you see what they looked like?"

He dragged his eyes away from Nora to focus on Camille. "Not really. No."

"Nothing?"

He shook his head. "Just that there were three of them, and they were big. I wasn't that close. And they ran away as soon as I started yelling."

"You yelled at them?" Nora said. She smiled, just barely. A twitch of the lips and then it was gone.

"Yeah." Adam wanted to see her smile again so badly that he said something stupid. "I have the whole thing on video."

"You *what*?" Camille said.

He regretted it instantly. To say that he had a video was to admit that he had been wearing a night-vision camcorder strapped to his head for the purpose of documenting himself hitting glow-in-the-dark Precision Impact Slugs on the golf course, for the purpose of making the varsity baseball team and proving to the world that he wasn't a geek—which was, in essence, confirming what a geek he was.

Crap.

They were both staring at him, waiting.

He had no choice but to explain. When he finished, Camille said, "Let me get this straight...you never turned it off?"

Adam shook his head. "I didn't realize I was still recording until this morning, when I watched the video. It's all there."

"And you didn't erase it?" Camille said.

"No. I mean...I didn't think I should."

"Oh my God," Camille said. "You brilliant, brilliant boy."

NORA

SHE DIDN'T WANT TO SEE THE VIDEO. SHE WANTED TO
leave. But Cam was the boss of the world, grabbing Nora's
elbow, pulling her up the stairs to Adam Xu's bedroom
without even stopping to ask if Nora wanted to see it.
Nora *didn't* want to see it, but she was so tired. She didn't
have the energy to fight.

"The video quality isn't what it would be in daylight,"
Adam Xu explained as he turned on his camcorder. "You
can only see black and white. But night-vision recording
has come a long way..."

He kept talking as he plugged a cord into his computer and pressed a few buttons, but Nora wasn't listening. Instead of looking at the computer, she was looking
around the room, pretending to be interested in what she
was seeing. Adam Xu's walls were white and bare. There
was a platform bed with a plain navy comforter, a freak-
ishly neat desk, and a bookshelf lined with the same
books Nora would be reading this year: *The Bluest Eye. The*

Crucible. Worlds of History. Adam Xu's room had about as much personality as a cardboard box.

Nora wasn't looking at the computer. She was looking at the bed again, those plump, white pillows. All she wanted was to lie down. As soon as she got home, that's what she would do. Sleep forever. With any luck she would wake up in a hundred years, like Rip Van Winkle, and the frat fair would be long gone.

Hahahahahahahaha!

"Nor," Cam said.

Nora turned to look. The video on the screen was grainy and wobbly like a bad home movie, but the sound was clear.

Hahahahahahaha!

Bouncing and shaking.

More bouncing and shaking.

Now she could see outlines...barely discernible bodies... three of them...no, four. One was lying down.

"Oh my God," Cam murmured. She squeezed Nora's elbow.

More bouncing and shaking.

Finally, the scene came into focus. One of the bodies was lifting an arm. Another was bending down.

Dude, she's completely out.

Silence for a second.

Cam moved in closer. "Is he *taking off his pants?*"

Nora closed her eyes.

Hey!

There was no point in watching this. None. Whatever happened last night was over and—

Ting xia lai!

Nora's eyes flew open. Slashes of light filled the computer screen.

Ting xia lai! Huai dan!

Slash, slash, slash.

"What the hell?" Cam said.

"It was instinct," Adam Xu said. "It's what my mom yells at the dog when he's bad."

"Is that *lightning*?" Cam said.

"It's my glow-in-the-dark baseball bat," Adam Xu said. "I was trying to scare them off."

The three bodies on the screen were gone. Just one remained: the one on the ground.

Hey . . . are you okay?

The camera moved closer.

A hand reaching out. Straightening clothes.

Nora found herself moving in for a better look. Her brain hadn't yet registered what she was seeing. She briefly considered the possibility that she was dreaming. This seemed unlikely, but she pinched herself anyway.

Nora? . . . It's me, Adam Xu . . . from school . . . Can you hear me? . . . Nora?

The room was suddenly too small and too warm. It was a cardboard box. She couldn't breathe.

"Nor," Cam said. "You okay?"

Nora shook her head. That girl lying there . . . it wasn't

her. It *couldn't* be her. That girl was practically naked. She looked dead.

A sound rose up from Nora's chest, half cry, half growl.

Cam reached out a hand, but Nora slapped it away. She didn't want to be comforted.

"Don't worry," Cam said quietly. "We'll find them."

Nora blinked. *Find them?* The three pixelated ghosts that had just evaporated into the night? She tried to laugh. The sound stuck in her throat, like a hairball caught in a drain.

She needed air.

But before she could leave Adam Xu's bedroom, there was something she needed to do. She had to erase the video. She couldn't take Adam Xu's word for it, either. She had to press the "delete" button herself. She had to check the camera to make sure the file was really gone.

"I thanked him," she said to Cam when they were standing on the sidewalk outside Adam Xu's house. "Okay? And I'm thanking you, too. Thank you for being there last night, for helping me. Now I never want to talk about it again."

"Nor," Cam said gently.

Nora did not like this tone.

"I'm not saying this to upset you," Cam said. "I'm saying this because I love you. You really need to go to the hospital. Or the police. You saw what those guys—"

"Shut up," Nora said. "It's over."

"But they—"

Nora stuck her hand in Cam's chest, a stiff-arm block. "It didn't happen to you. It happened to *me*. And if I say it's over, it's over."

"Nora—"

"I didn't *want* to see that video. You didn't even *ask* if I wanted to see it, you just dragged me upstairs. And now I have to get it out of my head."

"I'm sorry," Cam said. "But what those guys did—"

"I swear to God, Camille. If you say one more word about those guys, I will smack you in the face."

"You'll *smack me in the face*?"

"Yes."

"No you won't."

"I will."

"You don't *smack people in the face*. You're the least aggressive person I know."

"Please," Nora said, squeezing her eyes shut. "I am begging you. Just stop talking."

When Nora got home, her dad was at the end of the driveway. He was wearing his white FU baseball cap and his blue windbreaker with "Faber University Athletic Dept." emblazoned on the back. He was talking into his cell phone, pacing back and forth in front of the garage. Nora's dad was always in motion—talking, walking, gesturing. When he spotted Nora, he waved, and for a second, she had the crazy urge to sprint up the driveway and leap into his arms. When she was little, her dad had seemed as tall and strong as a redwood tree. She would scale him like a monkey.

Now, Nora's legs felt too wobbly to move. She was still nauseous, and she couldn't decide if food would make things better or worse.

You really need to go to the hospital. Or the police.

Please. Was there such a thing as a drama queen disorder? Because if there was, Cam needed serious treatment.

"I'm on it," Nora's dad spoke loudly into his phone. Even from the sidewalk, Nora could hear him. "I'm out here for you, kid."

This was classic Rhett Melchionda. Nora's dad was the most "on it" and "out here for you" person Nora knew. He had been that way his whole life. That's why his old fraternity brothers still called him "master of the universe," because they looked up to him. Everyone did. All the deans and coaches at Faber, hundreds of Division I athletes, the town council. Nora's whole life, she had watched her dad in action. There were pictures of him, cut out of the *Faber Gazette*, that Nora's mom had framed and hung in his office. Nora's dad in the middle of Crockett Stadium, helping his injured quarterback off the field. Nora's dad on the mound at the Faber–Yale game, throwing out the first pitch. Nora's dad in the stands at Tayte Rink, fists raised in the air.

That was Nora's favorite picture, because she had been there, too. If she looked closely enough, she could see the sleeve of her old checkered jacket. It was her tenth birthday. She and her dad had been watching the Faber University hockey game when a puck came soaring over the boards and through a hole in the net. If it had hit her in the head she could have died, but Nora's dad dove on top of her, making himself a human shield. There was a ton of blood. The Faber fan sitting beside them was wearing a white puffer coat, and Nora still remembered the splatter of red across the woman's chest, like one of Asher's paintings. Despite the blood, it wasn't a life-threatening injury—the puck merely grazed the length of her dad's eyebrow, slicing open the skin—but his eye swelled immediately, making him look like Arturo Gatti after his beatdown by Micky Ward.

When Nora was ten, she had three heroes: "Irish" Micky Ward, Zander Foy (goalie for the Faber University hockey team), and her dad. Nora's dad was the one who had introduced her to contact sports, a devotion they shared with no one else in the family. Nora's brother spent all his time in the garage, flinging paint onto old bedsheets and calling it art. Nora's sister was a bookworm whose idea of high-octane thrills was lounging in bed all day with Harry Potter. And Nora's mom thought sports were boring, which raised the question: Why did she marry an athletic director? Nora asked her once, and the answer she got was, "Animal magnetism, honey." Well, Nora knew a thing or two about magnets. She had been studying them in fourth grade. "The motion of electrical charge, resulting in attractive or repulsive forces between objects." Example: the electrical charge of Nora's eyeballs being attracted to Zander Foy's profile in the Faber hockey team's roster book.

Number: 32.

Position: goaltender.

Height: 6'4".

Animal magnetism was the reason Nora had been staring down at Zander Foy's killer smile instead of out at the ice when the puck came flying into the stands and split open her dad's face. He needed thirteen stitches, but the rest of him was fine. Other than a fat pink scar that would turn thinner and lighter with time, Nora's dad was unaffected by the experience. But Nora was changed forever. After that, whenever she looked at her father's eyebrow, she saw the arc reactor on Iron Man's suit. She saw Thor's hammer. When the whole fourth grade was asked to write an essay entitled "The Greatest American," Nora wrote about her dad: *Rhett Melchionda, athletic director by day, superhero by night.* Here was a man who had played rugby in college and—when he dislocated his shoulder during a nasty tackle—reset the joint himself and went back in the game. Here was a man who—when his wife unexpectedly went into labor in the middle of *Gran Torino*—delivered Nora's sister, Maeve, on the floor of the movie theater. Here was a man who—when faced with a flying hockey puck—sacrificed his own body to protect his daughter.

"Hey, ladybug." In the driveway, Nora's dad was off the phone. He was striding over, wrapping an arm around her shoulders. "How was your night?"

Nora pressed her face into her dad's jacket. She could smell his aftershave. For a second, it brought tears to her eyes.

"Good," she said.

He released her. "Win anything at the fair?"

Nora's mind whizzed and churned like a blender. Had she won anything at the fair? A goldfish in a plastic bag? A stuffed panda? She had no idea. Other than riding the Yo-Yo and drinking the root beer, her night was a sinkhole, a tunnel to nowhere. She shook her head.

"Cam win anything?"

"I don't think so," she murmured. She didn't want to lie to her dad, but she also didn't have the brainpower to explain that she and Cam had a fight and Cam didn't even go to the frat fair.

"You don't think so?" Her dad waggled his eyebrows one at a time, one of his many talents. This usually made Nora smile, but her smile muscles weren't working.

She shook her head again. "Those games are rigged."

"Well, it's all for a good cause," he said. "You'll be happy to know that we made a killing at the cotton candy booth. Thanks for swinging by."

Nora blinked. *Cotton candy booth.* Right. Her dad always worked the cotton candy booth at the frat fair. It was his thing. Had Nora actually eaten cotton candy, or had she just stopped to say hi? Was this before or after the root beer? She didn't know. Her brain was spun sugar on a stick, lighter than air.

"Hey," her dad said. His eyebrows were furrowed now. "You okay, kiddo?"

Was she okay? Nora looked at her dad, and for one crazy second, she thought about telling him the truth. *I don't remember anything about last night. I woke up on the golf course. Some guys took off my underwear.*

But no. No freaking way. Her dad would have a heart attack. He would never let her out of the house again. One time over the summer, when Nora had gone to the movies with Adam Courtmanche, she had forgotten to text her parents afterward to tell them she was stopping for a slice at NY Pizzeria. She had also forgotten to turn her phone back on after silencing it in the theater. When Nora's dad couldn't reach her, he walked all over town, asking everyone and their dog if they had seen Nora. When he finally found her eating a slice of cheeseless pizza with Adam, he made her get up and leave. On the walk home, he gave Nora his favorite line: *I'm your dad, ladybug. It's my job to protect you.* Then came the lecture: Did she have any idea what time it was? Did she know how worried he'd been? If she wanted to continue going on dates, she needed to remember a few things. (For the record, Nora and Adam had not been on a "date." What was this, 1987? They had just been hanging out.) But her dad's point was this: Nora had a curfew for a reason. She was a beautiful girl. Boys were going to want to spend time with her, and, while she might be flattered by their attention, she also needed to be smart. She couldn't stay out all night.

In case this message hadn't been clear enough, a few weeks later, Nora's dad asked her to come outside and play basketball. While they took turns shooting, he launched into a speech about how he knew she was growing up, and this was a different world from when he was a teenager, and maybe this was a conversation she should be having with her mother, but he was her dad; it was his job to protect her. And, well, he'd been in the garage yesterday, looking for the Master Lock, and...as her dad...he really didn't think Nora should be riding around town with her birth control pills in the seat pocket of her bike.

Nora had nearly fallen over. *"Birth control pills?"*

"Uh-huh." Her father kept shooting.

"Dad," she said.

"I know, ladybug, but—"

"I'm not having *sex*."

He palmed the ball and gawked at her. "Of course you're not. I assumed you needed the pill to...regulate your cycle. But this is a small town. People who don't know you like I do might get the wrong idea."

If there had been a hole in the driveway, Nora would have jumped through it, into the red-hot center of the earth. "It's not the pill, okay?" she said. "It's my retainer case."

"Your retainer case," he repeated.

"Yes," she said. "I was just at the ortho."

"Right...well...good."

The look on her dad's face would have been funny if the

whole thing hadn't been so mortifying. Nora was crazy to think that she could tell him about three random guys on the golf course yanking off her underwear. Her dad would lose his mind. He would love her anyway, of course. He was her father. But the image he had of her—his *ladybug*, riding around town with her retainer in the seat pocket of her bike—would be gone forever.

Nora knew there were girls her age, like Chelsea Machado and Anna Golden, who were already having sex—not just making out with someone in the back row of the movie theater—*legit sex*. Nora also knew how guys talked. She'd heard the names they used to describe Chelsea and Anna. Nora never wanted guys to talk about her that way, which was why she never let Adam get very far. There had been kissing, yes. There had been up-the-shirt action, yes. But Nora always drew the line there. Even though she'd considered going further a few times, she'd never crossed over.

"Nora?" Her dad was looking at her, waiting.

"I'm fine," she said. "Just tired."

"Not too tired, I hope," he said. He glanced at his big gold watch. "We need to go or we'll miss kickoff."

*Kickoff...Kickoff...*Nora scanned her brain.

"Here." Her dad handed her something she hadn't even noticed he was holding. "Change in the car."

Nora unfolded the something. It was her "Faber University Football" hoodie, soft and gray, smelling faintly of kettle corn. That's when the lightbulb went off. Today was the Faber–Colgate game. Nora and her dad went every year, and, normally, she would be thrumming with excitement. Blue Devils versus Red Raiders! The ultimate rivalry! But right now, all she wanted to do was sleep.

"Dev-ils, Dev-ils!" Her dad pumped his fist in the air and opened the car door for Nora.

"Dev-ils fight," she murmured.

Her dad grinned. He ruffled her hair. "Hop in, ladybug."

Well, what was she supposed to do? Break his heart?

—✒—

Nora was so tired she could barely keep her eyes open. Crockett Stadium was a scene. Usually she loved it— walking through those green metal gates with her dad, watching him raise his hand in greeting to everyone they met. Students, faculty, even the grouchy hot dog lady. Watching Nora's dad work a crowd, people didn't think *athletic director*, they thought *mayor*. He smiled. He cracked jokes. He clapped shoulders. Everyone knew who he was. And everyone knew who Nora was, too. She was Rhett Melchionda's girl. She had been coming to games with her dad since she was two, when she rode in on his shoulders like a circus performer, hair in pigtails.

Nora wished someone would carry her right now.

She wished the band weren't so loud.

She wished her dad didn't get stopped every three seconds by someone asking for a favor. Would he talk to the soccer goalie's English tutor? Would he weigh in on the proposed amendment to the code of conduct? Would he grand marshal the Faber Festival of Lights?

"The Festival of *Lights*?" Nora said when they finally broke free and made their way to the stands. "It's *September*."

"They plan these things months in advance," her dad said.

Nora and her dad sat on the frigid aluminum bleachers, watching the Faber offensive line take the field. She wished she were home in bed, not freezing her butt off in Cam's paper-thin sweatpants, surrounded by screaming Faber fans. She couldn't take the screaming. It made her head ache.

I'm pretty sure you got roofied.

No. She was not going to think about that. Pressing "delete" on Adam Xu's camcorder had been like flushing a toilet. All the crap from the golf course was gone, so there was nothing left to think about. Her mind was fresh and clean. It had only one job: watch football.

Beside her, Nora's dad cheered. The whole crowd cheered.

TD already? No. Just first down. Okay. Nora fixed her eyes on the field and tried to concentrate. White jerseys, blue helmets, crimson jerseys, black helmets, all arranging themselves into different configurations. Lines of bodies...clumps of bodies...

She couldn't do it. Her brain kept spinning off into another dimension. *Red cup. Golf course. Dude, she's completely out.*

Crap.

Nora's heart hammered in her chest. What if the three guys were on the field right now, running plays? Or sitting on these same bleachers, cheering? She felt a queasy panic rising in her throat.

"Dad?" she said. Her voice sounded strangled, but he didn't seem to notice.

"Yeah, ladybug?"

Nora wanted to tell him she didn't feel well; she might throw up. But she couldn't make herself say the words. He was in his element. If she told him she was sick, he would leave the game in a heartbeat. He would drive her home and tuck her into bed and bring her ginger ale and crushed ice in her Minions cup, circa fourth grade. He would do all this because he loved her more than he loved Faber sports, and that was saying something, because he was the proudest alum in the history of alums. But still.

"Never mind," Nora said.

"You sure?" Her dad's eyes were bright, his cheeks flushed. His feet were keeping time with the marching band.

Nora nodded. "Yeah."

"You want something? Popcorn? Hot pretzel?"

"That's okay," Nora said.

She fixed her eyes on the field and tried to concentrate. White jerseys, blue helmets. Crimson jerseys, black helmets.

CAM

KEEP IT ON THE CLOUD.

Cam had written the note on a gum wrapper she'd dug out of her pocket, with the pen she'd found on Adam Xu's desk while Nora was fiddling with his camcorder, trying to delete the file. Cam had written the note out of love and concern for her best friend. Because Nora clearly wasn't thinking straight—she hadn't even noticed the video uploading to the cloud—and as long as Nora wasn't thinking straight, Cam would do all the thinking.

She didn't have to be a heart surgeon to see that Adam Xu had a crush on Nora. It was cringingly obvious. And this, Cam felt, could only help her cause. Because what did every guy with a crush want? To demonstrate his worth. And what better way for Adam Xu to prove himself to Nora than to help Cam track down the three asshats who'd tried to hurt her? It was a no-brainer. Not that he stood a chance, of course. Cam felt bad, and she was sorry, but it was true.

Nora was one of those sought-after girls, and not just because she looked like a Hollywood pinup from the 1950s.

Even back in elementary school, when she had those awful bangs, and her knees were wider than her thighs, and her teeth grew in funny, Nora always had something—a blend of her dad's social ease and her mom's Montana farm girl purity—that drew people to her. Everyone at Faber High School wanted a piece of Nora. Guys wanted to hook up with her. Girls wanted to *be* her. Nora was beloved without even trying or caring. If Cam weren't Nora's best friend, she would find this highly annoying.

Cam was popular enough—she was a varsity athlete, and she hung out with some upperclassmen—but she wasn't golden like Nora. People didn't *flock* to Cam. They *certainly* didn't flock to Adam Xu. Adam Xu was serious and studious and quiet. He never went to parties. He wore T-shirts that said things like, "I paused my game to be here." And because, in the natural order of high school, like attracts like: the Nora Melchiondas of this world did not fall for the Adam Xus. Which, when Cam really stopped to think about it, made what had happened between her and Asher in Mrs. Tenhope's closet equally insane. Asher wasn't just a senior. He was a senior who had achieved an ironic level of coolness by being counterculture. He should be making out in closets with one of those senior girls in the art club—the ones who dyed their hair blue and wore boho tunics and smelled like patchouli. If Cam didn't have his texts on her phone as proof, she might think she had dreamed the whole thing up.

Wow

Still reeling

No regrets

Sitting on the couch in her living room, Cam deliberated. What should she text him back? *LOL? Ditto?* A smiley face emoji? She was out of her depth here.

Nothing, she decided finally. She would not respond to Asher's texts. She would do the opposite of responding. She would go for a run.

Running helped. This was something Cam had learned from her dad years ago. Michael Dodd ran five miles every morning before heading off to his job as a corrections officer at the Onondaga County Department of Correction. Running kept him sane. It cleared his head. Now, whenever Cam had a problem to solve, she would do the same thing: lace up her Nikes and go. She didn't need music. She listened to the rhythm of her feet. She listened to the rise and fall of her breath. Nine times out of ten, the super-oxygenated blood pumping through her veins, the endorphins or whatever, would work their magic. An answer would rise to the surface of her brain.

The town of Faber was 2.51 square miles. It was tiny but hilly. Runners could get a great workout if they knew where to go. Lebanon Street, for starters. Then Broad. Then Preston Hill Road; that's where Cam's cross-country coach,

Drews, always made them run incline sprints. Most of her teammates complained, but Cam never did. She liked to push herself. The more her legs burned, the more her heart hammered, the better she felt.

Cam was in the middle of her third incline sprint when she suddenly remembered something. It was before she and Nora had their argument. They had been up in Nora's room, just hanging out. Cam remembered Nora looking up from whatever she'd been organizing on her desk, and asking, "If you could invent any machine, what would you build?" It was a game they'd been playing forever, the "if you could" game. *If you could find a cure for any disease, what would it be? If you could kiss any boy at school, who would you kiss?* The day before, Nora had answered first: She would invent a LEGO vacuum. The night before, she had been babysitting the Delormes, and the kids had spewed about ten cubic feet of LEGO bricks onto the living room floor to play "trash compactor," and then they had refused to clean up. Nora had wasted an hour of her life picking up all those little pieces of plastic. If she'd had a LEGO vacuum, she told Cam, she could have done the job in three minutes.

"I'll never get that time back," she said.

It had been funny then, but Nora's words took on a different meaning after the golf course. If Cam could invent anything, it would be a time machine. *I will build a time machine, and I will go back to yesterday, and I will save Nora from getting roofied.* This was Cam's deep, illuminating thought as she ran. Ha!

By the home stretch, she still had no clue how to help Nora or how to answer Asher's texts. She dropped to the grass in front of her house to bang out forty-two push-ups. Cam always ended her runs with forty-two push-ups, ever since she'd discovered that the presidential physical fitness test had lower standards for girls than for boys. It bugged her. So she made sure, every time, to do more, not fewer, than the boys were expected to do. Real, military push-ups: chest to ground, full extension. Just on principle.

One and down. Hooold and up. Two and down. Hooold and up.

By twenty, her upper body was shaking, but she didn't stop. *Twenty-one and down. Hooold and up. Twenty-two and down. Hooold and up—*

"Not bad," a voice said.

Cam turned her head to the side and saw two bare feet, a bike tire, a flash of yellow. Holy shit. Her arms were weak. Her heart slammed against her rib cage.

"Don't get up," Asher said. "I'll come to you."

He lowered himself to the ground beside her. He was wearing a pair of ripped jeans and a faded blue T-shirt. He wore a darker blue bandanna on his head and the pirate earring. Who besides Captain Jack Sparrow could pull off this look? No one. It was ridiculous. And yet, strangely appealing.

Cam was suddenly aware of how hot and sweaty she was. She stank like the weight room at school. He had to be smelling her, right? She didn't know what to say or how to act, so she kept going. *Twenty-three and down. Hooold and up. Twenty-four and down. Hooold and up.*

With her peripheral vision, Cam could see Asher beside her, assuming the plank position, matching her rhythm. God, he was weird. Showing up here barefoot on his silly bike, suddenly doing push-ups.

Had the kiss in the closet really happened? Had Nora's brother actually cupped Cam's cheek and pressed his lips to hers? It seemed impossible, yet Asher was a foot away. So . . . what now? Did he want to kiss her again?

Thirty-six and down. Hooold and up. Cam's breath came in huffs. It was hard to look good while grunting like a pig.

Look good? In front of *Asher?* Since when did Cam care about how she looked in front of Nora's brother?

Cam finished her last push-up and collapsed onto the grass.

Asher collapsed beside her. "How many was that?"

"Forty-two," she said.

"The answer to life, the universe, and everything."

She blinked at him.

"Douglas Adams? *Hitchhiker's Guide to the Galaxy*?"

Who are you? Cam thought. She was about to ask when a voice behind them said, "We come bearing muffins."

There was Cam's mom, holding up a Blue Bird bakery box. There was her dad, grinning like a goofball.

"Blueberry, chocolate chip, or pistachio walnut?" Imani opened the box.

Cam didn't know whether to be annoyed or relieved

that her parents were handing out baked goods. Relieved, she decided. If they hadn't shown up, she might have been tempted to grab Nora's brother by the biceps and kiss him, right here on her front lawn. Instead, they ate muffins.

But as soon as Michael and Imani went inside, Asher said, "Follow me."

"What?" Cam said.

"Come on."

She followed him around to the side of the house where there was a tall row of forsythia bushes.

"You didn't text me back," he said.

"I didn't know what to write," she admitted.

"You didn't?"

She shook her head.

"Do you regret what happened?" he said.

Rather than answering, Cam pressed her body up against Asher's and kissed him, right there in the forsythia bushes. She didn't care if she stank. The urge to kiss him was stronger than her stench. They kissed and kissed. When they finally came up for air, she pulled away. "I can't do this."

"Why not?" he said.

"Nora."

"What about her?"

Cam hesitated. She should be with Nora, trying to convince her to go to the hospital, not making out in the forsythia. But Cam couldn't tell Asher what happened on the golf course. It would be the ultimate betrayal. So she decided to give him a different but equally valid explanation for why she couldn't kiss him.

"You're her brother," she said. "I'm her best friend. This"—she waved her hand vaguely in the space between them—"could get complicated."

Asher nodded. "I get it."

"You do?"

"Yeah."

"I just want to avoid..." Cam looked at his lips. The bottom one was fuller than the top. It was as plump and juicy as the inside of a peach. She wanted to bite it. "You know...," she said.

"You know...," he repeated.

"Unnecessary drama."

"Right." He nodded again. "I'll go."

He took one step out of the forsythia, and she yanked him back in. They made out like a couple of maniacs.

Who was Cam kidding? She was fifteen years old, and she lived in the smallest, most boring town on earth. Hiding in broad daylight under a cloak of yellow flowers, *making out with a senior*? Kissing Asher was the most exciting thing that had happened to her since the night of the Manischewitz. Nora's brother or not, she couldn't stop.

NORA

SHE'D LIED. FOR THE FIRST TIME IN HER LIFE, NORA HAD lied to her best friend. Well, technically it wasn't a *lie*—she really hadn't seen any bruises or blood or strange hair—it was more an omission of truth. What she had seen up in Cam's bathroom was a mark, maybe half an inch long, on the skin of her bikini area. Not purple like a bruise. Not red like a cut. Black. She'd tried to forget, but she couldn't stop thinking about it. When her dad dropped her at home after the game so he could go celebrate with the coaches, she went up to her room and locked the door. She took off her clothes again. Cam would have been proud of her this time; she used the camera on her phone so she could see what she was looking at.

Up close, it was pretty obvious. The black mark wasn't a birthmark or a scab or an engorged dog tick clinging to her skin. It was the number 9. (At first Nora had thought it was a lowercase "d" or a "6," but then she realized she was looking at herself upside down and backward, so it was actually a "9.") And she couldn't wash it off. She had gone into the bathroom and tried wiping with a soapy wash-cloth, but the mark wouldn't budge. Which meant it was probably Sharpie.

A black Sharpie 9 on her crotch.

The idea that someone had written it there—had branded her like one of the cows on her grandparents' cattle ranch in Montana—was creepy and embarrassing. Luckily, Nora wouldn't have to worry about anyone see-ing it the next time she put on a bathing suit to swim at the Faber University pool, because after she googled "How to remove Sharpie from skin," she discovered that rubbing alcohol was an effective solvent. It made her eyes water, but it worked. And she made a promise to herself as she hunched over, scrubbing at herself with an alcohol-soaked cotton ball, that she would never tell anyone about the 9. Not Cam, who—thank God—hadn't seen it when she put Nora's underwear back on. Not her parents. No one. Nora would carry on like nothing had happened. *Because, really*, she kept telling herself, *nothing happened. It* could have, *if Adam Xu hadn't shown up when he did, but it* didn't. So what if someone wrote on her? Hadn't something like that hap-pened to Asher once, back in middle school?...Yes, she remembered now. Her brother had gone on the seventh-grade overnight to Rogers conservation center and woken up with a Sharpie mustache on his face. Nora's mother had been horrified, but Asher had just laughed. He'd worn that mustache for days, like it was nothing.

The 9 was nothing.

Besides taking two Tylenol for her headache, Nora spent the rest of Saturday afternoon doing what she always did. She had a million Snaps to go through. Adam Courtmanche and Kevin Hamm and J. J. Fiorelli and that whole crew were always sending her funny TikToks and YouTube videos, so she watched those and responded. **LOL. Thx. LMAO.** She fielded a dozen texts from her friends:

> **Hey grrrrrl what happened last nite?**
> **Why'd u blow us off?**
> **Girl where'd u go?**
> **We lost u after the funnel cake**

Nora didn't remember seeing Anna or Chelsea or Becca at the frat fair, but she texted back anyway: **Went to get a soda and then I couldn't find u guys. Sorry. Super fun night!**

The lie didn't feel bad. It felt good. It felt like she was still herself.

She spent the rest of afternoon reading chapter three of *The Bluest Eye*. Conjugating French verbs. Studying for algebra. Fielding texts from people who needed help. **Totally don't get this. Can u FaceTime?**

At 5:07 PM, a text arrived from Cam. **Did u shower yet? I should have told u not to.**

?, Nora texted back.

Cam texted back: **Physical evidence.**

Physical evidence? What was Cam thinking? Nora wanted to throttle her. Because... what if someone saw those texts?

Someone with a big mouth, like Chelsea Machado? Nora had been friends with Chelsea forever, and Chels had many admirable qualities, but keeping information to herself was not one of them. She was like a BuzzFeed reporter, compelled to share any and all juicy tidbits with the world.

"Nora?" A knock at the door. "Can I come in?"

"Just a sec," Nora said. She sent a quick reply to Cam: **WTF I told you it's over. Delete this!!!**

When she opened the door, there was Maeve. Messy braids, black-framed glasses that were so geeky they were almost cool. Not that coolness ever registered with Maeve. She wore boys' Adidas track pants and oversize T-shirts with Harry Potter zooming across her chest on a broom. If she kept this up, she would be eaten alive in middle school. Nora, as the big sister, should be guiding her, steering her in the right direction, but she hadn't been doing that. She had been too caught up in the ludicrous details of her life, like reading stupid texts from her best friend who should know better than to put those things in writing.

"Dobby's dead."

"What?" Nora looked at her sister and realized her eyes were pink. Her bottom lip was quivering.

"Dobby!" Maeve raised the book in her hand and shook it. "Bellatrix *stabbed* him! To *death*!"

Right. Nora liked reading as much as the next person, but she didn't become attached to the characters the way Maeve did. She didn't buy T-shirts proclaiming her eternal love for them.

"Okay," she said gently. "But didn't you know that was coming? Haven't you read those books a million times?"

Maeve shook her head. "Only the first six. Not *Deathly Hallows*. I was *saving* it, *and* the movie. And now J. K. Rowling has gone and *ruined everything*!"

A part of Nora wanted to laugh. But another part, an inexplicable part, formed a knot in her stomach. Maeve was so young and clueless. There was a brown smudge on her face. Apple butter probably; she ate that crap by the spoonful. The smudge could stay there for a week and Maeve wouldn't know because she never looked in a mirror. Nora thought about herself standing in front of the full-length mirror on the back of Cam's closet door, scrutinizing her butt from ten different angles to make sure she looked okay in her miniskirt, in case there were any cute boys at the frat fair.

She wanted to barf.

She wanted to tell her little sister to *stay just like this forever*, with brooms on her shirts and apple butter on her face.

"What's wrong?" Maeve said.

Nora shook her head.

"Do you even *know* who Dobby *is*?"

Nora shook her head again. "I think I saw one of the movies, but it was a while ago. I don't remember names."

"Oh my *God*," Maeve moaned. "How can you be fifteen and not know anything about Harry Potter?"

Nora shrugged. The knot in her stomach was still there. Her throat ached. "I'm sorry," she said.

Nora's mother was standing at the kitchen counter, cranking out pasta from the pasta maker. Nora's dad was at the Blue Bird, buying a round for his coaches, the way he always did after a big win. Any minute now he would burst through the front door, singing the Faber fight song. Then he would twirl and dip Nora's mother all around the kitchen. *Victory mambo!*

Nora glanced at the chore chart taped to the side of the refrigerator. Before the frat fair, her job had been dinner prep. She remembered chopping red and green peppers while her dad grilled steaks. They'd been out on the deck, and he had been instructing her on marinades. *The key, ladybug, is to enhance the flavor of the meat.* Now she was supposed to set the table, but she couldn't bring herself to do it. She watched her mother drape ribbons of pasta over her arm, seamlessly transferring them into a pot of water on the stove. How did she make everything look so graceful? Her mother did a pirouette away from the stove and gave Nora a startled smile. "Oh, hi, honey. I didn't see you there."

Nora's arm twitched, an awkward wave.

"Are you okay?"

Her mother had asked her the same question earlier, when Nora first got home from the football game and they passed each other on the stairs. Diane had been holding a basket of dirty laundry, which she had shifted to one hip so she could touch the back of her hand to Nora's forehead. She had suspected a fever, but Nora told her she was fine, just tired; she was going up to her room to rest. A blatant lie. She had been going up to her room to pull down her pants and stare at the Sharpie 9.

"You look pale," her mother said now.

"I'm fine," Nora said. Because, really, what was she supposed to say? *No, Mom, I'm not okay? I got roofied last night and barfed steak and peppers and funnel cake all over the golf course? P.S. Someone took off my underwear and wrote on my crotch?*

Nora's mother would curl up in a ball and die from shame. Diane Melchionda was as upstanding as a citizen could get, even more upstanding than Nora's dad. People were always asking her to join their committees. The Faber PTO, Friends of the Faber Public Library, NY Moms Demand Action. You name it, Diane was on it. She didn't exactly look the part—most Faber moms had the same layered-bob haircut and a closet full of cardigans, but Nora's mom had long, windswept hair and a closet full of peasant blouses and floor-length denim skirts. Cam called Diane's look "farm chic." For jewelry, she wore her wedding band and a tasteful gold cross around her neck. For makeup, a little brown mascara and clear lip gloss—that was it. As Nora's dad would say, Diane didn't need to paint her face because she was a "natural stunner."

Nora's parents met in college. Not just any college, either. Faber. Nora had heard the story so many times she could tell it by heart. Her dad, who had just spent eight agonizing days in the student health center, recovering from pneumonia, was walking, slowly and weakly, across the quad toward his fraternity house. Then, suddenly, there was this girl.

She was sitting on a bench.

She was wearing jeans and a checkered shirt.

Her hair was piled on top of her head, held in place with a pencil.

Nora's dad was a senior. He'd seen hundreds of pretty girls on the quad, but he had never seen anyone like Diane. It was fall, and the trees were red and orange and gold. The sun, glinting through the leaves, lit her up like a candle. But that wasn't the only reason he stopped. He stopped because she was crying. And he said, "Excuse me. Would you like a tissue?" That was the famous line, the one that made Nora's mom look up.

Nora's dad offered her a pack of mini Kleenex that the nurse at the student health center had given him, and she said, "Thank you."

And he said, "What's your name?"

And she said, "Diane."

And he said, "I'm Rhett. Do you mind if I sit down?"

And she said, "I don't know."

And he said, "I'm a pretty good listener."

And she said, "Okay."

That was the beginning of the Rhett-and-Diane story: an eighteen-year-old natural stunner from Whitefish, Montana, who had come out east for college because she thought it would be an adventure, but who was actually terribly, horribly homesick, and a hotshot senior, treasurer of his class, president of his fraternity, who happened to be crossing the quad, carrying a pack of mini tissues in his pocket, at the exact moment she burst into tears. Rhett knew, even before Diane started talking, that he was going to marry her.

Nora looked at her mother, standing there in her boho peasant dress. Even if she were fifteen, Diane would never go to the frat fair by herself, let alone wearing a miniskirt. She would never let some random guys drug her root beer, drag her away to the golf course, and pull off her stars-and-stripes underwear. Nora's mom would never *buy* stars-and-stripes underwear. She only wore practical white, the kind that came in a six-pack at Target. She wanted Nora to be just like her, to wear flowy clothes and barely there makeup and a gold cross around her neck. Lately, all they seemed to do was argue, like they had at the Sangertown Mall the week before school started.

> **NORA:** I would like to buy this skirt.
> **HER MOTHER:** I don't think so, honey.
> **NORA:** Why not?
> **HER MOTHER:** Because it barely covers your
>   bottom. I can't have you parading around
>   town in a scrap of denim that leaves nothing
>   to the imagination.
> **NORA:** I won't be *parading around town*. I'll be
>   going to school.

HER MOTHER: Either way, it's not a message you want to send.

NORA: What *message*? That I have legs? Didn't you wear miniskirts when you were fifteen?

HER MOTHER: Actually, I didn't. That was a simpler time.

NORA: How?

HER MOTHER: I grew up on a ranch, not in a college town.

NORA: What does growing up on a *ranch* have do with anything?

HER MOTHER: [Silence.]

NORA: Mom. Come on. Every girl my age wears skirts like this.

HER MOTHER: If every girl your age jumped off a bridge, would you follow?

Sometimes, her mother's cluelessness made her want to scream. Diane was the reason Nora had to bum rides to the mall with Anna Golden's sister, Julie, and use her own babysitting money to buy things. Diane was the reason Nora had to hide miniskirts and electric-blue eyeliner in the back of her closet. Nora's mother didn't want Nora to be Nora. She wanted Nora to be a mini Diane. *Why don't you wear this dress, Nora? Why don't you start a cooking club at the high school, Nora? Why don't you stay home on Friday night and play a board game instead of slutting it up at the frat fair, Nora?*

In the kitchen, Diane was holding up a spoon so Nora

could taste the tomato sauce simmering on the stove. "Gravy," Nora's mother called it, because that's what Nora's dad had called it when he was growing up.

"Tell me if this needs more salt," she said, cupping one hand under the spoon.

Nora shook her head. The smell made her stomach lurch.

Oh God, steak and peppers.

Oh God, funnel cake.

"I'm not hungry," she murmured, taking a step back.

Her mother frowned and lowered the spoon. "You're coming down with something."

Coming down with something? Maybe her mother was right. Maybe Nora had one of those crazy-high fevers she used to get when she was little and she thought her dolls were floating on the ceiling. Was it possible the frat fair had never actually happened? Was it possible she'd imagined the 9?

"Don't ask," Maeve announced, sweeping into the kitchen. She was still wearing the Harry Potter T-shirt, but she had traded in her reading glasses for oversize sunglasses and added a black hat with a veil.

"Well, hello, Jackie Kennedy," Nora's mother said.

"I'm in mourning," Maeve announced, grabbing a roll from a plate on the counter and ripping into it. Even in her grief, she ate like a pig.

"Maeve," Nora's mom said, placing a bowl of salad greens on the table. "Manners, please."

Now Asher was clomping in from the garage, paint-splattered as usual, in a ratty, pit-stained T-shirt and ripped jeans. But did Nora's mom say anything about the "message" he was sending with his outfit? No. She just smiled.

"Hi, sweetheart."

"Hey, Mom. Smells great," Asher said.

"Taste this, would you?" Nora's mother said. She repeated the sauce-and-spoon routine on Nora's brother, who opened his beak like a good baby bird and said, "Mmmm."

"You don't think it needs more salt?"

"No. It's perfect."

God. Could Asher be any more annoying? Lately, when Nora looked at her brother, she wished she had a pair of scissors. She would chop his ponytail right off. Maybe this made her a terrible sister, but wasn't Asher the one who had stood in her doorway just a few weeks before and basically told her to stop dressing like a slut because seniors were starting to notice?

They used to be friends. A long time ago, when they were little, they had built forts in the living room. They had played spit and crazy eights and Monopoly; they had listened to CDs on their dad's ancient boom box; they had made Rice Krispies Treats in a bowl in the microwave. Nora and Asher had sat in the back seat of their mom's old Volvo wagon and made pulling motions with their arms out the window to try to get truckers to honk. They used to make each other laugh.

"Would you dress the salad, sweetheart?" Nora's mother said.

And Asher said, "Sure. Just let me wash up first."

Watching the two of them was like watching a 1980s sitcom, all gee-whiz and lollipops. Asher and Diane never argued. They were always in sync. Okay, maybe once in a while, Nora's mother would try to convince Asher to go to a game with Nora's dad, to spend some "guy time" together. Asher always resisted. He would say something weird that no teenager would ever say, like, "Homework is a jealous mistress," or "My muse is calling." Sometimes, Nora's mother would push harder: "Please go to the game. It would mean the world to him," and Asher would say, "Maybe another time." To Nora, who loved being with her dad—who, in fact, *sought out* time with him—her brother's attitude was baffling.

"What's up with you and Dad?" she had asked Asher once.

"What do you mean?" Asher said.

"I mean, how come you never hang out?" Nora said. "You never do stuff together."

"We are who we are," Asher said. This was the kind of nonanswer that drove Nora nuts. Asher was full of these little bumper stickers. *It is what it is. Live and let live.*

"Come on, Ash," Nora said.

"He's just..." Asher's shoulders rose and fell. "Hard to get along with."

Hard to get along with? Nora had stared at her brother in disbelief. Were they even talking about the same person? Rhett Melchionda was the easiest person in the world to get along with. He was the most outgoing, most generous, most fun person Nora knew.

"Fight, fight, fight, fight, fight on for Faber!"

Nora pivoted her head and saw her dad in real time, marching through the doorway, pumping his fist in the air.

Here we go, she thought.

Now he was swiveling his hips across the kitchen floor. "Victory mambo!"

Nora's mom whooped as Nora's dad grabbed her around the waist and dipped her so low, her hair touched the floor. Her dad had all kinds of moves. When Nora was little, she used to stand on his feet and he would dance, twirling her around the room. It felt like she was flying.

Asher was just jealous, Nora thought. Across the kitchen she could see it in her brother's eyes, in the hard set of his jaw as he tossed the salad. Nora almost felt sorry for him. Because how could anyone look at their dad and not feel a twinge of envy? For his dance moves alone.

"Stop, Rhett," Nora's mother squealed. She was breathless and laughing. "You're making me dizzy."

Nora's dad stopped and waggled his eyebrows. "What can I say? I have that effect on women."

"*Women*, huh?" Nora's mom said. She patted her hair into place, straightened the top of her dress.

"Just one woman," her dad said, bending his neck to kiss her.

"Gross," Maeve said.

Nora didn't love watching her parents make out in the

middle of the kitchen, either. It was awkward. But it was also a good distraction.

Nora needed a good distraction.

When her parents stopped kissing, she set the table. Plates. Cups. Forks to the left. Knives to the right. She took her seat and helped herself to a roll.

Soon, her dad took charge, passing around the pasta and salad. Then he raised his water glass. "A toast. To the Devils' offensive line."

"Congratulations, babe," Nora's mom said, squeezing her dad's hand.

"Thanks, babe."

Everyone clinked glasses.

"Did you call about the roofing guy?" Nora's mom said.

"Not yet," her dad said. "I'll call tomorrow."

"He didn't have to die," Maeve said fiercely, apropos of nothing. "It was bad enough she killed Dumbledore. The least she could have done was save Dobby. I mean… woman, you're the author! You have a *responsibility* to your *readers*!" Maeve plunged her fork into the serving bowl and lifted a dripping pile of pasta up under her veil and into her mouth.

"Maeve," Nora's mother said. "Manners."

Who cares about Dobby? Nora suddenly wanted to shout across the table. *I got* roofied *last night!* But she couldn't do that because her dad would use all his powers to track down the three guys and beat the crap out of them, and then he would get thrown in jail for assault and battery, and then Nora's mother would have a breakdown from the shame of it all, and then—

"I think I might have a girlfriend."

Nora looked up. "What?" She was picturing her dad in an orange jumpsuit, her mother crying in a courtroom.

"I think I might have a girlfriend," Asher repeated.

Nora stared at him. Asher had a girlfriend? *Asher.* Her ponytailed, perpetually paint-splattered brother had a *girlfriend.* Nora's brain scrambled to process this new information. She wasn't the only person at the table who was surprised. Everyone was staring at him. At least she assumed everyone was staring. She couldn't see Maeve's eyes through the veil and sunglasses.

"You do?" Nora's mom said.

Nora's dad clapped Asher on the shoulder. "Way to go, chief."

"Yeah," Asher said.

"Who?" Nora said.

Asher looked at her. "What?"

Nora said, "Does she have a name?"

Asher hesitated. He took a sip of water, then set his glass back down. "I'd rather not say."

Nora studied her brother across the table. His face was as still and calm as a lake. She felt a surge of irritation. Why would he announce to everyone that he had a girlfriend and then not tell them who she was?

"It's still early," Asher said. "I don't want to jinx it."

"Jinx it?" Nora's dad laughed and clapped him on

the shoulder again. "You'll be fine. You're a Melchionda man."

Asher looked at Nora's dad. "Thanks," he said, his face breaking into a grin.

A *grin*? Asher didn't *grin*. He looked weird, showing all those teeth.

Nora's mother propped her chin on her hand like she was posing for a school photo. "I think that's romantic, Ash. Keep her to yourself for a little while."

"Like Ron and Hermione," Maeve said.

Nora looked around the table at her family and thought, *None of you know anything about anything.*

Bedtime. Teeth brushed. PJs on.

Nora stood in front of her dresser, staring into the mirror.

"I got roofied," she said softly. She watched her mouth form the words, lips stretching wide on the *I* and puckering on the *oo*, like a kiss. "I. Got. Roofied."

Normal girls flipped out when this happened to them, right? They sobbed like soap opera actresses. They pounded the walls of their bedrooms, screaming in righteous outrage. But Nora just stared at her mouth in the mirror and thought about how, when you say a word over and over again, it starts to lose meaning. *Roofied. Rooooof. Eeeeeeed. Rrrrrroof-ied.* When it sounded ridiculous enough, she went to bed.

ASHER

I THINK I MIGHT HAVE A GIRLFRIEND. **THE WORDS HAD JUST** slipped out of his mouth at dinner. Why? Asher had only kissed Cam twice. He'd sent her only three texts. He knew this didn't make her his "girlfriend," not even close, but he'd made the announcement anyway. And announcing it had certainly gotten a reaction. Asher's father had clapped him on the shoulder and said, "Way to go, chief"—a response so rare that Asher had nearly choked on the ice cube he'd been sucking.

Asher was his father's greatest disappointment, though it hadn't started out that way. When Asher was young, even before kindergarten, his father had put him in every youth sports program the town of Faber had to offer. Mini Mite hockey. Tiny Mite football. Future Stars basketball. Junior lax. Rhett had been normal and dad-like at first, maybe a bit more enthusiastic than the other dads, but fine. Then Asher started showing "potential," whatever that meant for a five-year-old. Hand-eye coordination and speed—the hallmarks of a great athlete, his father said—made Asher stand out from the other kids. Basically, Asher could throw and catch and shoot and score. So his father began spending hours with him in the backyard, and out on Taylor Lake when it froze, setting up cones and running drills. His father invited Faber coaches over to the house and said, *Watch this*, as he threw the football, a long bomb across the length of the yard, and Asher made diving catch after diving catch, like a performing seal. Every weekend, his father brought him to the college games, instructing him on the finer points of football and hockey and basketball and lacrosse. *You see that pass, Ash?* he would say. *You see that finesse?* He introduced Asher to all his best players, the superstars. *Shake his hand, Ash. Look him in the eye. That'll be you some day.*

The better Asher got—the more goals and touchdowns and baskets he scored, the more his father instructed him and picked apart his games on the ride home—the more he hated sports. Not just one sport—all sports. Asher developed an allergy to cleats and mouth guards, pucks and balls. He began making up excuses to avoid practicing. He was tired. He had shin splints. He was behind on his homework. But his father had an answer for everything: *Have a PowerBar. Pain is just weakness leaving the body. Do your homework in the car on the way to the field.*

The irony was, Asher's father wasn't even that great of an athlete. Not now, not ever. Everyone assumed that he had been, because he was the AD of a Division I university, but the truth was that Rhett Melchionda had been only a third-string high school quarterback and JV hockey player. He had never been recruited. The only collegiate sport he'd played was club rugby. But Rhett Melchionda did have a gift—this Asher would acknowledge: His father could walk the walk and talk the talk as if he were Tom Brady or Bobby Orr. He was handsome and charming; he drank Budweiser; he bench-pressed 335; he'd been president of his Faber fraternity; he'd won the NCAA Award for Administrative Sportsmanship, not once but twice; he'd held a seat on the Faber town council for the past decade; and he didn't take no for an answer. Rhett Melchionda was convinced of his own greatness—and he accepted no less from the people around him.

The day Asher quit sports, he was twelve years old. He and Nora and their father had been at a Faber football game, and Asher had gotten up to use the bathroom. On his way back from the field house, he wandered under the stands. He had seen other kids running around down there, oblivious to the game, just having fun. When he stepped inside, he saw that it was a treasure trove. He found rocks and bottle caps, pom-poms, coins, chess pieces, Matchbox cars, even a deck of cards. It was better than the beach. He collected everything in an empty popcorn tub, and, when the game ended, he showed Nora and his dad.

"Look at all this stuff I found," he said.

Asher could still see the look on his father's face. It was a WTF look, although he hadn't said WTF. What Rhett had said was, "You missed the fourth quarter to pick up *trash*?"

"It's not trash," Asher said. "I'm going to make something out of this."

"Make something out if it?" His father frowned.

Nora looked confused.

"Yeah," Asher said. He already had a vision. "We have wood glue at home, right?"

His father glanced at his big gold watch. "You have practice in twenty minutes, bud. Your gear's in the car."

"I'm not going to practice," Asher said.

"Of course you are," his father said.

"No." Asher shook his head. "I'm not."

"If you don't go to practice," his father said, "you can't play in the game tomorrow."

"I don't want to play in the game tomorrow," Asher said. "Or any game. I'm done with football. I'm done with hockey, too. And basketball, and lacrosse."

Looking back, he always considered the moment significant. It was the first time in his life that he looked at his father and saw something other than pride in his eyes.

"You don't mean that," Rhett said dismissively.

"Yes," Asher said. "I do."

That wasn't the end of it, of course. There were many more discussions, not just between the two of them. Coaches called the house. They showed up at the front door with milkshakes and pleas, telling Asher how talented he was, how uniquely skilled, one in a million and all that. What could they do to keep him on the team? The answer was always the same: nothing.

"You'll regret being a quitter," his father warned him. "You'll regret it more than anything in your life."

That was the funny thing. Asher hadn't regretted quitting sports. He *still* didn't regret quitting sports. In fact, from the age of twelve on, Asher had taken pleasure in being different from his father in practically every way. Instead of throwing passes into the end zone, he threw paint onto old bedsheets. Instead of playing golf on the weekends, he taught himself to juggle. Instead of cutting his hair short, he grew it long. Instead of eating hamburgers, he ate salad. Instead of driving a souped-up Ford F-150, he rode a bike he'd found at the dump. Instead of wearing a gold Apple watch, he wore a hoop earring. Instead of being gregarious and authoritative, he was reserved and thoughtful, like Ferdinand—the bull from the children's book his mom used to read to him—who chose not to impale people with his horns but rather to sit quietly under the cork tree and smell the flowers.

Did this drive Asher's father up a wall?

Yes.

Did Asher care what Rhett thought of him?

Sometimes. Not often, but sometimes.

There was a time, when Asher was fourteen or so, that he had been home alone, and he went out to the driveway to shoot hoops. He was just curious. Besides gym class, he hadn't picked up a basketball in years. He wanted to know if he still had the touch. Asher stood at the free-throw line and took a practice shot. *Swish.* And another. *Swish.* He didn't know why it came so easily to him. He just locked his eyes on the little red hooks that held the net to the rim, and his body knew what to do. Toes to fingertips, one fluid motion. *Swish.*

At some point while Asher was shooting, his father showed up. He had forgotten something at home—some paperwork for a player—and he stopped at the end of the driveway to watch Asher shoot.

"You've been practicing," Rhett said.

Asher fumbled the ball, startled. "No." He turned to face his father. "Just messing around."

"You've still got it," Rhett said. He held out both hands. "Here."

Asher shrugged, shooting his father a chest pass. "I guess."

"It's not too late." Rhett half smiled as he passed the ball back. "You could try out for the high school team this year. You'd make JV. Maybe even varsity. I could give Coach Blackford a holler."

"Nah," Asher said. He caught the ball, flipped it into the ball holder behind the hoop. "I was just messing around."

"Jesus, Ash." Rhett's whole face changed. "You could play any sport. *Any* sport, and be exceptional. You have God-given athletic talent, and you're pissing it away. For what? Finger painting in the garage?"

If Asher were very honest with himself, he would admit that those words had stung. If Asher were very honest with himself, he would admit that his father clapping him on the shoulder at dinner and saying, "Way to go, chief," had felt good. Asher was used to that kind of encouragement from his mom. She gave it constantly. *Wow, sweetheart. You're so creative, so talented.* But Rhett didn't say those things—not anymore, certainly not about art. He had given up on Asher a long time ago and replaced him with Nora.

Whenever Asher stopped to think about this, it made perfect sense. His sister worshipped their dad. She would go to every game, hang on every word, laugh at every joke. Nora never disagreed with him. She never pushed back. She was like the son their dad had always wanted but didn't get. Asher would be lying if he said this didn't bug him.

He'd asked Nora once, "Why do you go to all those games? Do you actually *like* football?"

And Nora had said, "It's fun being with Dad."

Fun being with Dad? Asher couldn't remember the last time he'd had *fun* with his father. Without sports, there seemed to be nothing between them, no mutual interests. They didn't go to museums or the theater. They didn't play cards or watch movies or discuss current events. They barely spoke at all, except about logistics, like when Asher had to be home on Thursday night to watch Maeve because Asher's mom had her book club and Rhett and Nora were going to the Faber hockey game.

His mom had tried talking to Asher about it. *I know Dad can be tough on you, sweetheart, but it's coming from a good place. It's only because he cares.*

Asher loved his mom. Diane was the kindest, most genuine and supportive person he knew. But she was dead wrong. Rhett didn't care about Asher. Rhett cared about Rhett, and how having an artsy-fartsy son who was pissing away his God-given athletic talent reflected on Rhett.

Maybe, deep down, that was why Asher had blurted out those words at dinner. *I think I might have a girlfriend.* Because he knew his father would approve. God, was that really it? Asher certainly hadn't thought through the consequences.

Who? Nora wanted to know. *Does she have a name?*

Asher had wanted to blurt out everything: *Camille Dodd. No, he hadn't planned on hooking up with her; it just happened. Yes, he knew she was Nora's best friend.* But to say any of those things—to try to explain that Cam hadn't *felt* like Nora's best friend up in Mrs. Tenhope's closet—would have opened a can of worms that Asher wasn't sure he wanted to open. And so, he'd pled the Fifth. He hadn't told anyone in his family how alive and exhilarated kissing Cam had made him feel. He couldn't. Not with Nora shooting one of her penetrating looks across the table. Her *How are we even related?* looks.

So he'd said, "It's still early. I don't want to jinx it."

And then, amazingly, Asher's father had clapped him on the shoulder *again* and said, "Jinx it? You'll be fine. You're a Melchionda man."

Asher must have stared at his father for a full ten seconds. He knew Rhett was riding high, both from the win and from the victory beers, but still, Asher didn't know what to think. *You're a Melchionda man.* Was this sarcasm? No. Rhett wasn't sarcastic by nature. He was a straight shooter—a say-what-you-mean, mean-what-you-say kind of guy.

You're a Melchionda man.

Asher felt his mouth break into a grin. "Thanks," he said. He hated himself a little, but there it was.

CAM

@ashersimages
started following you. 14m

Cam stared at her phone. She'd started following Nora's brother back in seventh grade when she first got Instagram and, like a total lemming, was trying to get as many followers as possible. For three years he had been too busy, or too cool to follow her back. But now...

Cam tapped on Asher's name. Scrolling through his feed, she felt a rush of excitement. Asher and a bunch of other art clubbers standing in front of the mural in senior hall, holding paintbrushes. Asher's bare feet, walking across a canvas. Asher's mouth, wide open, four Atomic FireBalls dissolving onto his tongue. Suddenly, it was obvious. She was hot for him.

Hot!

What if Cam had been attracted to Asher Melchionda her whole life, but she was just now realizing it? How could she be attracted to her best friend's brother? It was not good. Not good at all. Cam knew what she had to do. To preserve her friendship with Nora, to maintain her own moral compass, she had to nip it—whatever *it* was—in the bud.

11:02 PM

CAM
You awake?

ASHER
Yup

CAM
Thanks for the follow

ASHER
You're welcome

CAM
I like your feed

ASHER
Yeah?

CAM
Yeah. Cool pics

ASHER
I like you

Cam hesitated. What did he *mean* by this? She wasn't sure how to respond.

96

ASHER
**I can't stop thinking about you…
kissing you**

Oh my God, she thought. *OhmyGod, ohmyGod, ohmyGod.*

ASHER
Cam?

ASHER
You there?

ASHER
Hey sorry if I'm making you feel weird

Cam's fingers hovered over the phone. She didn't feel *weird*. She felt…

ASHER
**I can completely back off if you're
uncomfortable. Just give the word**

CAM
I like you too

NORA

IT WASN'T THAT SHE WAS BEING A DRAMA QUEEN. IT was that the image of her lifeless, half-naked body was burned on her brain, and the fact that she couldn't unsee it bugged her. Two days after watching the video, Nora woke to the image in her head. All weekend, she had been telling herself that nothing bad had happened—because, really, she was fine—but on Monday morning, she was struck again by the reality of her Friday night.

They'd removed her *underwear*.

They'd branded her, like a *cow*.

Nora used to think that Faber was a safe place, maybe the safest place on earth. But now…what? Was she supposed to start carrying pepper spray? Her family never even locked their front door.

Nora stood in front of her closet, feeling untethered. She yanked a white jean miniskirt out of her hiding place and considered slicing it to shreds with her mom's good sewing scissors. That's how she felt, now, about miniskirts. But no, she would not destroy a perfectly good American

Eagle mini that she'd bought with her own babysitting money, because that is what a drama queen would do, and she was not a drama queen.

Relax, Nora. She had a closet full of clothes that were not revealing. There were plenty of those "classic cuts" that her mother approved of, that Nora had worn basically her whole life. Straight-leg khakis, button-down shirts. Classics were classic!

No one else in the house was up. Normally, Nora liked to wake early to get herself organized for school. But for the past two nights, she hadn't slept. She had laid in bed, stiff-limbed under her comforter, staring up at the black ceiling, listening to herself breathe. She was exhausted, but her brain was so amped, so busy trying not to think, that sleep never came. Tired and wired. That's what she was. Tired, wired, and dressed like a freshman boy.

Nora made herself eat something. In an hour, everyone would be up and her mom would be cooking. Eggs and turkey bacon. Multigrain pancakes. But now, Nora sat alone at the kitchen table, coaxing food into her mouth. One, two, three bites of banana. One, two, three walnuts. Potassium and omega-3s. *Chew and swallow, Nora.* Breakfast was the most important meal of the day!

She brushed her teeth. She scraped her hair into a ponytail. She grabbed her backpack and her field hockey stick from the front hall. If anyone tried to jump her on the way to school, she would slap-shot him in the teeth.

If anyone tried to jump her on the way to school. She couldn't believe she'd just thought that.

Out the front door, onto the sidewalk. The sun was just starting to rise. The air smelled crisp and leafy. The day before, Nora's dad had been outside, raking. There was a huge pile in the middle of the lawn. When Nora was younger, she used to leap, joyfully, into the leaves her dad had raked. She would toss them in the air like confetti. Now, she stared blankly at the pile. She couldn't imagine jumping in it. She couldn't access that impulse. She felt like... she felt like *what*?

She felt like hitting something.

Nora gripped the field hockey stick in her hands. She wanted that feeling she got in a game, every time she took a shot. The crack of the wood. The adrenaline rush.

She knew where to go.

The high school wasn't a real high school. It was just a wing of Faber Central School, grades K through twelve. It sat on a rolling, grassy plot that used to be farmland. Behind the elementary wing, there was a wooden playground that all the adults in town, including Nora's parents, had helped build. It had towers and turrets and a splinter-filled pirate ship that Asher had once dive-bombed off and broken his arm. There were three athletic fields in the back: a football field, a baseball field, and a hybrid soccer / lacrosse / field hockey field that confused everyone with its many spray-painted lines. On a typical school morning, there would be kids everywhere. But not at 6 AM.

Nora made her way to the back of the school, to the equipment shed at the far end of the hybrid field. Unlike the Melchiondas' house, the equipment shed was locked. Nora debated jimmying the lock with a paper clip—she'd learned that trick from Cam—but decided against it. There were always balls in the woods, from overshooting the goal. She used her field hockey stick to dig through the brush. She found three. They weren't hockey balls; they were baseballs, moldy and waterlogged. But so what? She lined them up on the shooting circle and fired.

Bam. Bam. Bam.

—⁓—

Walking across the blacktop to the locker room, sweat beads shimmying down her spine and into the waistband of her khakis, Nora heard footsteps behind her, the *clank-clank* of metal on asphalt. For a second, she froze. She clenched her field hockey stick. It felt solid in her hands, like a sword. She whipped around, the weight of her backpack shifting and throwing her, momentarily, off-balance.

It was Adam Courtmanche, bowlegged in football cleats, a gray "FCS Athletics" T-shirt clinging wetly to his chest. He reached out a hand to steady her.

Nora pulled away, air catching in her throat.

"Hey," he said. "Didn't mean to scare you."

She lowered her stick, exhaled. It was only Adam. "Hey."

He smiled. His fingers raked damp, blond hair off his forehead. "Team have an early practice?"

Nora's ponytail swung, back and forth. "Just me."

"Same," he said, walking alongside her. "I was running suicides."

"Not my favorite," she said.

"No." He laughed, that perfect guy laugh, deep and rumbly. "Mine neither. But I need to get faster."

Nora knew what Adam meant. One time freshman year, they'd sat astride the monkey bars on a Friday night and he'd told her about how his older brother, Trey, had won the Faber-2-Faber Scholar Athlete Award, and how he wanted to win it, too. Because, obviously, who wouldn't want a full ride to Faber and a spot on a Division I team—but also, because the Courtmanches didn't have money for college. Adam's dad was on disability after the construction accident back when they were in seventh grade, and the medical bills were a gift that kept on giving. Adam wanted that Faber-2-Faber scholarship. He *needed* that Faber-2-Faber scholarship. But FCS only awarded one a year, so Adam had to be stronger, faster, hungrier than anyone in their grade.

"Hey," he said. "You go to the game on Saturday?"

"Yeah," she said.

"You see Trey score?"

She racked her brain. The Faber–Colgate game was a blur of helmets and jerseys. "Uh-huh," she said. It wasn't a lie. She had been there the whole time; she must have seen Trey score.

"That's gonna be me in three years," Adam said.

"Trey two-point-oh?"

"Better," he said. "Just wait. You'll be begging for my autograph."

"Oh, really," she said.

"Guaranteed."

Nora smiled. She couldn't help herself. Adam Court-manche was one of the cockiest people she knew, but she could never hold that against him. Nora had known Adam almost as long as she'd known Cam. He'd peed in the sandbox next to her in kindergarten. He'd walked her to the nurse in fifth grade when she got hit in the face with a dodgeball. He'd kissed her, for the first time, by the flagpole in front of the school—and another twenty times after that.

They walked together to the gym entrance, but the door was locked.

"Shit," Adam said. "I guess we have to wait."

"Yeah," Nora said.

"You wanna...take a load off?"

She realized, the way he was smiling at her, that she was a hot mess. A sweat ball. She could feel her ponytail stuck to the side of her neck.

"Yeah, okay," she said.

She should probably feel embarrassed. When she took off her backpack to join Adam on one of the benches in front of the school, she could feel her button-down shirt plastered against her skin. But so what? At least she was *dressed*. At least her underwear wasn't hanging from a *flagstick*.

No. Nonononono. She was not going to think about that. She was going to sit on the bench in front of the school, and chug from her water bottle, and listen to Adam Courtmanche talk about what a superstar he was going to be in three years.

"Hey," Adam said. He was smiling again.

"What?" Nora said.

He leaned in, kissing her lightly on the lips.

She pulled away.

"What's wrong?" he said.

"Nothing," she said, heart thudding in her chest. "I'm just gross right now."

"You're not gross."

"I am. I'm all sweaty."

"So am I," he said. "We can be sweaty together." He leaned in again, his breath hot on her neck.

This time, Nora pushed him away. "No."

"Fine," he said, holding up both hands. "Geez. I thought I was irresistible to you."

He was, normally. Adam was gorgeous. Every time he kissed her, he made her feel all melty inside. But now... how to explain? Thinking about his tongue darting inside her mouth made Nora think about other tongues darting inside her mouth, other hands touching her body. And thinking about that made her feel like she wasn't sitting on the bench. She was floating in the air, higher than the flagpole, looking down on herself.

Adam whistled through his teeth.

"What?" Nora said.

He jutted his chin toward the parking lot.

Nora watched as Ms. Sauce shut the door of her shiny red Prius and began walking toward the school. *Special Sauce.* That's what all the sophomore boys called her because, even though she had to be almost Nora's mom's age, they thought she was hot. They made excuses to go to the counseling office to talk to her. They made jokes behind her back about what kind of sauce she would taste like—Honey mustard? Chipotle?—and how they'd like to spread her on a sandwich. Nora hated when they said things like that, but whenever she told those guys to be more respectful, they told her to lighten up.

Ms. Sauce was wearing a dress. A short, tight dress with multicolored splotches all over it, and a pair of kelly-green knee-high boots. Nora thought she looked pretty—like a tropical bird—the opposite of most of the teachers in this school, who dressed to blend in with the walls.

"Happy Monday!" She smiled at Nora and Adam as she waved her teacher badge in front of the sensor to open the door.

"Happy Monday," they repeated.

"Damn," Adam murmured, watching Ms. Sauce walk inside.

"Are you checking out her *butt*?" Nora said.

"Yeah."

"She's a *teacher*."

"Technically," Adam said, "she's a guidance counselor. And you don't dress like that without knowing exactly what message you're sending. She wants it bad."

She wants it bad.

A thought rose, acid-like, in the back of Nora's throat. What if, at some point after drinking the root beer from the red cup, she had, in fact, *wanted it bad*? In her conscious state, Nora didn't know, exactly, what wanting sex was supposed to feel like. With Adam, she always kept her clothes on. But who knew what she had been like on Friday night? What if she'd flirted with those guys? What if Asher was right, and she'd given them an invitation—

"Hellooo."

"Hm."

"Earth to Nora."

Nora saw the hand waving in front of her face and blinked.

"You want to hang out this weekend?" Adam said.

"Hang out," she repeated.

"Yeah. I know it's only Monday, but, hey, I'm a planner."

Nora shook her head. She willed her brain to reset.

"Come on." Adam reached out and squeezed her thigh. "We always have fun when we hang out."

Did they? Have fun? Looking at his hand, feeling his

fingers pressed into her skin, she couldn't process his words. All she could feel was that strange, floaty sensation.

"I can't," she said, shifting her body on the bench so they were no longer touching.

"Why not?" he said.

"I have plans."

Adam frowned, looking both confused and irritated. "The whole weekend?"

Nora nodded. She reached for her backpack, trying to remember how to act normal. "Pretty much," she said. "Yeah."

~

"What happened to you?" Cam said. She was waiting outside American lit, holding a Big Gulp.

"Sorry." Nora shook her head. "I forgot."

"You forgot."

"Yeah."

Cam gave her a look that said, *We've only been meeting at 7-Eleven every Monday since sixth grade.*

"I woke up early," Nora explained, "so I decided to shoot on goal for a while."

Cam raised an eyebrow. "Since when do you work out before school?"

Nora shrugged.

"You hate getting sweaty in the morning."

She shrugged again.

"Okay." Cam nodded slowly. "Are you thirsty?"

"Yeah," Nora said.

Cam handed her the Big Gulp. "Blue Shock–Wild Cherry combo. Pace yourself."

Nora took a sip. She felt the icy sweetness coat the back of her throat. "Thanks."

"You're welcome," Cam said. Then, dropping her voice an octave: "Are you okay?"

"Yeah."

Cam took a step closer. Nora could smell her Juicy Fruit. "Did you, you know . . . *remember anything?*"

Nora shook her head.

The bell rang.

She responded automatically, the way her body was programmed, by turning and walking into the classroom.

ADAM XU

CAMILLE HAD ASKED HIM TO KEEP THE VIDEO ON THE
cloud, so he had kept it there. He hadn't watched the foot-
age since Saturday morning when she and Nora were in
his room. He wasn't sure, exactly, what he was supposed
to do.

Then, during study hall on Monday, Camille walked
into the library. Adam was sitting at one of the back study
carrels, doing his Spanish homework, when he heard his
name.

He looked up, and there was Camille.

"We need to talk," she said. "Come outside with me."

In the hallway, she reached out and touched his arm.
Adam wasn't used to girls touching him. Despite his best
effort to stay cool, he felt his cheeks flush.

"They were going to rape her, Adam. You know it, and
I know it."

Adam closed his eyes and felt the full weight of those
words crash over him.

"We need to find them," Camille said.

"Find them?" he repeated.

"Yeah. Nora's in complete denial. It's like she thinks if she pretends nothing happened, then they did nothing wrong. Which is bullshit. It's still on your computer, right?"

He nodded.

"Will you help me?"

He didn't know what she meant by "help."

"We can't let them get away with it," Camille said.

She's braver than I am, Adam thought. Or stupider.

"You saved her. I can barely stand to think about it. If you hadn't shown up when you did..." Her voice trailed off.

He nodded. She didn't need to say more.

"Help me find out who they are," she said. "Please. Before they do it to someone else."

To fight Camille Dodd on this would be pointless, he realized. He had heard her argue with Mr. Kavanaugh, the gym teacher, once, over the number of push-ups in the presidential fitness test. The girl was relentless.

"Okay," he said.

"Really?" she said.

"Yes."

~~

He was "bright," "gifted," a "rapid learner." He was all the things teachers had been saying about him since kindergarten. At the Shuang Wen School, Adam and a group of his classmates had taken part in an after-school STEM club. That was a good thing, because they'd gotten to do cool projects.

They'd calculated the cost to construct the St. Louis Arch. They'd built organ models. They'd blown up balloons with baking soda and vinegar. Then he moved to Faber, where there was no one like him. Once a week in fourth grade, Mrs. Osternek pulled Adam Xu—and only Adam Xu—out of class to do prealgebra worksheets. That was a bad thing. Because suddenly, he was different from everyone else. Suddenly, he was the nerdy, studious Asian kid. Okay, yeah, so he was good at school, but what if he didn't want to be a mathematician or a scientist? What if someday he wanted to be a record producer? Or an actor? Or an entrepreneur?

The problem with being smart, besides the obvious typecasting, was that everyone assumed things that weren't necessarily true. If you were good at science, you must also know the entire mythology and history of the DC and Marvel universes and have a closetful of Star Wars action figures. If you were good at math, you must also be the next Mark Zuckerberg.

Adam Xu was not the next Mark Zuckerberg.

Besides the basics of uploading a video and saving it to the cloud, he knew little about computer technology. It just wasn't his area of interest. So when Camille suggested that he "increase the resolution," to "find identifying clues" and then "track down suspicious social media accounts," he was at a loss. Honestly, she sounded more qualified for the job than he was.

But then he thought about Nora—the twitch of her lips when he told her he'd yelled at those guys on the golf course—and he wondered, if he did something even more dramatic, could he make her smile for real? He wanted that. He wanted to be the reason Nora Melchionda's face lit up.

"Okay," he told Cam. "Yes."

After school, the house was quiet. The only sound came from the kitchen, his mother clanging pots around on the stove. His father was still at the university. Monday was his late night.

Adam's fingers hovered above the keyboard on his desk. He opened Google, took a deep breath, and typed: "How do I increase the resolution of my video?"

It was a multistep process. First he had to download and install some video-enhancing software. Then he had to select a codec—whatever that was—and choose a higher resolution to re-encode the original video. After it was re-encoded, he had to convert the new file. He had no idea, really, what he was doing—he was just following instructions—but finally, the upgraded video was ready to play.

Adam plugged his earbuds into the computer and angled the screen sideways, just in case his mother decided to walk in. He couldn't imagine having to explain to her what he was watching. He didn't ever want her to know. Better for her to think that he spent every night of his life asleep in his bed for ten uninterrupted hours.

Hahahahahahaha!

Adam leaned forward in his chair and squinted. At first, the video quality didn't seem any better. The camera bounced and shook, bounced and shook. Then it stilled. He could see the bodies on the screen just as he had seen them before. He clicked the track pad, freezing the image. He was about to zoom in when his phone pinged. He thought it might be Camille, but it wasn't. It was the JV baseball team's GroupMe.

Dudes, u have to see this.

CAM

CAM HADN'T CHECKED HER MESSAGES SINCE BEFORE cross-country practice. Her battery was low, so she'd powered off her phone and left it in her locker while she ran. Now, when she powered it back on, her phone started buzzing and dinging like an arcade game.

The first text was from Adam Xu: **Did you just get sent what I just got sent?** Which confused her.

And then.

Then there were a bunch of texts from sophomore girls—Becca Bomberg and Anna Golden and Chelsea Machado—all sent within the last twenty minutes.

> **Omg did you see sup faber?**
> **Check out sup faber. WTF?**
> **Please tell me this is photoshopped**

Cam stood in the middle of the locker room, staring at her phone. What the hell was happening? she wondered. And then she tapped to enlarge the image.

NORA

WHILE SHE WAS RUNNING SUICIDES, SHE DIDN'T HAVE TO think about anything. Not red cups, or golf courses, or Sharpies, or Adam Xu, or Adam Courtmanche, or Cam, or anyone. She didn't have to answer anyone's questions. *Nora, will you pass with me? Did you do the chem homework? What are you wearing to homecoming?* All she had to do was listen for Coach Schepps's whistle telling her where to go.

Shooting line, back.

Twenty-five-yard line, back.

Center line, back.

Nora's throat ached and her quad muscles burned, but she didn't care. When the whistle blew—one long blast to signal the end of practice—she wanted to keep going. She would have, but there was Cam, sprinting across the field, waving both arms like a lunatic. What was Cam doing? She looked like an air-traffic controller chasing down a plane.

"Nor." She sounded breathless. Cam never sounded breathless. Cam had the lung capacity of a blue whale.

"What?" Nora said. She grabbed one ankle, pulling it to her butt for a stretch.

"I need to—talk to you."

"You are talking to me."

Cam clamped a hand on Nora's arm, pulling her off the field, away from the other girls. "I'm assuming—you haven't—seen this." Cam paused to cough.

"Seen what?"

"This is—huge."

"What?"

Cam took a deep breath. She bent over her phone, tapping and scrolling. "There's a post on Sup Faber."

Nora shook her head. Whatever it was, she didn't want to see it. Sup Faber—@supfaber—was an Instagram page where kids at FCS posted embarrassing photos of one another and left comments using anonymous handles. Freshman year, there had been a photo of Anna hooking up with a senior in the wrestling room during the homecoming dance. Anna had never found out who posted it, but she remembered the hashtags; they all did: #froshslut #jailbaitbang #homecumming #classicfaber.

"Look," Cam said.

"No, thanks," Nora said.

"You have to, Nor," Cam said. "I'm sorry, but you do."

Before she could turn away, Cam's phone was in her face. And there was a photo—of herself. She recognized the clothes right away. Black scoop neck, jean miniskirt. Her back was to the camera, and her head was resting on someone's shoulder—a big blond guy in a gray hoodie. His arm was wrapped around her waist. A dark-haired guy in a red shirt was on the other side of her, laughing. His hand was on her butt, lifting her skirt.

Oh God. OhGodohGodohGod.

Nora's heart sped up, faster than when she was running suicides. His hand was on her *butt*. He was *laughing*. A third guy, a redhead, was holding open a car door. Had she gotten in? Was that how she'd ended up on the golf course?

"Nor."

Nora shook her head. She had no memory of a car. None. Her hands were starting to shake.

"Look at his shirt."

She blinked at Cam.

"Look at the guy's shirt. The red shirt."

Nora looked down at the red shirt. Slowly, the image came into focus. The skull and crossbones. The three letters: AΨB. Her brain clicked. "That's my dad's fraternity."

"No," Cam said. "That's evidence."

PART
TWO

NORA

SHE HAD HEARD STORIES ABOUT THE FRATERNITIES. OF course she had. No one could live in Faber and not hear about the frat boys and their drinking, their theme parties, their kooky initiations. One time when Nora was in middle school, a bunch of pledges from Alpha Psi Beta had appeared on the Melchiondas' front porch. They were handcuffed together and dressed as cheerleaders. When Nora's dad came to the door, they serenaded him with the Faber fight song. Nora remembered feeling embarrassed, not just for them, but for herself. They were wearing lipstick and bras. Their legs were so hairy. But then she saw her dad laughing and singing along with them. He told Nora that pledging was an important part of the Greek experience; it bonded the brothers for life. That's what he called them, his "brothers," like they were a part of the family.

Sometimes the frat boys would do funny things—like stealing all the town's Christmas decorations and building a giant elf on the quad, or hitching porta potties to the backs of pickup trucks and spinning doughnuts around the hybrid field behind the high school—and then the town would complain to the university. Sometimes, if there was a formal report and the frat boys were Nora's dad's players, they would ask him to support them at a disciplinary hearing, which he was always happy to do. Because he understood this better than anyone: being a Division I athlete was a pressure cooker. Building elves and spinning doughnuts was just harmless fun—a way for players to blow off steam. These were good guys, Nora's dad always said. Stand-up guys. He would give the shirt off his back to any one of them.

Which was why Nora had never given much thought to the other things she'd heard. Like when Anna's sister, Julie, warned Nora and her friends, "Don't walk by Greek Row alone at night." There was a story about a girl who'd graduated from FCS years ago, Julie said. One night after an orchestra concert, she had been walking past the frats on her way home. Some of the brothers from Alpha Psi had been sitting outside on lawn chairs. They'd called her over. The next thing she knew, she woke up on the quad in a Faber football jersey with a Blue Devil tattoo on her boob. Nora didn't know if this was true or just an urban legend, but everyone seemed to have heard some version of the same story: The girl didn't wake up on the quad; she woke up on the town green. She wasn't wearing a football jersey; she was wearing a toga. The tattoo wasn't a Blue Devil; it was the Alpha Psi insignia.

In any case, "Don't be frat bait" was a running joke among the girls at Faber Central School, and that was how Nora had always thought of it—as a joke. Because the fraternities did so many good and charitable things. Because her dad was the AD and he stood behind his guys. Because every time Nora and her dad were on campus and they ran into one of his athletes, one of the Alpha Psis or Sigma Taus, her dad always put his arm around her and said, "Do you see this beautiful girl? This is my daughter. You will look out for her like she is your own sister. Do you understand?"

And they always said, "Yes, sir."

Because this mere fact had made Nora feel invincible her whole life. And by feeling invincible she had gone to the frat fair alone, wearing a miniskirt, and she hadn't thought a thing about it. Not a single thing.

Until now.

Now there was an Instagram photo of her and three frat brothers, and one of them had his hand on her ass—the AD's daughter's ass. Was it possible they hadn't recognized her? Nora looked so different now than she had a year ago. She was practically a new person.

@yobitchez33
Looks like little miss perfect isn't so perfect @noramelchionda

@ncrdiblhulk7
FCS girls gone wild #classicfaber

@ctch_me_if_u_can
Hey nora show me ur tits

@invisigirl2019
#slut #fratbait #classicfaber

@ragin_cajin69
Who knew melchionda's sister was a frat ho?

Nora powered off her phone. She stuffed it in her backpack.

～

"I've been hearing things," Asher said on Monday night. He was standing in Nora's doorway, holding a half-eaten banana. "Tell me they're not true."

"They're not true," Nora said.

～

"Don't listen to the noise," Cam said on Tuesday morning. She was waiting at Nora's locker, holding a bag of green apple Airheads. "Eat these and hold your head high today. You have done nothing wrong.

"Not now," Cam said to anyone in the hall who tried to approach Nora. "Give her space. She'll talk when she's ready."

Amazingly, Nora made it through the morning. She didn't look at her phone. She pretended all the *Hey girl*s and *Hi Nora*s and eyes watching her were business as usual. She pretended to be completely engrossed by her classes—taking notes on symbolism in *The Bluest Eye*, parallel lines and transversals, atoms.

And then everything blew up.

She was in the cafeteria, sitting at her usual table with Cam and Anna and Chelsea and Becca, because Cam had insisted on it. *You will not hide in a corner! You will sit among your people!*

Nora's people.

She could feel it, the sideways glances from all around the caf. She was trying to look like she was eating, but the idea of food was making her sick, so really she was dunking Tater Tots in ketchup and sliding them around on her plate. Conversation at the table was strained. Chelsea was talking about open-toed sandals. Becca said her rice cakes were stale. Why were rice cakes called *cakes*, Anna wanted to know, if they tasted like Styrofoam?

Finally, Nora couldn't take it anymore. "Okay," she said. "I know you all saw the post—"

"Oh my God," Chelsea said. "I'm so glad you said something. I've *totally* been there with the slut shaming."

And Anna said, "Remember that post of me last year, from homecoming? Jailbait bang?"

"Yeah," Nora said. "But this isn't what it looks like."

The questions came hard and fast, like pelting rain. What happened? Who were those guys? Were they her dad's players? Was this over the weekend? Was this at the frat fair? Who posted the picture? Whose car was that?

Nora looked at Cam, expecting her to shut down the

questions like a good press secretary. But Cam said, "She doesn't remember."

Nora stared at Cam in disbelief.

"You were drunk?" Becca said.

"No," Nora said sharply. "I was not drunk."

"She was roofied," Cam said.

"OhmyGod." Anna's hand flew to her mouth.

"Seriously?" Chelsea said.

And Anna said, "It's just like that story about the girl and the Alpha Psis. Where she woke up on the quad in a football jersey and she couldn't remember anything."

"It was a toga," Chelsea said.

"Maybe it was two different girls," Anna said.

"Nor," Becca said softly. "Jesus. Are you okay?"

But Nora couldn't respond. She was angrier than she had ever been in her life. Her blood was hot lava. *Judas!* she thought. *Benedict Arnold!* She wanted to throw her lemon seltzer in Cam's face. She wanted to crumple her napkin into a ball and shove it into Cam's mouth.

But a hand was on her shoulder. "Nora?"

She whipped around. There was Ms. Sauce in her tight blue pencil skirt and scarf with the little FCS badgers all over it, tied in a jaunty bow around her neck like she was an old-timey stewardess.

"Would you come with me, please? You may bring your lunch if you'd like."

Nora was so angry, she couldn't even look at Cam. She

couldn't look at any of them. She just stood up, pushed her chair in, and followed Ms. Sauce to the guidance office.

—✓—

"Sit wherever you'd like," Ms. Sauce said to Nora. She gestured to a worn leather couch and three overstuffed armchairs the color of eggplant. Nora remembered these chairs. Freshman year, she had been nominated to join peer advocates, and she had been called into the guidance office to receive the good news. Then, Ms. Sauce had been all smiles and congratulations, talking about what an honor it was for Nora to have earned the respect of both classmates and teachers, what a testament to her integrity and emotional intelligence.

Nora sank into the leather couch. Ms. Sauce repositioned one of the eggplant chairs and sat down to face her. She looked at Nora with a furrowed brow.

"I've asked you here, not because you're in trouble, but because I've been hearing some things around school."

Things. What *things*? Nora willed herself to stay calm, to give nothing away.

"It could be just gossip," Ms. Sauce said, "but in my experience, most gossip contains at least a seed of truth. So I wanted to check in.... How are you doing?"

"Fine, thank you. And you?" The words came out automatically, just the way Nora's mother had taught her. She directed her attention to the stain on the wall above

Ms. Sauce's right shoulder. It looked like a rabbit. No...it looked like a duck. It reminded Nora of the optical illusion she had seen once, at the children's museum in Utica. Rabbit...duck...rabbit...duck.

"Nora?"

She shifted her gaze to Ms. Sauce's eyebrows. They were so dark and thick. They looked like two fuzzy brown caterpillars inching along her forehead.

"I want you to know that this room is a safe space. A confidential space. Everything you share in here...about friends, boys, whatever...stays between us....Is there anything you'd like to tell me?"

Nora might have told Ms. Sauce to mind her own business, but it was easier just to sit there, numb to questions, numb to Cam's blabbermouth, numb to @supfaber and all the comments and hashtags.

"Nora?"

She shook her head. "No, thank you." She let the silence stretch out between them like a blanket.

"I grew up in Faber," Ms. Sauce said finally. "Did you know that? I went to FCS, just like you."

Nora's head bobbed without her permission. Even though her brain was numb, she remembered freshman year, when some of the boys had found a photo of Ms. Sauce in one of the old Faber yearbooks in the library. *Josephine Sauce.* Sometimes, when they weren't calling her "Special Sauce," they called her "Jo-so-fine."

"Back then," Ms. Sauce continued, "we didn't have

smartphones and social media to spread rumors. We had bathroom stalls and Sharpies."

Sharpies? Nora's stomach clenched. Did Ms. Sauce know about the 9? No. No possible way.

"Nora." Ms. Sauce leaned forward in her eggplant chair, resting her elbows on her knees. A stack of silver bangle bracelets slid down her arm. "There is nothing you could say right now that would shock me or make me think less of you. Believe me. I know what it's like to be a girl in this town."

Nora let out something between an "oh" and an "uh-huh." It was such a weird comment. *I know what it's like to be a girl in this town.*

Ms. Sauce looked at her, head cocked.

Nora lowered her eyes to her sneakers. In eighth grade, she and Cam had bought the same ones, white Converse low-tops that they'd relaced with blue and gold ribbons for Faber spirit. Nora still wore hers, but Cam never did anymore. She said she'd outgrown them.

"When I was thirteen," Ms. Sauce said, "I remember the boys at school had a contest. They called it butt tag."

Nora looked up.

"The object of the game was to grab as many girls' backsides as possible, in the hall, in the cafeteria, in the bus line. This went on for days. They kept a running tally, names of the girls and the number of times they'd been grabbed. Finally, my friends and I went to the principal. Not Mr. Hicks, but the principal at the time, Mr. Fisher. And do you know what he said?"

Nora shook her head.

"He said we should be *flattered*. He said it was the boys' way of showing they *liked us*."

Nora said nothing. She wondered if Ms. Sauce knew that butt tag was an enduring Faber middle school tradition. Except, when Nora was in seventh grade, the boys called it ass tag and posted their tallies on Insta.

"I promise you, Nora," Ms. Sauce said, " 'you should be flattered' is not the response I would give if a student came to me with a similar complaint."

A similar complaint. Nora thought about the frat boy's hand on her ass. She thought about strange hands taking off her underwear, writing on her skin while she was passed out.

"Nora—"

The bell rang.

Like a trained monkey, Nora stood up.

"You don't have to go," Ms. Sauce said. "I can write you a pass."

"I have a chem quiz," she blurted. It wasn't exactly a lie. Mr. Bond gave a pop quiz almost every day.

"Okay…" Ms. Sauce stood up, too. "But come back any time you feel like talking. My door is always open."

Nora's head bobbed, a buoy on the wide-open ocean.

～

At the end of the day, Adam Courtmanche was waiting at her locker. "What the hell?" He was holding up his phone.

Nora didn't even have to look.

"Explain this to me," he said.

"I can't," she said.

"You can't."

"No." She opened her locker.

"You can't explain to me why there's a picture of you and three Alpha Psis and one of them has his hand on your ass."

"No," Nora said. She took out her backpack.

"You realize that's Trey's fraternity. Those are my brother's brothers."

She turned to look at him.

"Do you know how humiliating this is for me? I thought we had something. I thought we were…" He laughed, a short *ha*. "I guess the joke's on me."

Nora opened her mouth.

"Save it," he said. "Don't even bother." And he walked away.

——

Nora, hey, are you okay?

Do you want to talk?

Everyone's worried about you.

Do you still want to be on the homecoming committee?

Hey, Nora. You too good for us high school guys now? You only have foursomes with frat boys?

It was photoshopped, right? Nora?

Oh my God, Nora, I know this is the last thing you want to think about right now, but did you do the French homework?

CAM

"IS SHE OKAY?" ASHER ASKED CAM.

They were standing in the hall outside Nora's locked bedroom, listening to music blasting from Nora's speakers. It was her Fierce Femmes playlist, circa eighth grade. Cam should know; they'd made it together. Dua Lipa. P!nk. Beyoncé. *When you hurt me, you hurt yourself...*

"She'll be fine," Cam told Asher. "She's processing."

Cam knew Nora was mad at her; of course she did. Nora had been ignoring Cam all afternoon, ever since Cam told the truth to their friends at lunch. Nora wanted to live in denial about what happened, which had been understandable at first. But the fact was, they didn't just have Adam Xu's grainy video, they had a photo that clearly showed Nora, the three guys, and the incriminating AΨB T-shirt. Now they could actually *do* something.

"Should we knock?" Asher said.

Cam shook her head. "She'll come out when she's ready."

Under the hall light, Asher's hair glowed. With his

pirate earring and his "Eat Local" T-shirt and his bare feet, which were long and bony and pale and reminded Cam of some prehistoric bird, he was the last person on earth she would expect to be attracted to. And yet...

"Is it true?" Asher said.

"What?" Cam said.

"What people are saying about her?"

Cam shook her head. "Don't believe everything you hear."

"I don't," Asher said. "Usually."

"Did you see the post?" Cam said.

"Yeah. I wish I hadn't, but yeah."

"Did you ask her about it?"

"I tried, last night. She wouldn't talk to me."

"Well," Cam said carefully. It was one thing for her to speak the truth to their closest friends. It was another for her to speak the truth to Nora's brother, who Cam had been secretly hooking up with behind Nora's back. "She's a private person."

When you diss me, you diss yourself...

The music was so loud, Cam could feel the bass in her chest. She was sure Asher could feel it, too. He was just standing there, looking at her. One step closer, and his breath would be on her face. One tip of the chin, and his mouth would be on hers. His hands, gripping the back of her head. His lips, his tongue. It took Cam a few seconds to come to her senses, to realize the music had stopped. Thank God they hadn't started kissing, because the door flew open, and there was Nora. She wasn't crying, exactly, but her eyes were pink.

"Great," she said, looking from Cam to Asher and back to Cam. "You told *him*, too?"

"Told me what?" Asher said.

"I didn't tell him," Cam said. "I came to check on you. I looked for you after cross-country, but Anna said you never went to practice."

Nora's face twisted. "You think I'm going to *field hockey* after you told everyone?"

"Okay," Asher said, holding up both hands. "Sounds like you two need some time to talk."

"No," Nora said. "We don't."

But Asher backed away anyway, into his own room.

"Look," Cam said to Nora. "I get that you're mad, but I didn't tell *everyone*. I told our three closest friends, who care about you."

"Right. And they're so good at keeping secrets."

"They won't tell anyone," Cam said. "Not about this. They actually agree with me, that we have an opportunity. No, we have a *responsibility*—"

"*We?*" Nora's eyebrows shot up.

"Yes."

"This has nothing to do with you!"

"It does, actually," Cam said. "I live in this town, too. It could have happened to me. Or Anna. Or Chelsea—"

"But it didn't!" Nora's voice was strangled. "It happened to *me*!"

"Yes. And it could happen again, to any one of us."

"You don't even know if it's true. You just did some stupid Google search!"

"You want to know if it's true?" Cam said. "Give me a piece of your hair."

"What?"

"I'm serious. We'll get it tested. One of my uncles can do a tox screen."

"Jesus, Cam!" Nora cried. "You told your *uncles*?"

"No," Cam said. "But I did some research on Rohypnol. We have ninety days until—"

"Wait," Asher said sharply, stepping out of his bedroom. He looked from Cam to Nora and back again. "Rohypnol? The *date-rape drug*?"

Nora let out a burble of hysterical laughter. "Oh my God! This just keeps getting better!"

Asher looked like he'd been punched. "Nora. Did those guys rape you?"

"No, but—" Nora was suddenly laughing so hard, she could barely get the words out. "They—branded me—like a cow!"

NORA

SHE COULDN'T BELIEVE SHE'D SAID IT OUT LOUD. *THEY branded me, like a cow!* The words sounded ridiculous to her ears. She couldn't stop laughing. She was laughing so hard, tears were spurting out her eyes. Was she having a mental breakdown?

But no, she wasn't. The words *were* ridiculous.

"What?" Asher said. He looked stunned.

"What do you mean," Cam said slowly, "they *branded you*?"

Nora's laugh sputtered to a stop. What was she supposed to say now? That she was just kidding? That she was losing her marbles? It wasn't a big deal, she reminded herself. It was just a number. But to tell Cam—God, that would be a disaster. Cam could turn a drop of water into a tsunami. It was her superpower. Like that time in eighth grade when Anna wore a camisole to school and was cited for a dress code violation. Principal Hicks made her put on a sweatshirt because he could see her bra straps. Anna wasn't that upset—she didn't get suspended or anything—but Cam was so fired up she convinced half the girls in the middle school to wear camisoles to school the next day and stage a protest outside the principal's office, chanting, "Yes, we wear bras! Deal with it, bruhs!" Luckily, Nora had woken up with strep throat that morning, so—even though she *had* been planning to show her solidarity for Anna—she was saved. She never had to mortify herself by chanting about her bra in front of Principal Hicks.

"Never mind," she said now. She should have known better than to tell Cam she'd been branded. She should have kept her mouth shut.

"Nora."

Nora did not appreciate Cam's tone, or the hand on her arm. "Forget it," she said. "Forget I said anything."

"*Nora.*" Cam was very, very serious now.

"Tell us," Asher said. "Please."

Nora glanced at her brother. He looked genuinely upset, which threw her. Nothing fazed Asher.

"It's not a big deal," she said. And she told them. It wasn't a *brand*. It wasn't like they'd used a hot poker and seared the number into her flesh forever. It was just Sharpie, and she'd gotten it off fine.

"Jesus Christ," Asher murmured.

And Cam said, "Please tell me you took a picture."

"No, Camille," Nora said. "I did not take a picture."

Asher shook his head, over and over, like he was trying to shake something off. "I need the whole story, from the beginning."

There was no way Nora was telling her brother the whole story from the beginning. She had spent the past four days trying to forget it ever happened. She didn't have the bandwidth.

"Nor," Cam said.

Nora looked at her.

Cam raised her eyebrows.

"Fine," Nora said. "You want to tell him, tell him."

ASHER

THEY ROOFIED HIS SISTER.

They took off her clothes, and they wrote on her body, and they hung her underwear on a stick like some kind of trophy.

Asher was shocked. He was—how else could he describe it?—stupefied. He looked at Nora, and he had no words.

"Go ahead," she said.

"What?"

"Say, 'I told you so.'"

Asher shook his head.

"You tried to tell me. *When you wear things that are too short*"—she shook her finger and made her voice deep—"*guys think it's an invitation.*"

"You said that to her?" Cam stared at Asher.

He shook his head. "I said *some* guys. I didn't mean—"

"No," Nora said. "You were right. And I didn't listen, and I should have, and now..." She raised both hands in the air and let them flop to her sides. "It's all I can fucking think about."

Asher wasn't sure what shocked him more—that his sister thought he was right, or that she'd just used the word "fucking."

NORA

"LISTEN TO ME," CAM SAID FIERCELY. SHE GRABBED NORA by the shoulders. "What those guys did to you had nothing to do with what you were wearing. *Nothing.* Even if you'd been wearing a string bikini, you did not ask for it. You did not invite it. You did not deserve it. Do you hear me?"

Nora felt a stinging sensation behind her eyeballs, which surprised her. "Yes," she said.

"Do *you* hear me?" Cam stuck her finger in Asher's chest.

"I hear you," Asher said.

"Good. When does your dad get home?"

"What?" Nora said.

"Your dad. He can ID the guys in the photo. The frat boys are all athletes, right?"

"No," Asher said.

"There are two sports fraternities," Nora explained. "Alpha Psi recruits football, hockey, and lacrosse. Sigma Tau recruits soccer, basketball, and baseball. The rest are open."

"Okay, whatever," Cam said. "The shirt's an Alpha Psi shirt. If that's one of the sports frats, your dad should know who they are."

"No," Nora said.

"Why not? They must be his players."

"Yes, but I'm not telling him."

"Are you kidding?" Cam said. "You have to tell him."

Nora stared at Cam. "You have *met* my dad, right? You know how protective he is."

"Yes," Cam said.

"I'm his *daughter*."

"Exactly."

"He would die."

"He would not *die*, Nora. He would be outraged. He would do everything in his power to take those guys down."

"No." Nora shook her head. "I'm not getting him mixed up in something like this."

Asher gave Nora a funny look.

"Something like what?" Cam said.

"Some"—Nora waved a hand in the air—"sex-related scandal—attempted—whatever. It would look bad for him. And the university."

"Are you serious?" Asher said.

"What?" Nora said.

"Dad deals with this kind of thing all the time."

"No, he doesn't."

"Well, not with his own kid," Asher said, "but come on. Remember that hockey player? Peyton something?"

"Peyton Mallory?"

"Yeah. He sexually assaulted a sorority girl at a frat party."

"What?" Nora said. "No, he didn't."

"She filed a report with the university saying he did. There was a disciplinary hearing."

"I don't believe you," Nora said.

"Why would I make that up?"

"I don't know. But I never heard about it."

"Neither did I," Cam said. "Was it in the news?"

Asher shook his head. "I don't think so."

"Why not?" Nora said.

"Because the guy got off. He was never expelled. He was never even suspended from the team."

"How?" Cam said.

"What?" Asher said.

"How did he get off?"

"I don't know," Asher said. "But Dad was his adviser at the hearing. Just like he was for that football player from LA. The quarterback. A girl said he raped her behind the Iron Jug. He said it was consensual. Dad helped him get off."

"What are you talking about?" Nora was getting annoyed now. "How do you know all this?"

"Come on, Nora," Asher said. "You've heard Dad talk on the phone. His voice only has one volume. Open your ears."

"You shouldn't eavesdrop," Nora said. "It's rude."

"Why was none of this in the news?" Cam said.

"Good question," Asher said.

"Why did you never say anything about this before?" Nora said.

Asher looked at her. "Because you wouldn't have believed me."

"Did you tell *Mom*?"

He shook his head. "No. I only talked to Dad."

"And what did he say?"

"He told me I misunderstood the situation."

"Well, then," Nora said, "you misunderstood the situation. Because he would never do something like that."

CAM

ON HER WAY HOME FROM NORA'S, CAM TEXTED ADAM XU.

Sorry I went dark
Assuming you saw the post but there's more
U free?
Come over, 37 hickory ct

ADAM XU

HE WAS STANDING ON THE DODDS' FRONT PORCH BECAUSE Camille had asked him to come over. It had been a whole day since the baseball team GroupMe sent him that photo. He couldn't stop thinking about it. The AΨB shirt. That guy's hand lifting up Nora's skirt. The way her knees buckled and her head flopped to the side, like she could barely stand.

He wanted to know that she was okay, but the only class they had together was American lit. This morning, she had not been sitting at her usual spot in the front row, where she got called on constantly. At first, Adam had thought she might be absent—maybe because of the photo and what people were saying—but then he spotted her in the back-right corner of the room, near the door. She was wearing a gray hooded sweatshirt that looked two sizes too big, and her hair was loose around her face. Camille was, as always, in the seat beside Nora. At that moment, Adam wanted to switch places with Camille. He just wanted to know that Nora was okay. While Mrs. Bell was taking attendance and writing on the board, Nora was talking to Camille. Adam was in the same row, but he was eight seats over, so he couldn't hear their conversation. Nora's head was ducked. Trying to gauge her emotional state from his vantage point was impossible. He could see only a sliver of her face.

That's when Adam had an idea, one he'd never had the nerve to contemplate before. For as long as he could remember, he had sat in the same spot in every class: back row, left corner. He felt comfortable there. The only exception had been freshman biology, when Mr. Mahoney assigned not only seats but also lab partners, and Adam had been forced to endure an entire year of sitting front and center with Kevin Hamm. Kevin Hamm, linebacker on the football team, who enjoyed stabbing their frog specimen repeatedly with the scalpel and flinging its eyeballs across the room like lacrosse balls. Incredibly, Mr. Mahoney never seemed to notice. Or, if he did, he looked the other way. Maybe because he couldn't be bothered to discipline Kevin, or maybe because he was one of the football coaches. In any case, Adam preferred, in every class where he had a choice, to sit in the back-left corner of the room. He believed in self-preservation. Why invite scrutiny if he could avoid it?

But then he thought about what a good person Nora was—the kind of person who would reach out her hand and pull the new kid up when he was splayed on the cafeteria floor, covered in milk. He thought about Nora on the golf course, just lying there, and he decided he had to do it. Right then. Before he chickened out. Adam stood up, pivoted, and walked seven paces to the right. He pulled out the chair beside Camille. He sat down, one desk over from Nora. He cleared his throat, and said, "Hey."

"Hey," Camille said, like it was no big deal.

Nora did not look happy. Her eyebrows bunched together, like his presence either confused or annoyed her.

"Hey," he said again. *Again*, like a moron. Like he'd forgotten he already said hey.

Luckily, Mrs. Bell saved him. "Okay, critical readers," she said, "assuming you have all done your homework and finished reading *The Bluest Eye*...Why do you think this work of American literature has been challenged and banned so often?"

Adam opened his notebook. He tried to concentrate on the question. He wondered what Nora was thinking. He wondered what she was feeling. When Sarah Hecht raised her hand and said, "Because it's sexually perverted?" he wondered if those words made Nora blush the way they made him blush, or if she felt any eyes shift, ever so slightly, to the back-right corner of the room, or if she heard someone in the class mutter, through ventriloquist lips, the word "slut."

"Because," Camille said loudly, "it makes people uncomfortable."

Camille had heard it, Adam could tell. She was sitting straight up in her seat, and her chin was raised.

"Because," she said, "it makes them face things they don't want to admit about themselves, like how racist they are."

Adam thought about that as he stood on the Dodds' front porch—what a good friend Camille was. How she'd heard the word "slut" in the middle of class and immediately deflected attention away from Nora and onto herself. Camille had stepped right out in front of the firing squad.

"Are you calling us *racists*?" Sarah Hecht had said.

And Camille had said, "If the shoe fits."

Adam still couldn't believe she'd done that.

"Hey there," she said, opening the door wide. Her hair was piled on top of her head, wrapped in a strip of khaki-colored fabric.

"Hey," he said.

He had never been inside the Dodds' house before. He had never sat at Camille's kitchen table or tried one of her smoothies.

"The emerald goddess," Camille called it, as she dropped a bunch of kale into a blender. "My specialty."

Adam had told her not to go to any trouble; he was happy with water. But Camille had insisted. And so Adam was now holding a glass of green sludge.

"Trust me," she said. "It looks disgusting but tastes amazing."

He lifted the glass and braced himself for the first sip. It tasted like grass. A grass smoothie. It made him think of the golf course.

He swallowed and set the glass down. "I enhanced the video."

"Yeah?" Camille said. She took a sip of her smoothie. "And?"

"It's still not great," he said, "but if you zoom in, you can see the shirt now. The skull and crossbones, and the Greek letters, just like in the photo."

He'd recognized the AΨB right away. He had seen those letters before, on his many walks through the Faber campus. Across from the tree-lined row of sorority houses that his mother cleaned each week was the row of fraternity houses—a half dozen redbrick, Southern-style mansions set against a backdrop of less spectacular academic buildings. AΨB was one of those frats.

"Alpha Psi Beta," Adam said to Camille. "I searched it on the Faber University website. They have a Facebook page."

"A *Facebook page*?" Camille said.

"Yeah."

"Who under the age of forty has a Facebook page?"

He shrugged. "I don't know, but they do."

Adam had tried to look up the names of the likers and followers, but he couldn't, not without a Facebook account. So he'd made one up. It was just a generic profile, no photos, with the name "Adolf von Baeyer II," since "Adolf von Baeyer" was already taken.

Adolf von Baeyer II.

The Adam Xu of three days ago would never have done that. The Adam Xu of three days ago would not have created a fake social media account—named after the German chemist who had discovered the blue dye used to color jeans—for the sole purpose of uncovering a list of 2,124 names, any of which could belong to three college guys big enough to beat the crap out of him.

This was the new Adam Xu, who would not think about getting the crap beaten out of him. Because he was on a mission.

"Do you want to see it?" he asked.

"What?" Camille said.

"Their Facebook page."

"Not right now," she said. "There's something else. Nora tried to downplay it, but..."

"What?" he said.

"They wrote on her with Sharpie. A number nine, on her bikini line."

He stared at Camille. *"What?"*

"Yeah. She saw it the next morning, but she didn't tell me until today. I wish she'd taken a picture, but—"

"Wait—" he said.

"What?"

Adam was remembering something. Gym class, last week. Monday. Or was it Wednesday?... Either way, he had been in the locker room, changing his clothes for badminton because, although no one really worked up a sweat batting a shuttlecock over a volleyball net, a quarter of their grade was "appropriate attire," so everyone was changing. The locker room was packed. Adam was pulling on his shorts when Kevin Hamm materialized, hair flopping in his eyes, mouth smirking the way it always did. Kevin Hamm hadn't changed a bit since fourth grade, when Adam forgot to touch first base and Kevin let everyone know it. If anything, he was worse now. Since freshman year, Kevin had developed a bloated, crushing ego. Adam knew enough about the social hierarchy of high school to understand that, in the eyes of his classmates, Kevin's talent on the football field and his friendship with Adam Courtmanche outweighed his pea-size brain and cystic acne. Whether people actually liked him was irrelevant. When Kevin Hamm spoke, they listened. In the locker room, when Kevin stood on a bench, held up his phone, and said, "Who wants to see some prime FU titties?" they looked up. Adam had looked up, too, before he could even process what Kevin had said. And of course, because Kevin had the newest iPhone with the biggest, brightest screen, the photo was right there in HD for everyone to gawk at. A pair of breasts barely contained by a lacy white bra, with something black scrawled between them.

"What is that?" Adam heard someone ask. The whole locker room was crowded around Kevin, jostling for a closer look.

"It looks like a four," someone else said.

And Kevin smirked. "More like thirty-four double D, am I right, fellas?"

Adam had looked away, embarrassed. He'd tried not to

think about it, someone writing a number on that girl. He *hadn't* thought about it, until now.

"There's a four," he said.

"What?" Camille said.

"There's a girl with a number four written on her chest," he said. "I saw it last week." He told her the story.

"Oh my God," Camille said. She grabbed his arm. "Where did Kevin get that picture?"

Adam shook his head. "I don't know. He just said it was an FU girl."

Camille's eyes widened. "Holy shit, Adam."

"Yeah."

"You know what this means, right?"

"What?"

"It means there are more numbers. It means..." She threw back her emerald goddess like it was a shot of whiskey and banged the glass down on the table. "We need to go black ops."

"Black ops," he repeated.

"Yeah."

"I don't...know what that is."

Camille raised her eyebrows. "Covert operations? Employing measures not generally authorized?"

"Oh." He nodded. "Uh-huh. So..."

"So we need to find some hard evidence. The video and the photo are a start, but they don't actually prove a crime was committed. I asked Nora for a piece of her hair so we could get a tox screen, but she didn't go for it, so..." Camille must have read the look on his face, because she grimaced. "Sorry. You must think I'm a whack job. My dad's whole family is in law enforcement. You should spend a Thanksgiving with us. My uncles spend the entire time trying to one-up each other with their knowledge of forensics. It's like a *Bones* convention."

"Oh," he said. Then, "What's a bones convention?"

"You've never seen *Bones*?"

He shook his head.

"It's this old crime show," Camille said. "It's good. But *anyway*, Nora doesn't want to get her dad involved, and I need to respect that, even though he's the perfect person to get involved because he's the AD. But I have to do something. I *have* to."

"You're a good friend," Adam said.

"I don't know about that."

"You are," he said. "In class this morning, I know you heard it, when someone called her a slut. And you changed the subject right away. You took the hot seat."

Camille laughed, a short *ha*. "Yeah, calling the class a bunch of racists went over real well."

"I think it did, actually," he said. "I think people listened to you. And now, you're trying to find those guys."

Camille frowned. "I owe her. I should have been there."

"You *were* there," he said. "You came when I texted you."

"No. I should have been with her the whole night. We

had a stupid argument, and I went to Kyle's party without her, and she went to the frat fair alone, and now..." Camille's voice trailed off.

"It wasn't your fault," he said.

"Yeah, well. I'm also hooking up with her brother behind her back."

"*What?*"

"Yeah."

"*Why?*"

"I don't know. Pheromones?"

"No," he said. "Why behind her back? Why don't you tell her?"

"I don't know. It's..." Camille hesitated.

He waited.

"She'd hate the idea of us together."

"Why?" he said.

"You're an only child, right?"

"Yeah."

Camille said, "Me too. I don't really get the sibling-rivalry thing, but I've spent half my life at Nora's house, so I can tell you this. She and Asher are *completely* different. She's a daddy's girl, he's a mama's boy, and...what's that expression? 'Never the twain shall meet'?"

He said, "It's also a movie."

"What?"

"*Never the Twain Shall Meet.* I used to watch all these old movies with my grandmother, when she was still alive. It's pretty racy. I think you'd like it."

Camille gave Adam a look that said, *You are more interesting than I had originally thought.*

"Fee fi fo fum!" a voice called out.

"Oh God." Camille rolled her eyes. "My dad's home. He's doing his giant impression. He's been doing it since I was three."

Adam smiled. He couldn't help himself.

"Hey," Camille said. "You want to stay for dinner?"

He looked at her.

"My dad's a total cheeseball, but he makes a mean sloppy joe."

"Okay," he said. "Yeah."

Sloppy joes at Camille Dodd's house. It was a first.

NORA

ON TUESDAY NIGHT, MAEVE CAME TO NORA'S ROOM IN her pajamas. "Tatum said that Ella D said that her brother, Ethan, said there's a pervy picture of you going around school."

Maeve, eleven-year-old *Maeve*, just said the words "pervy picture of you." Nora was horrified. She wanted to hand her little sister a graham cracker and a juice box and send her back to bed.

"Is it true?" Maeve demanded. "Did you have sex with three frat boys?"

Nora opened her mouth, then closed it.

"What? I'm in fifth grade. Sheesh, I know about *sex*."

Maeve knew about sex, and the pervy picture of Nora and the three guys from the golf course was traveling around Faber Central School like the stomach bug. Probably parents were hearing about it, too. Their Facebook pages must be lighting up—#classicfaber. Probably the next time Nora's mother went to Price Chopper, some PTO officers would come up to her in the organic produce section and say, in hushed tones, "You really need to get your slutty daughter under control, Diane."

"Well?" Maeve said.

Nora felt like if she tried to speak, something crazy would come out, like hysterical laughter or screaming. Maybe smoke. But she had to tell Maeve something, or Maeve would never leave the doorway.

"No," Nora said. "It's not true."

"I knew it!" Her sister raised a fist in the air. "You're like Harry Potter in *The Chamber of Secrets* when everyone assumes he's the heir of Slytherin just because he can speak parseltongue, but just because he *can* doesn't mean he *is*. Right?"

"Um," Nora said.

"I figured." Maeve nodded, shoving her glasses higher up on her nose. "That's all I needed to know."

"Hi, honey," Nora's mother said. She was home from her PTO meeting and standing in Nora's doorway. Everyone, it seemed, felt compelled to stand in Nora's doorway and make pronouncements she did not want to hear.

Even if you'd been wearing a string bikini, you did not ask for it.

Dad deals with this kind of thing all the time.

I'm in fifth grade. Sheesh, I know about sex.

"How was your day?" her mother said.

How was her day? Nora felt her lips twitch.

"What's funny?" her mom said.

What was funny? Nothing was "funny," except for her mother standing in the doorway in her peasant blouse, asking how Nora's day was, like everything was normal. Even if Nora told her dad what happened to her, even if he used all his AD power and found out who the guys were and got them kicked out of Faber—no one would forget the vision of that frat boy's hand on her ass. That wasn't how high school worked.

"Sweetheart?"

Nora shook her head. Her mom was so naive. It wasn't her fault; it was because she had grown up on a ranch in Montana, where the biggest problem a girl ever faced was whether to feed the chickens or milk the cows first.

"My day was fine," Nora said.

~~~

She loved her dad more than anyone in the world. She *trusted* her dad more than anyone in the world. So why was she hovering outside his office door at ten thirty at night, like some kind of undercover spy?

This was all Asher's fault. *Open your ears, Nora,* he'd said, in that patronizing way of his. Well, here she was, ears wide open, and she didn't hear a thing.

"Dad?" She knocked. "Are you working?"

And he said, "Just got off a call. Come on in."

Nora's dad's office was her favorite room in the house. It smelled like Murphy's Oil and aftershave. It wasn't fancy—just a wood-paneled cube with a matching oak desk and swivel chair that her mom had picked up at a yard sale, refinished, and given to her dad for his birthday. There was an oak shelf lined with sports books—*Gridiron Genius, Hockey Tough, The Boys of Winter*—and a blue shag rug. But Nora's favorite part was the stadium seats. There were three of them—numbers 56, 57, and 58—salvaged from the original Faber football stadium after a rich alum donated a boatload of money to tear it down and build a whole new field named after himself. Nora's dad had anchored the three seats to the floor. Whenever Nora, Asher, and Maeve came into his office, they always had a place to sit.

"Hey there, ladybug." Her dad smiled at her from behind his desk. He was wearing his "Faber Hockey" hat, the one with the silly pom-pom.

"Hey," she said, rubbing the bronze number plaque—57—with her thumb. She had sat in that seat more times than she could count. When she was little, she would sit there while her dad was doing paperwork and pretend she was doing paperwork, too. She would flip through his old Faber University yearbook, *The Mirror*, and look at the pictures. "What was your call about?"

"Oh, you know," her dad said. "Just putting out fires."

Putting out fires. That's what he called it whenever he had to fix something for a player. Trouble with coaches. Grades. Injuries.

"What kind of fires?" Nora asked.

"Oh, the usual," her dad said. He was clicking a ball-point pen with his thumb. *Clickclick. Clickclick.*

"Dad?" she said.

"Yeah, bug?" *Clickclick. Clickclick.*

"Did Peyton Mallory sexually assault a sorority girl at a frat party?"

The clicking stopped. Her dad cocked his head to the side. "Where did you hear that?"

"Oh, you know," she said, pulling at a stray thread on her bathrobe. "Just around school."

In the silence that followed, Nora could feel her heart thump. She wondered if she had made a horrible mistake.

"No," her dad said finally. "Peyton Mallory did *not* sexually assault a sorority girl at a frat party, but a sorority girl did accuse him of assaulting her."

"Oh." Nora nodded. "Okay…What about Jason Mann?" He was the quarterback from LA Asher had been talking about. She'd just remembered his name.

"What *about* Jason Mann?" Nora's dad looked at her evenly.

"Did he rape a girl behind the Iron Jug?"

"No. But a girl did accuse him of raping her."

"Oh," Nora said. She pulled on the stray thread again, pulled and pulled until it snapped. "How do you know?"

"How do I know what?"

"Who's telling the truth?"

Nora's dad stood up. He walked around his desk and across the shag rug. His shoes were off. He was wearing the socks Maeve had given him for Christmas, with the maroon and gold stripes for Gryffindor. Nora would never have remembered this, except that Maeve had made such a big deal about those socks. She'd written a whole speech about the qualities of a Gryffindor. *Nerve, chivalry, daring.*

"I know my athletes," her dad said. He sat in Maeve's seat—number 58. "That's how I know who's telling the truth. I've been doing this job a long time, and I've seen a lot of things, and I always come back to the same place. I know my athletes. I know each and every one of them. And I trust their word. If they look me in the eye and tell me they didn't do something, they didn't do it."

"Oh." Nora nodded.

"Here's the thing about D-One athletes, ladybug. They're just like the pros. Everyone wants a piece. The media, the public. These girls...they want to get close to the players. They'll do anything, really. Dress up for them, go to their parties, have too many drinks, and...well, events can be misinterpreted in the light of day. Feelings get hurt. Do you understand what I'm saying?"

Yes, Nora understood what he was saying. Her brain was moving faster than her mouth could respond. "What if...the girl's your athlete?"

Her dad blinked at her.

"What if the girl...accusing the boy...is your athlete, too?"

Silence for a second. Then he shook his head. "That would never happen."

"It wouldn't?"

"Not on my watch," he said. "No. That's not the kind of program we run."

Nora looked at her dad. The pom-pom on his hat. The stubble on his chin. When she was little, she used to watch him shave. She would stand beside him at the bathroom sink, and he would blow up his cheeks like a chipmunk, and he would squirt Barbasol onto her nose, and she would crack up.

Nora shook her head. This didn't make sense. None of this made sense.

"Ladybug?"

She willed herself to look him in the eye.

Her dad glanced at the wall over her head. "It's almost eleven. I'd love to keep talking, but you have school tomorrow."

Almost eleven.

School tomorrow.

"Right," she said. "I should go to bed."

They both stood up.

"Hey." Her dad reached out his hand. He ruffled her hair. "I love you, kiddo."

"I love you, too," she said.

━━ ✍ ━━

In the morning, Asher offered Nora a ride. "Mom's letting me take the minivan. I have a bunch of canvases I need to drop off at the art room."

Nora looked at her mother.

Diane looked back at her and smiled. She was wearing rubber gloves and one of Nora's dad's old "Faber University Athletic Dept." T-shirts with a hole in the armpit, which meant it was a cleaning day. "You look nice," Diane said.

Nora was wearing the least slutty thing she owned. It was a blue flowered dress with a high neck, straight off the prairie. Her mother had made her wear it to her cousin Jane's first Holy Communion the year before, along with some tall, lace-up boots that felt like fifty-pound weights on her legs.

"Thank you," Nora said. She had woken up early. She had braided her hair and eaten half a piece of toast. She had made her bed and brushed her teeth.

"You ready?" Asher jangled the car keys.

"Yes," Nora said. She grabbed her field hockey stick and slung her backpack over one shoulder.

She was playing her part. She wouldn't think about her dad, because he was at work. Earlier, he had swung through the kitchen on his way out the door. "Hey, ladybug. Men's soccer is playing Bucknell, Friday under the lights. You in?"

"I don't know," she'd said. "Maybe."

"*Maybe?*" Her dad had smiled at her. "Faber men's soccer hasn't beaten Bucknell since 1987. You don't want to miss this game. Trust me."

Trust me.

No, sorry, no, she couldn't think about that right now.

She couldn't think about Faber men's soccer or anything else. She had to go to school.

———

"So," Asher said, as he backed the minivan out of the driveway. "How are you feeling about...everything?"

"Fine," she said.

"Nor," he said, glancing over at her. "Come on. You can be real with me."

"I can be *real* with you?"

"Yes."

"Okay," she said. "Why did you tell me all that stuff about Dad's players?"

"What stuff?"

Nora shifted in her seat so she could face her brother. "You *know* what stuff."

"Because it's factual and relevant information," he said.

"*Because it's factual and relevant information?*" Why couldn't he talk like a normal person? Why did he always have to sound so superior?

"Yes," Asher said. "What those frat boys did to you was not okay, Nora. And it was not an isolated incident. Neither was Peyton Mallory, or...whatever his name is... that quarterback. It happens every year. Everyone in town knows it. The university knows it. *Dad* knows it. And they all look the other way because they're athletes."

Nora shook her head. "It's not like that. I talked to Dad last night. It's not...there's no way he would..."

"There's no way he'd what? Try to protect his players? Try to protect the university?"

"I didn't say that," she snapped. "Don't twist my words. Just…stop talking, okay? Stop talking to me about Dad. You don't even know him."

"Oh, *I* don't know him?" Asher said. "*You* don't know him."

Nora glared at her brother. "If all that's true, then why did you never call him on it?"

"I told you, I tried. You think he listened to me? He said he didn't do anything wrong."

"Then he didn't do anything wrong."

"Wow." Asher shook his head. "He really has you brainwashed."

"I am not *brainwashed*."

"You know, people who are brainwashed never actually know they're brainwashed until someone points out—"

"Shut up!" Nora shifted her body as far away from her brother as possible. She stared out the window. "Just… shut your piehole."

Nora rested her head against the window and stared at the passing scene, the *whipwhipwhip* of houses and trees and gray, gray sky. She wasn't mad at Asher—not really. If she were completely honest, she would admit that she was embarrassed for herself. She had known that her dad fixed things for players—a disagreement with a coach here, a failing grade there—but those were small things, inconsequential things.

Nora's own cluelessness mocked her.

I know my athletes.

Events can be misinterpreted.

Feelings get hurt.

Her dad's words bounced around in her head like pinballs. She thought, *My feelings aren't* hurt. She thought, *I woke up on a golf course with a Sharpie 9 on my crotch.* She thought, *I didn't misinterpret anything.*

A few minutes later, Asher pulled into the senior lot and he turned off the engine and he gathered up his canvases. Nora opened the door and stepped out. She grabbed her field hockey stick. She slung her backpack over one shoulder. And then, like effing Little Red Riding Hood, she went skipping out merrily into the woods where all the wolves were waiting.

CAM

MAYBE SHE SHOULD HAVE TOLD NORA WHAT SHE AND
Adam Xu were planning, but she knew that if she did, Nora
would shut the whole thing down. Nora wanted to protect herself, and Cam could understand that. Nora wanted
to protect her dad, and Cam could understand that, too.
She loved Nora. And she loved Mr. M—of course she did,
everyone did. But still. Finding the three guys from the golf
course was about more than just Nora and her dad. It was
about justice. It was about what those three guys could do
to other girls, if Cam and Adam Xu didn't stop them.

At least that's what she told herself.

Adam Xu wasn't sold on the idea at first. "My parents
work at Faber," he said to Cam, as they sat on the couch
in her living room on Wednesday afternoon. "If they keep
working there while I'm in college, I go tuition-free. I can't
do anything to jeopardize that."

Adam Xu told Cam a bunch of stuff she'd never known
about him. How his mother had grown up in China. How
she had been studying at the culinary institute in Shanghai

when she met his father, a graduate student at Columbia who had been traveling around Asia as part of his dissertation research. How his mother had moved to New York to marry his father and gotten pregnant right away, so she never finished school. College was important to her, he told Cam. She wanted to give him every opportunity to succeed in this country.

"I get it," Cam told Adam Xu. "My mom grew up in Haiti. She was the first person in her family to graduate from high school, let alone become a doctor."

"Really?" he said.

"Yeah," Cam said.

She promised him she wouldn't do anything to hurt his chances of going to Faber tuition-free. "Trust me," she said. "No one will even know who we are."

When she first came up with the idea, Cam had considered, briefly, making it a social experiment. If she and Adam Xu presented themselves as they really were—supercool, biracial feminist who ran like the freaking wind, and supersmart, baseball-bat-wielding, Chinese American Clark Kent—how would the Alpha Psi Beta brotherhood respond to them? Would they respond at all? Then Cam reminded herself that to convince three frat boys to reveal their crimes, she and Adam Xu would need to do everything right, which meant presenting themselves as generically as possible.

Katie J, a Colgate student (@katiegategrrrl), and Matt R, a high school junior from Michigan (@mattyrtouchdown24)—who "yo, just started talking to recruiters about playing FU football" and was "juiced to pledge APB"—were about as exciting as two slices of Wonder Bread. For Katie J's and Matt R's profile pics, Cam scrolled through her photo gallery and chose the two most Abercrombie-looking counselors from her track-and-field camp in Florida two summers ago. To protect the innocent, she and Adam Xu zoomed in and cropped artfully. Half a lip-glossy smile and tan shoulder; one blue eye, square jaw, and bare, manly chest. They created Gmail accounts and linked them to Katie J's and Matt R's shiny new Instagram accounts.

"Wait—" Adam Xu said, "is this even legal?"

He was sitting on the couch, watching her take and post a bunch of random photos from around the house. Katie J wanted to be an interior designer (**#designgirl #throwpillows #ineedthisinpink!**). Matt R loved bananas (**#potassium #mybodyisatemple #touchdownbreakfast**).

"Creating fake profiles isn't illegal," Cam told Adam Xu. It wasn't; she'd checked. Neither was clicking on those shady "100 free followers" links. Anna had been the queen of fake followers back when they first got phones.

"What's illegal," Cam said, reaching over Adam Xu's shoulder to click another link, "is sexual assault."

He nodded. "Right."

It was cute how Adam Xu knew nothing about social media. When Cam asked why he didn't have Snapchat or Insta, he shrugged and said his mom had strong opinions; she thought social media turned teenagers into narcissistic zombies, and she paid for his phone, so...

Cam had to teach him *everything*. How to post a pic, how to hashtag, how to follow professional athletes and Hollywood celebrities, how to take a list of 2,124 followers from the "Alpha Psi Beta—Faber University" Facebook page and find their Instagram handles so Katie J and Matt R could follow them like normal teenagers.

"They have a lot of followers," Adam Xu said.

"They don't, actually," Cam said. "Serena Williams has thirteen million."

"Thirteen *million*?" Adam Xu gaped at her.

She laughed. "Welcome to Insta." Then she said, "Don't worry about every name. We don't need the alumni, just the students."

"How will I know the difference?" he said.

"Just look at their profiles," Cam said. "You'll know. I'll help you in a sec. I just want to get us some food."

While she was in the kitchen, digging snacks out of the cupboard, her phone pinged. She thought it might be Nora, ready to be friends again, but then she looked at the screen.

ASHER
Are you still mad?

Was Cam still mad? She had been pissed, when she heard what he'd said to Nora. *When you wear things that are too short, guys think it's an invitation?* Jesus. Cam knew people who thought that way, but she had always assumed Asher was different. She needed him to be different.

171

She texted back:

> **Myth #1, it's a victim's fault if she wears revealing clothes**
>
> ASHER
> **Yeah I know, but she's my sister. I don't like hearing guys talking about hooking up with her**
>
> CAM
> **Ur discomfort is on you, not her**

She could see his text bubble, the three little dots that meant he was responding, but she cut him off: **Words matter Ash. Check ur misogyny**

> ASHER
> **I hear you & I'm sorry. It won't happen again, in this lifetime or in any parallel lifetime**

Cam had to smile at this. *In any parallel lifetime.* It was such a classic Asher thing to say. She wondered, briefly, what he would think about what she and Adam Xu were planning. He would probably think she'd lost her mind, but she wasn't going to let that stop her right now.

Cam carried a bag of pita chips and a tub of hummus into the living room. She sat on the couch beside Adam Xu.

"Okay," she said. "Let's do this thing."

NORA

AFTER SCHOOL ON WEDNESDAY, SHE HAD A HOME game, and, even though it wasn't sunny out, she put eye black on her face. She double-knotted her cleats. She put in her mouth guard and sneered at herself in front of the mirror.

The rain started about ten minutes into the game. It matched Nora's mood. All day, she had been trying to ignore people, like the three senior girls who passed her in the hall, laughing at her dress.

Nice frock, Mary Ingalls.

Which one was she again?

The one who went blind, remember? The fire?

Nora wouldn't have minded being blind today. She wouldn't have minded being deaf, either. She knew her friends were trying to be supportive, but it came out wrong. Like Chelsea, at lunch: *Why are you covering yourself up like that? It's like letting those guys win.* And Anna: *You shouldn't be hiding, Nor. You have such a great body. I wish I had* half *your body.*

Anna could have half her body. Anna could have *all* her body. Nora didn't want a body.

Up and down the field she ran, slipping on the wet grass every time she tried to steal the ball from one of the Mount Markham players. She was soaked through, rain was dripping into her eyes, but she didn't stop. Finally, one of Nora's jab tackles dislodged the ball. She had control of it and was dribbling toward the goal. She was almost at the striking circle, pivoting into her backswing for a drive, when Brittany Carr, her own teammate, who was playing right wing, suddenly reached out and hooked the toe of her stick around Nora's ankle. Nora did a full-body flop onto the ground. She face-planted. She could taste the grit on her tongue, and she could hear the ref blow his whistle and call a time-out, but she couldn't breathe. The air was knocked out of her.

Nora just lay there on her stomach until someone flipped her over and Coach Schepps's face was inches from her own. Nora gasped air back into her lungs.

"You okay, kiddo? You hurt? What hurts?"

"Wind," Nora choked.

"Got the wind knocked out of you? It happens." Coach Schepps guided Nora to a seated position.

"Britt—" Nora paused to suck in a breath. "Tripped—me."

Coach Schepps turned to Brittany. "Carr?"

Brittany shook her head. "It was an accident, Coach. I slipped...I said I was sorry." She looked around. "Didn't you guys hear me say I'm sorry?"

Yes. Everyone heard her say she was sorry.

The thing was, Nora didn't believe her. Nora didn't believe it was an accident, and she didn't believe Brittany was sorry. And she didn't know why Britt would do something like that.

"Come on," Coach Schepps said, helping Nora to her feet. "Let's get you some water."

～

"Hey. I saw your game."

Nora was standing outside the school, waiting for her mother to pick her up, when a boy materialized beside her.

"That was quite a fall you took," he said.

Dark wavy hair. Straight nose. *Jonah Hesse*, she thought. The week before freshman year, Nora and Cam and Chelsea and Anna and Becca had gathered around Asher's yearbook and made a list of the upperclassmen they would flirt with when they got to high school, and Jonah Hesse was on it. That list was still in Nora's room somewhere, buried under all her awards and half-finished diaries.

"I'm Jonah," he said. He reached out his hand.

Nora took a step back.

His smile faltered.

Nora felt stupid. He wasn't trying to grab her; he was trying to introduce himself. "Sorry," she said. "I'm dirty." She *was* dirty. Even though the rain had stopped, she was still soaked and covered in mud. She could have changed her clothes in the locker room, but she hadn't. She'd just grabbed her backpack and left.

Jonah's smile returned. "Nice to meet you, Dirty." Then he cringed. "Sorry. I didn't mean— That was stupid. I know who you are."

"Right," Nora said. Of course he knew who she was. Everyone knew who she was now. She turned her gaze to the yellow PICK UP HERE sign and willed her mother's car to appear.

Jonah cleared his throat.

Nora sent telepathic messages to her mom. *Hurry up hurry up hurry up.*

"I took a fall like that once," he said, "flat on my face. Third grade. I fell off the pirate ship on the playground. Knocked out two teeth."

Without her permission, Nora's mouth opened. "My brother broke his arm jumping off the pirate ship."

"Asher?"

"Yeah."

"He's a good guy."

Nora shrugged. "I guess."

"No, he is. He helped me with precalc a bunch of times last year. I didn't even ask. He just saw I was struggling and offered."

"Huh," Nora said.

"Speaking of offers..."

She looked at him sharply.

"How do you feel about ice cream?" he said.

"How do I feel about *ice cream*?"

"Yeah."

"I'm lactose intolerant."

"Oh." Jonah grimaced. "Well…how do you feel about those giant cookies from the Blue Bird?"

Nora shrugged. "They're pretty good."

"Let me guess…you're a chocolate chip girl?"

"M&M," she said.

"M&M." He nodded. "Okay. So, let me buy you one."

"Why?"

"Because…" He hesitated. "Your team lost. And I'm offering you a consolation cookie."

"A consolation cookie."

"Yeah. I'll even throw in a glass of milk. Oh, wait, shit. You're—"

"Lactose intolerant," they said together.

He laughed. "Wow. I'm really striking out here."

He was cute, Nora decided. Not *Thor: Ragnarok* cute like Adam Courtmanche, but cute in a self-deprecating, prepster sort of way. When he smiled, a dimple appeared in his right cheek. Nora was actually considering saying yes to the cookie. Some other time, obviously. She was covered in mud, and her mom was on her way. But sometime.

And then a car slowed down in front of them. A car full of guys with their heads out the windows, whooping and whistling. They yelled things like, "You da man, Hesse!" And "Close the deal!"

Nora's heart thudded in her chest. Suddenly, she felt exposed. Her jersey was white and wet, clinging to her chest, and her legs were bare. Why hadn't she taken the time to change? Why did field hockey players have to wear *kilts*? A kilt was basically a miniskirt that girls ran around in, trying to score goals. None of the football players had to run around in kilts.

"Sorry," Jonah said, shaking his head at the car as it passed. "My friends are boneheads."

"Uh-huh," Nora said. "They think if you buy me a giant cookie, I'll have sex with you."

"No! That's not...I wouldn't..."

At least he had the decency to stutter.

"I gotta go," she said. Because, by some miracle, her mother had arrived.

"Wait—" Jonah said.

But Nora didn't wait. She opened the door to the car, threw in her backpack and field hockey stick, and told her mom, "Drive...please."

CAM

BY FRIDAY, KATIE J FROM COLGATE WAS BLOWING UP Cam's phone. Apparently, her half a smile and one tan shoulder were enough to inspire ninety-eight new followers. Already, she had comments from guys she'd never even met.

@jb_kuziak
Ur cute

@dantheman007
Nice pillows

@hanleeknowzall
Tell me about katie j

@leodalion34
Hey, want 2 come 2 a party?

It couldn't be that easy, could it? Or could it?

@katiegategrrrl
I love parties!

@leodalion34
Well we love gate girls so win-win.

@katiegategrrrl
When & where

@leodalion34
Sat night, alpha psi beta, university ave

@katiegategrrrl
Great!

@leodalion34
Oh and it's a graffiti party so wear white

@katiegategrrrl
?

@leodalion34
What, you've never been 2 a graffiti party?

@katiegategrrrl
Nope

@leodalion34
No way, r u a freshman?

@katiegategrrrl
Yup

@leodalion34
Even better :). When u come 2 the door someone will hand u a highlighter so u can write on whoever u want and they can write on u. The whole house will be black lit

@katiegategrrrl
Cool!

@leodalion34
Definitely. Bring ur cute friends. The more gate girls the merrier

@katiegategrrrl
Yay!

NORA

ON FRIDAY NIGHT, SHE WENT TO THE FABER–BUCKNELL soccer game with her dad. She needed to show him she wasn't acting weird. Everything was normal. When they stood for the national anthem, he wrapped his arm around her shoulders the way he always did. Nora's dad loved the national anthem. Every time he sang it, he got tears in his eyes. Under the lights, they shared a carton of nachos drenched in orange cheese and a tub of buttery popcorn. "Fan dinner," her dad called it.

Because Faber men's soccer was finally decent, and because they hadn't beaten Bucknell since 1987, the stands were packed. Nora was aware of all the bodies pressed in around her. At one point, a guy tried to push past her to get to an empty spot. Nora could smell him. Beer. Sweat. For a second, she panicked. She felt her breath go short and fast in her chest. But Nora's dad reached out his arm, creating a barrier around her. *I'm your dad, ladybug. It's my job to protect you.*

The nervous feeling passed.

Nora looked out at the field, at all the shiny shorts and

muscular legs running around. She would enjoy this game, she decided. She might not be the world's greatest soccer fan, she might not even care who won, but she was under the lights with her dad—her favorite person in the world—on a Friday night. Where else would she want to be?

CAM

ADAM XU—A.K.A. "MATT R FROM MICHIGAN"—HAD HEARD about the party, too. He texted Cam about it on Friday night. Cam had never known Adam Xu to use emojis, but his latest text was a string of thumbs-up and frothy beer mugs and exploding fireworks. She understood his sudden burst of enthusiasm. This was their big break. There was just one problem: They looked nothing like Katie J and Matt R.

Wait, Cam thought. *Was* this a problem? "Bring ur cute friends," @leodalion34 had said. Cam qualified as "cute," right? And surely, at five nine, she could pass for a Colgate freshman, a "gate grrrl" like Katie J. Even though she *wasn't* Katie J, Cam would have no trouble getting into the party.

The real problem was Adam Xu. Cam was sorry, but it was true. He might be almost as tall as Cam, but unlike Cam—and unlike Matt R—Adam Xu still had a baby face. He looked fifteen, and no fraternity was going to welcome some random fifteen-year-old boy inside. Because it didn't work that way. Just like homecoming at Faber Central School didn't work that way. It was only an unspoken rule, not an official law, but still, freshman boys weren't welcome at the homecoming dance. Only freshman *girls* were welcome at the homecoming dance, and that was so junior and senior guys could drool over their bodies in short, tight dresses and rank them for hotness. It was stupid and sexist and disgusting. Which is precisely why Cam had boycotted the homecoming dance last year, and why she would be boycotting it this year, too. Just on principle.

Cam had never set foot inside a frat house, but she would bet money on two things:

1) This Alpha Psi Beta "graffiti party" would be as stupid and sexist and disgusting as a Faber homecoming dance.

And, 2) Adam Xu would not be welcomed at the door with open arms.

—

"I've been thinking," Cam said when she and Adam Xu met at the Blue Bird on Saturday morning, to review the plan. "I need you to run backup ops tonight."

"Backup ops," he repeated.

"You know...dress in black and hide in the woods outside the frat house with your phone at the ready."

"You want me to hide in the woods?"

"Well, it's more like a little patch of trees," Cam said. "But yeah."

"You don't want me to come in with you?" Adam Xu said.

"It's not that I don't *want* you to come in with me. It's more like...we don't want to draw any more attention to ourselves than we have to."

Adam Xu raised his eyebrows.

"I'm just saying...you don't exactly look like Matt R."

"And you don't look like Katie J."

"No," Cam said. "But I can pass for a college freshman. And you...look young."

"Ouch."

"No offense. Honestly, it's more that you're not a girl. They'd probably let you in if you had a vagina, even if you looked thirteen."

"That's disturbing," Adam Xu said.

"Completely," Cam said. "But the point is, we don't want to arouse suspicion. We want to extract information, and I think we'll have our best shot at doing that if I go in alone."

Adam Xu lifted half a grilled corn muffin from the plate to his mouth. He chewed, swallowed, looked at Cam. "So, you're offering yourself up as bait?"

Cam pictured herself hooked to the end of a fishing line, dangling over a room full of sharks in white T-shirts. "Yeah. I guess I am."

"For the record," he said, "I think that is a really bad idea."

"Why?" she said.

"*Why?*"

"I'm bringing my own drink, so it's not like anyone can roofie me. And I bought some Mace."

"You bought some *Mace*?"

"Mace Triple Action Police Pepper Spray," Cam said. "I found it at Ray's Hardware, in the home-safety section. And I have a switchblade."

"A *switchblade*?" Adam Xu's eyebrows shot straight to the top of his head. He looked like a cartoon character.

Cam laughed. She reached into her backpack and pulled out the switchblade, lunging across the table like she was about to stab him.

"Jesus!" Adam Xu jumped back in his seat.

"Relax," Cam said. "It's not actually a knife." She pressed the silver button with her thumb. "It's a *comb*, see? Isn't it brilliant? My parents bought it for me at the Spy Museum on our trip to DC when I was in fifth grade. When we went to the US Mint, to see how money gets made, I actually got stopped by security. So if I need a deterrent tonight, I'll just whip this bad boy out and say, 'Touch me and I'll stab you, asshole.' "

Adam Xu shook his head.

"What?" Cam said. "I know what I'm doing. And if we run into trouble, I have all my uncles on speed dial."

Adam Xu stared at her. "They know about this?"

"Of course not." Cam shook her head. "They'd never let me do this in a million years."

"Maybe that should tell you something."

"Excuse me?" Cam said.

"Maybe this is above your pay grade."

"Why?" She narrowed her eyes at him. "Because I'm a *girl*? You think I can't handle myself at a frat party because I don't have a *penis*?"

"Hey." Adam Xu held up both palms, surrendering. "I don't think *I* could handle a frat party. I'm not even going in. I just want to make sure you've thought it all through."

"I've thought it all through," she said.

"Okay, then," he said.

"Okay, then. Ten o'clock. We'll meet in front of the bell tower on the quad."

"The bell tower on the quad," Adam Xu said. "I'll be there."

Cam didn't love lying to her parents. As parents went, Imani and Michael were pretty cool. They didn't saddle Cam with digital citizen contracts or curfews or reminders to wear her retainer. They trusted her to make smart decisions. So when Cam told them she was sleeping over at Anna Golden's house, they didn't even blink. They just told her to have fun.

Cam couldn't lie to Nora, though. And even though Nora was still mad and probably wouldn't be inviting her over to watch movies and eat Chunky Monkey in the next three hours, Cam sent a preemptive text: **Doing work tonight, fu library.** Because, technically, she *did* have work to do tonight, *undercover* work, and the Faber University library *was* where she was going right now, to hone her plan and kill time until she met Adam Xu.

By 10:12 PM, Adam Xu was successfully hidden in the patch of trees behind Alpha Psi Beta, dressed in head-to-toe black. Cam was standing alone on the sidewalk out front, in her plain white T-shirt, looking up at the darkened windows of the frat house and feeling her fight-or-flight response kick in. Adam Xu was right. This was a really bad idea.

Abort mission. Abort! Abort!

But then a sea of laughing, white-shirted Faber University girls appeared on the sidewalk beside Cam, maybe fifteen of them, and they didn't look nervous. In fact, they rolled right up the front steps like they owned the place, and Cam, almost without thinking, let herself be swept along with them.

"Thanks," she said to the glowing, white-shirted guy at the door, who handed her a highlighter.

"You're welcome," the guy said. "Have fun." When he smiled at Cam, his teeth glowed purplish white.

Cam followed the group of girls to the back of the frat house. It was dark and hot and crowded and loud, and everything around her glowed. Not just people's hats and teeth and shirts—many of which, Cam realized, had been graffitied with genitalia and suggestive, though not particularly clever messages like "Eat me"—but also the drinks they were holding.

What kind of drink glows under a black light? Cam wondered, as the bodies and the heat and the music throbbed all around her. Surely these people weren't drinking milk.

"Hey!" a voice shouted.

Cam turned. It wasn't easy to see what anyone's skin really looked like in here, because everyone appeared dark, but the guy in front of her was Black. And he was tall, with broad shoulders and slim hips. His glowing white T-shirt read, "Talk to me."

"Hey!" she shouted back.

"I'm Malik!"

"I'm Michelle!" Cam shouted. This was the name she had decided on, her alias. It had come to her when she was hiding out in the library stacks, killing the time until ten by reading the first seven chapters of Michelle Obama's autobiography.

"You don't have a glowy drink, Michelle!" He lifted the cup in his hand, taking a sip of neon green—what? Toxic waste? Battery acid?

"I have this!" Cam shouted back, holding up her Snapple iced tea, which wasn't glowy at all.

"It's not glowy!"

"No! But *I* am! See?" Cam grinned, knowing that her teeth were giving off purplish white light.

He bent down. Cam could feel his breath on her cheek. She could smell the tang of alcohol. "You have a great smile, Michelle!"

"Thanks! You have great shoulders!"

"Thanks!"

Were they shout-flirting? Cam laughed at the thought. The music thumped. Bodies and swooshes of light moved all around them. It reminded her of those laser tag parties that were all the rage in sixth grade. Only it was laser tag on steroids: the kind of scene that made people feel drunk even when they weren't. Or like they were about to have a seizure. Was the feeling in Cam's chest excitement or claustrophobia? It could go either way.

"Hey, Michelle!"

"Hey, what?" Cam shouted.

"You want to go somewhere we don't have to shout to hear each other?!"

"Like where?!"

"My dorm room?!"

His *dorm room*? Cam felt a little thrill. Was this what college would be like? Cute boys flirting with her at parties? Asking her to go somewhere private to talk? A cute frat boy had just asked Cam to go back to his dorm room. Obviously he wanted to hook up. With *her*. But then she thought, *Holy shit. Cute frat boy? Dorm room?* She'd almost fallen for it. It scared her how quickly she'd lost all common sense, and she wasn't even drinking. She shouldn't be *flattered*, she should be *pissed*—how presumptuous could this guy be? But she couldn't be pissed, because then she would blow her cover. Oh my God, she had to focus.

"Actually!" Cam shouted. The music suddenly got even louder. "I'M HOT! LET'S GO OUTSIDE!"

He nodded and reached for her hand. "C'MON!"

Cam hesitated. Was she really letting some college guy she'd just met lead her out into the night?

Yes, she decided. Outside was not a dorm room. There were plenty of people around.

And somehow, like Moses parting the Red Sea, Malik managed to make space appear for the two of them to walk through, past the lights and the bodies and *thumpthump-thump* of the bass.

"Dude!" Some guy in a backward baseball cap stopped them on their way out the door. "Open your mouth!"

Cam watched as Malik tipped back his head and the guy lifted a bottle in the air, pouring something down Malik's throat. Pouring and pouring.

Jesus, she thought. If anyone did that to her, she would throw up. Just like Nora threw up the night of the Manischewitz.

Nora. Cam felt a twist of guilt in her gut.

"Drink?" The guy with the bottle grinned at Cam.

"No, thanks," she said quickly.

"Come on," Malik said, pulling her by the hand.

Out of the black light, under a string of Christmas lights that Cam imagined had been hanging there since last December, she could see Malik clearly. Big brown eyes. Chin dimple. He was even better looking than she'd suspected.

And drunker.

"You okay?" Cam said, when he stumbled on a patio stone, grabbing her elbow for support.

"Yeah." He straightened up, smiling lazily at her. "These puppies are strong. You want?" He lifted his cup, sloshing some of his drink onto the ground.

"I'm good," Cam said. She had to stay focused. "So," she said, taking a seat on an old, ripped-up couch sitting randomly on the grass—how cool was that? A couch outside on the grass? "You're an Alpha Psi Beta?"

Malik flopped down beside her. "I'm a pledge."

"And what does that mean, exactly?"

"It means..." He slugged down the rest of his drink, then shifted his body on the couch so they were face-to-face. "I'd like to kiss you, if that's okay?"

Whoa! Forward much?

He was waiting, actually waiting, for Cam to respond. She thought for a moment. She was sober. And he was *asking*. And maybe kissing him was the way to extract the information she needed. Also, if she was being completely honest with herself, she was curious. She'd only made out with high school guys. There wasn't anything wrong with a little experiment, was there? A little compare and contrast in the name of science? It's not like she was planning to have *sex* with him.

The next thing Cam knew, they were kissing. She told herself to stop, she was crazy, what about Asher? But this *was* for research. Intellectually, she wanted to stop—she did—but her hormones had suddenly taken the wheel, and Malik was a great kisser. Like Asher—maybe even better because he was in college and he had probably had more experience. Malik had definitely had more experience. The circles he was making with his tongue. The way his hands were holding her hips, lifting her up to meet him.

Wow, Cam thought. Just...*wow*.

And then he pulled away, breathless. "Hey," he said.

"What?" She was breathless, too.

"Can I write on you?"

"Write on me?" Cam said.

"On your shirt. No one's written on you yet. I want to be the first one."

It was cute, in a way, that he'd suddenly interrupted their make-out session because he wanted to be the first person to graffiti her white T-shirt.

"Uh, okay," Cam said. "As long as you don't write anything gross."

"I won't," he said. "I'm just gonna write a number."

"Your phone number?"

He shook his head.

"What number?"

He pulled a Sharpie out of his back pocket and snapped the cap off with his teeth.

"Don't worry about it."

"I'm not *worried about it*," Cam said. "I just want to know what you're writing."

"A seven."

"A *seven*?"

"Mm-hm."

Oh my God, Cam thought. *Ohmygodohmygodohmygod.* She watched as Malik pulled her T-shirt straight out in front of him, so he wasn't actually touching her body as he scrawled a sloppy black "7" across the middle.

"I wanna take your picture."

Cam sat straight up. "Why?"

"Just 'cause." Malik reached into his back pocket and pulled out his phone.

Are you seeing this? Cam sent a telepathic message to Adam Xu. *Please tell me you're seeing this.*

"Wait," Cam said. "I want to ask you something first."

"What?"

She took her phone out of her pocket. The photo was right there on her home screen. "Do you know these three guys?" She zoomed in.

"Lemme see." He reached clumsily for Cam's phone, and she let him have it.

He brought the screen close to his face. "Riz."

"Riz?" she said.

"Riz."

"Okay." Nicknames. Guys loved to give each other nicknames. "What's his real name?"

Malik shook his head. "Dunno."

"Do you recognize anyone else?"

He squinted at the screen. "Sully?...maybe. Mac. Thaz Mac."

"Who's Mac?" Cam said. "The redhead? The guy in the sweatshirt?"

"Hey." He looked up from Cam's phone. "Lemme take your picture. Lemme take two pictures."

"Two pictures, huh?" She snatched her phone out of his hand and started tapping out a note to herself. **Riz, sully, mac.**

"Hey, thaz my phone."

"No," she said. "This is *my* phone. *This* is your phone." She grabbed his phone off the couch where he'd dropped it.

"Hey," he said, swiping his hand through the air. "Lemme take a picture."

Cam hopped backward. "Of this?" She pointed to her shirt. "You want a picture of this?"

"Gimme that." He swiped the air again.

"Tell me why you need a picture of me," she said. "What's the seven for?" She was playing keep-away. He reached; she hopped. He reached; she hopped.

"Izza pledge thing," he said finally. "Iztupid." His slurring was getting worse, Cam realized.

"What kind of pledge thing?" she said.

"Jussa game."

"What kind of game?"

He reached again for the phone, and when Cam hopped away once more, he slumped back against the couch and sighed. "Can't tell."

"Why not?"

He shook his head, raising one uncoordinated hand to his lips, to lock them and throw away the key.

"I'm not going to tell anyone," she said. "I don't even go to college here."

His eyebrows moved up, but his eyelids stayed half-closed.

Cam was afraid he would fall asleep. She had to think fast. "Actually, I'm in high school."

"Ha."

"What do you mean *ha*?"

He lifted a sloppy finger to his mouth again. "Shhhhh-hhh. Izza secret."

"I like secrets," Cam said. "Tell me a secret."

"Shhhhhhhh." He sprayed spit through the air. He didn't look so cute anymore, spraying spit through the air. "Eighteen holes."

"What, like golf?"

He didn't answer. His head drooped.

"Like *golf*, Malik?"

"I donwanna play," he mumbled into his chest.

"You don't want to play *golf*?"

He didn't answer.

"Malik?"

He let out a loud, rumbly snore. Cam couldn't believe it. She was just starting to get somewhere, and now her only source for information was snoring like an old man.

ADAM XU

WHAT IS SHE DOING?

Camille was bonkers, he realized as he crouched behind a tree, watching her make out with some frat boy on a couch. He shouldn't have been surprised, of course. This whole thing was bonkers. The Mace? The *switchblade comb*? Jesus. He'd tried to talk her out of it, but she wouldn't listen. And now, she was making out with a college guy right in front of him. She *did* remember he was on backup ops, right? She knew he could see everything she was doing. Or maybe she had forgotten he was there. Adam was used to people forgetting he was there. Most of the time, he didn't mind. It was better than being the center of attention, like everyone pointing at his tomato face the one time he'd tried alcohol. *Dude. What's wrong with you? Look at Xu! He's plastered!*

He was relieved when Camille stopped making out with the guy on the couch. Other things were happening. They were talking...the guy was doing something to her shirt...and now they were—what? Playing keep-away?

Adam's feet were starting to tingle. He had been squatting for too long. He needed to move. He marched quietly in place. He did a few stretches.

Finally, Cam came walking toward the trees, shaking her head. She hadn't forgotten him.

"C'mon," she said. "Let's go."

"What—now?"

"Yeah. This was a bust."

Adam glanced over at the couch. The guy was still there, slumped to one side. "Is he okay?"

"He's fine. Just passed out."

Adam waited until he and Camille were walking along the sidewalk, a safe distance from the fraternities. Then, he asked, "What happened? You couldn't extract any information?"

"I asked if he could ID the guys."

"And?"

"I got a few nicknames," Camille said. "Maybe. I don't know. He was so drunk. I'm not sure he's a reliable source."

"What were they?"

"What?"

"The nicknames."

Camille bent over her phone. She tapped the screen a few times. "Riz. Sully. Mac."

"Okay." Adam nodded. "I'll check the Facebook page when I get home, see what I can find."

Camille told him about the number 7. She told him about the frat boy asking to take her picture for some pledge game. Something about golf. *Eighteen holes*, he'd called it.

"Google it," Adam said.

"What?"

"Google 'eighteen holes.'"

Camille shrugged. "I doubt we'll find anything."

They stopped under a campus security light and she took out her phone. She spoke the words aloud as she tapped them out with her thumbs. "Ayyy...teeen...hoooles."

Adam waited.

"*Eighteen Hole Round: Scottish Golf History*," Camille said. "'Why Golf Courses Have Eighteen Holes,' Snopes dot com. 'Why Do Golf Courses Have Eighteen Holes?' NBC Chicago. Want me to keep going?"

He shook his head. "Try a hashtag."

Camille smiled. "Adam *Xu*."

"What?"

She clutched her phone to her heart in a mock swoon. "My little social media wizard. I am so proud of you."

"Okay, okay," he said gruffly. "Just try it."

Camille started tapping on her phone again. "Hashtag... one...eight...hoooles."

Adam waited. He watched Camille scroll and tap, scroll and tap.

"Anything?" he said.

More scrolling and tapping.

"Nah," she said. "Just golf stuff...Let me try 'hashtag eighteen holes Faber University'..."

More tapping and scrolling.

Nothing.

Camille tried "#18HolesAlphaPsiBeta."

Nothing.

Adam Xu tried "Numbers game Alpha Psi Beta Faber University."

Nothing.

Camille tried "Pledge games Alpha Psi Beta Faber University."

This turned up an article. She read out loud: "'The chapter was in trouble when it was suspended after a freshman pledge nearly died of alcohol poisoning in 2003. Two years earlier, Faber's Sigma Tau fraternity was suspended after a hazing episode contributed to an inebriated pledge falling off the roof of an academic building and suffering a fractured skull. "Hazing is a complex issue," says dean of students Barton Hodge'...blah blah blah. It's all about drinking. Nothing about sexual assault...Keep searching. I'll find their Insta. Maybe they posted something there..."

Adam tried "APB FU pledge game." He tried "APB FU 18holes."

"Found it," Camille said, holding up her phone. "Alpha PsiBetaFU." She scrolled and tapped. "Soup kitchen... Meals on Wheels...red T-shirts...picture of old dudes...blazers and ties...more blazers and ties...nothing. Damn it."

"Huh." Adam rubbed his forehead. He looked at the time on his phone. "I have to go," he said. "Can we talk about this tomorrow? I have to sneak back into my house before my parents realize I'm gone."

"Shit," Camille muttered.

"What?"

"I told my parents I was staying at Anna's."

"Let me guess," he said. "You didn't tell Anna."

"Nope." She looked around. "I guess I can sleep here. Plenty of benches."

"Are you crazy?" he said. "You can't sleep on the quad."

"Why not?"

He gave her a look.

"I have Mace, remember? And a switchblade."

"It's a *comb*."

"Do you have a better idea?"

"No, but…"

"Hey." She nudged his arm with her elbow. "Can I sleep at your house? I'll sneak out before your parents wake up. I promise."

Adam hesitated. It was a horrible idea.

"Please?" Camille folded her hands and propped them under her chin. "We can check the Facebook page together."

"Okay, fine," he said. "But you have to be *really* quiet. My mom has bionic ears."

CAM

SHE WAS IMPRESSED. THEY'D HAD TO CLIMB A TREE, scale a roof, and sneak into Adam Xu's room through a window. "I had no idea you were such a badass," she whispered.

"Yeah, well." Adam Xu shrugged. "I didn't know you were, either." He handed her a pair of sweatpants.

Cam mouthed her thanks. She looked around for somewhere to change.

Adam Xu pointed at a door to the left of his bed. "Don't flush," he whispered.

Cam tiptoed into the bathroom to put on the sweatpants, pee, and splash water, very quietly, onto her face. When she came out, Adam Xu's computer was on. "Check it out," he whispered. "There's a new post on their Facebook page."

Cam leaned in.

FU Alpha Psi Beta Fraternity

9:36 PM

Big congrats to the fall pledge class for helping to raise more than $3,400 for local charities, including the Boys and Girls Club of Chenango County!

Under the caption was a photo of thirty or so smiling guys in red T-shirts and jeans, standing on the front steps of the fraternity house. Cam inhaled sharply. "Please tell me they're tagged."

Adam Xu moved the cursor over a spiky-haired guy in the back row. A name popped up: *Trip Meister*.

"Yesss," Cam said. "Keep going. We're looking for... hang on..." She consulted her phone. "Riz, Sully, and Mac."

Adam Xu worked his way from left to right. Ryan Stern. Nate Engelhart. Jonathan Washkowitz. Tom Rizzoli.

He glanced at her. "Rizzoli?"

"Click on him."

Adam Xu clicked. Cam squinted at the profile. *Tom Rizzoli*. Dark hair winging out from under a backward baseball cap, mirrored sunglasses. Cam scrolled through her phone to find the photo of Nora and the three guys. She zoomed in on the laughing guy with the dark hair and placed him next to Tom Rizzoli's head on the computer screen.

"Riz," she whispered. "You can run, but you can't hide."

Adam Xu went back to the group photo and kept going, moving the cursor from face to face.

Liam Sullivan matched the blond guy in the gray

sweatshirt. Alec MacInerney matched the redhead holding open the car door.

Tom Rizzoli, Liam Sullivan, Alec MacInerney.

Thank you, Malik, Cam thought. She had seen his name when Adam Xu skimmed briefly over his face. Malik Jones. He was one of them, yes, but he had also helped.

"Maybe this is all we need," Cam said. "The video, the photo, and the names. We can hand everything over to campus police. And if you come forward as a witness—"

"What?" Adam Xu looked startled.

"You saw what happened on the golf course. You can make a report."

"No." He shook his head. "No way."

"Adam—"

"I told you. My parents work at Faber. I can't get involved."

"You're *already* involved."

"I can't get *publicly* involved."

Cam huffed out a long stream of air. "Fine. So we send it anonymously and hope that's enough."

"How?"

"Katie J's email. And we take the sound off the video. Can you live with that?"

Adam Xu nodded slowly. "Maybe. But we have to ask Nora first."

"Do we?" Cam said.

"We absolutely do."

In her heart, she knew he was right. She wished he

wasn't, but he was. "Okay, fine," she said. "We'll ask her tomorrow."

"Tomorrow," he agreed.

"First thing," she said.

"First thing."

ADAM XU

CAMILLE HAD SET AN ALARM ON HER PHONE FOR 6:00 AM, but neither of them heard it. They just kept sleeping.

"Xǐng lái!"

Adam woke to the sound of his mother's voice.

"Nimen zai gan shenme?!"

He opened his eyes and saw her and immediately wanted to rip the comforter off his bed and throw it over Camille. But it was too late for that. His mother was already gesticulating at the floor. Her Mandarin was so fast that the only words Adam Xu could make out were "girl in the bedroom."

Camille sat up and gave a little wave. "Oh, hey, Mrs. Xu." She stretched both arms above her head and yawned, like there was nothing strange about this at all; she was used to waking up on the floor of guys' bedrooms. (For the record, Adam had offered her the bed, but she had insisted that the floor was fine; she was just happy to have a place to sleep.)

"Adam. What's going on?"

Great. His father had arrived.

"Hey, Mr. Xu," Camille said. She stood up and walked across the room—in her white T-shirt with the Sharpie number 7 and a loaner pair of Adam's sweatpants—to shake his father's hand. "Camille Dodd. Nice to meet you. You have an awesome son, by the way."

Adam's parents looked from Camille to Adam and back again.

"It's not what it looks like," Adam said weakly. Even though it *wasn't* what it looked like—even though it was only Camille, and she was on the floor—he felt his cheeks flame. His parents were looking back and forth between them. Their eyes saw things. The fact of Adam's maleness and Camille's femaleness. But more than that, the bed. Adam knew that his parents were making the natural, although not-remotely-accurate assumption, that boys and girls and beds meant only one thing.

"I needed a place to crash," Camille explained.

She was trying to help, of course. But there was no helping this. Adam's mother did not want an explanation. She wanted to gesticulate and spew angry words that Camille couldn't possibly understand. "Gun chu qu!"

—~—

"Sorry about that," Adam mumbled as he walked Camille outside. His mother was standing on the porch behind them. Watching, judging.

"No worries," Camille said. She was still wearing his

sweatpants, the crumpled ball of her jeans clamped under one arm.

"She sees a girl in my bedroom and she thinks…you know."

"Yeah, well," Camille said, "if it were *my* mom she'd be telling us sex is a beautiful thing, and we should be using spermicidal foam with our condoms."

Adam cringed. He glanced over his shoulder to make sure his mother hadn't heard that. She probably didn't even know what spermicidal foam was, but still.

"I'm going to see Nora," Camille said.

"What?" he said.

"You heard me," she said. "Are you coming?"

Adam looked back at his mother. Her arms were folded.

He looked at Camille. He felt torn. "I can't," he said. "I want to, but my mom would kill me."

Camille nodded. "I get it. I'll talk to Nora for both of us."

"Text me after," he said. "Let me know what she says."

"I will."

NORA

IT WAS EIGHT O'CLOCK ON SUNDAY MORNING WHEN THE doorbell rang. It kept ringing and ringing. At first Nora was annoyed, then confused. Why wasn't anyone answering the door? Finally, she remembered: She was the only one home. Her dad was in Massachusetts, for a Patriot League athletic directors' meeting, and her mother was driving Asher and Maeve into Syracuse so Asher could walk around the College of Visual and Performing Arts and Maeve could see some goblin exhibit. They had planned the trip weeks ago, and Nora was supposed to go, too, but she had pleaded her case. She was behind on her homework, she said. She had a chem test on Monday. And her mother had agreed to let her stay home alone, which was a relief.

Until now.

This infernal ding-donging.

Nora groaned. Whoever was at the door, Girl Scouts, Jehovah's Witnesses, she didn't want to deal. She was still half asleep. But she got out of bed anyway. Because…what if this was an emergency?

She staggered down the stairs and swung open the door.

There was Cam.

"What?" Nora said. Her voice sounded froggy.

And Cam said, "I texted you on my way."

"I was *sleeping*," she said.

And Cam said, "I need to talk to you."

Nora looked at Cam. Her hair was mashed down on one side, like she had just woken up. She was wearing a white T-shirt with something scribbled on it and holding a pair of jeans. "Why are you holding jeans?" she said.

"Can I come in?" Cam said.

"No."

"Please? It's important."

"Fine." She rolled her eyes and stepped back into the hall.

"Where is everyone?" Cam asked, as the two of them walked into the kitchen.

"Out," Nora said. "It's just me."

"Good," Cam said. She pulled out a chair at the breakfast bar and sat down.

"Why *good*?"

"Will you sit down? Please?"

"Jesus Christ, Camille, what is it? Just tell me!"

"Okay." Cam took a deep breath. "I know who they are."

"Who?"

"The guys from the golf course. I know their names.

And you're not the only number. It's a whole game. A pledge thing."

"What are you talking about?" Nora said.

"Alpha Psi Beta. I was there last night, for a party, and—"

"Wait—what?" Nora said. "You said you were doing work."

"I was. Not for school, though. For you. Undercover work."

Undercover work. Nora's brain spun.

"There was this graffiti party," Cam said. "Adam Xu went with me. Well, he hid out back, and I went in alone. But that's not the point. The *point* is, I met this frat boy, this pledge named Malik, and he was drunk, and he wrote a number seven on me. See?" Cam pointed to her white T-shirt, the black scribble that Nora had thought was random but now could see was a 7. "He said it was for a game, some pledge thing, and then I showed him the photo of you and those three guys and I asked if he recognized any of them, and he did, so—" Cam paused for a breath.

Nora stared at her.

"Adam Xu and I looked them up on the Alpha Psi Facebook page. Weird, I know. Who under the age of forty is on *Facebook*? I'm sure it's just for the old fogy alumni. But wait..." Cam took out her phone and started tapping. "I have pictures."

Cam's phone was in her face.

"Tom Rizzoli. Liam Sullivan. Alec MacInerney."

Nora shook her head and pushed the phone away. "I don't care who they are."

"What do you mean *you don't care who they are*?"

"I mean," Nora said, "their names don't change anything."

"Their names don't change anything?" Cam threw up her hands in disbelief. "Their names change *everything*! Now we can turn them in. We have the photo. We have the video—"

Nora looked at Cam sharply. "We don't have the video."

"Okay...don't get mad at me...I asked Adam Xu to save it to the cloud that day, when we were up in his room. I passed him a note while you were trying to delete it."

"Camille!" Nora wanted to throttle her.

"I'm sorry. I thought we might need it for evidence."

Nora made her voice calm and measured. "We do not need it for *evidence*. Because we are not going to do *anything* with it."

"We have to," Cam said. "Adam enhanced the video, so now you can see the T-shirt. We have to turn those guys in. It's a *game*, Nor. All the Alpha Psi pledges are playing. Someone has to stop them."

Nora shook her head. Shook it and shook it. This was the ultimate breach of friendship, right? Cam had trampled Nora's wishes; she had disregarded Nora's feelings. And for what? For some undercover mission on the campus where Nora's dad worked, in his old fraternity house, no less? This was classic Cam, plowing ahead without thinking, under the guise of justice, just like the bra-strap protest of eighth grade.

"Look," Nora said. "I get what you're saying. But it's just not worth it."

"What do you mean *it's not worth it*?" Cam said.

"I mean," Nora said, "my dad has enough to deal with in his job. I told you. I don't want to drag him into something like this. I won't."

"You're killing me, Nora," Cam said. She put her head down on the breakfast bar. "You know that? You're absolutely killing me."

Nora smacked Cam lightly on the head. "You're killing me, too."

—✑—

When Nora was alone in the house, she had a guilty pleasure. She liked to curl up on the couch under Grandma Merrill's ugly brown afghan and watch *The Fighter.* If any of her friends could see her right now, they wouldn't get it. Why was she watching sweaty old men pummel each other when she could be binge-watching rom-coms on Netflix? Nora would never be able to explain. For her, it wasn't just about the boxing. It was about the story. It was about everything that had happened to Micky Ward in his life—from the moment he was born into his crazy family to the moment he stepped into the ring—that made him want to prove something. "People think boxing is about brute strength," Nora's dad had told her once. "But really, it's about heart. It's about getting knocked down and standing up again." Watching *The Fighter* allowed Nora to disappear, the way reading did for Maeve or painting did for Asher. "Irish" Micky Ward was Nora's drug of choice, and right now, who could blame her? After Cam left earlier, the reality of what she'd told Nora hit hard. The nameless, faceless guys on the golf course had names and faces. They were real. Nora could no longer pretend they weren't. But she *could* redirect her attention to the ring, to the sweaty backs and cocked fists and dancing feet.

Nora pulled the afghan up under her chin. She closed her eyes and listened to Micky Ward. *I'm the one fighting, okay? Not you, not you, and not you...*

"Nor."

Her eyes snapped open. A hand was on her shoulder. For a second, her heart stopped. Who was shaking her?

"Nora."

But it was only Asher.

"What the hell?" she said. She sat up, trying to get her bearings. He was home already? What time was it? She must have fallen asleep.

"I told Mom," Asher said.

Nora blinked. "You told Mom what?"

"About you getting roofied. She's on her way in. I wanted to give you a heads-up."

"*What?*"

"I'm sorry," he said. "I've been sitting on it for days, and I couldn't just... I had to."

Nora exhaled in one long stream. She hated her brother. Hated him! Asher had told their mother she was roofied. Their mother! Nora wanted to stuff Grandma Merrill's ugly brown afghan into his mouth so he couldn't say anything more.

"Ash?" Nora could hear Diane calling from the kitchen. "Would you stay here with Maeve for a little while?"

"Sure," Asher said.

"Nora." Her mother's head, poking into the living room. "Put your sneakers on."

Nora looked at her mother. "What?"

"Put your sneakers on and meet me outside in five minutes."

Five minutes. Diane meant business. Although what putting on sneakers had to do with anything, Nora didn't know.

She got her answer five minutes later, when she went outside with her sneakers on. Her mother's hair was in a long side braid. She was wearing a flannel shirt and a pair of beat-up cowboy boots. "What are we doing?" Nora said.

And Diane said, "We're going for a hike."

A *hike?* Nora knew better than to ask why. She knew better than to invite a conversation she didn't want to have. But come on. A *hike?*

She said, "Where?"

Her mother said, "Mount Aggie."

Nora nodded. Mount Aggie wasn't really a mountain. It was more like a high, wooded hill at the far end of the Faber University campus, with a huge outcropping of rocks at the top. The trailhead was a mile from their house, a twenty-minute walk before they even got to the hiking part. Nora felt tired just thinking about it, but she wasn't in a position to argue. When her mother started to walk, she started to walk, too. Nora wondered what would happen when they got to the top. What would Diane say? *Privates are private, Nora. You can never take back your reputation, Nora.* Her mother guarded Nora's reputation like it was some precious jewel, hermetically sealed behind bulletproof glass.

Nora fought the urge to run in the opposite direction. She wasn't going to allow herself to wimp out. She was going to do this: have a perfectly mortifying conversation with her perfectly perfect mother about sexual assault—*attempted* sexual assault, but still. It felt to Nora like a death march.

They walked in silence until they reached the quad, and then Nora's mother said, "I'm going to tell you a story."

Okay, weird, Nora thought. When was the last time Diane had told her a story? Kindergarten?

"It starts over there..." Her mother pointed. "On that bench, where I first met your dad."

Right. The Rhett-and-Diane story. Nora had heard it a million times. Her mother did realize this, right—that Nora could tell it herself? *It was fall, and the trees were red and orange and gold. The sun, glinting through the leaves, lit her up like a candle.*

"I lied."

Nora looked at her mother. "What?"

"I wasn't crying that day because I was homesick."

"You weren't?"

Diane shook her head. "I've never told anyone this.... It's hard."

Nora's brain scrambled. What hadn't her mother told anyone? What was hard? "Do you want to sit down?" she said.

"Yes," her mother said. Then she changed her mind. "Actually, no. Let's get to the trail."

This was fine with Nora. If things were going to get weirder, she would rather be moving.

Her mother said, "My freshman year roommate was a girl named Amy. Amy Bachman. She was from Sandpoint, Idaho. Sweet. Funny. We hit it off right away. Because we were both from out west and we both felt out of place at Faber, we spent all our time together. Amy was shy, but when rush week started, I convinced her to rush with me. We went to all the socials and learned about the sororities, and when we were both tapped to pledge Kappa Kappa Nu, we were thrilled."

Wait, Nora thought. Since when was her mother a sorority girl? Nora's dad loved talking about his fraternity days. On alumni weekend, his Alpha Psi brothers filled the house—Aldo, Pinchy, Joey D, Keefer—all Nora's surrogate uncles telling their wild stories. They called Nora's dad "master of the universe" and laughed about the time he got stuck in the laundry chute trying to capture a runaway ferret. But Nora's mom had literally never mentioned a single sorority sister or told a single Kappa Kappa Nu story.

Yet here she was, telling one.

"The pledge season lasted, oh, maybe six weeks. And toward the end, there was a party at the Alpha Psi Beta house. The theme was King Tuts and Egyptian Sluts."

Nora's eyebrows jumped. *Seriously?* She didn't know what surprised her more, the name of the party or the fact that Diane Melchionda had just said the word "sluts."

"Amy and I both dressed like Cleopatra," her mother continued. "Thick black eyeliner. Rope belts. Sandals. When we got to the party, all the brothers were painted gold. Faces, chests, legs. They had black shoe polish in their hair. They were handing out shots of Goldschläger, with 'flecks of real gold,' they told us. Amy and I had one drink. That was our rule: one drink. We thought we were being smart."

"Right," Nora said. But inside, she was thinking, *Really?* Her mother was an *underage drinker?*

"Our other rule was to stick together," Diane said. "But at some point I had to go to the bathroom, and Amy was talking to one of the frat brothers about books. They were having a pretty deep discussion, and she didn't want to leave. She told me to go ahead. So I went to the bathroom, and when I came back I couldn't find her. The party was so crowded. All those King Tuts and Cleopatras...We didn't have cell phones yet, so it's not like I could text her...all I could do was wander around....I..."

Nora had a sinking feeling in her stomach. This story was not going to end well.

"You don't have to tell me," she said. They were on the far end of the quad now, almost to the trail head. "Really."

"No," her mother said. "I do. I want to." She paused for a moment and then continued. "I looked and looked, but I couldn't find her. I figured she and the guy she'd been talking to had hit it off. So I went back to the dorm. I fell asleep. The next morning, Amy was in her bed. She said she didn't feel well, and I should go to breakfast without her. I offered to take her to the health center, but she said no. It took her a few days to tell me...she'd been raped at the party by two of the frat brothers. She had no idea who they were because they looked like every other King Tut."

Nora stared at her mother. *Raped?* Why was her mother telling her this? Well, she knew why, of course she did: because Asher had spilled the beans about the guys on the golf course. It occurred to Nora that Asher telling their mother that she had been roofied might have made Diane assume that Nora had been raped, too.

"Mom," she whispered.

But her mother shook her head. She paused at the trailhead, pointing to the wooden sign: MOUNT AGGIE. OPEN SUNRISE TO SUNSET. "Come on."

Nora felt stunned and a little sick. But she followed her mother onto the dirt path.

"I told Amy she should call her parents, tell them what happened. But she said no. She said they would pull her

220

out of school, make her move back home. So I said we should tell her big sister. That's who you're supposed to tell when you're in a sorority. They slam you over the head with it from the minute you start rushing. *Strength in sisterhood.* So we went to Amy's big sister, a senior named Lauren, and Amy told her she'd been raped by two Alpha Psis, and Lauren said...I'll never forget this...she said, 'Don't worry about it. We all drink too much and do stupid things.' And Amy said, 'I only had one drink.' And Lauren said, 'Still. We all do things we regret at parties. It's part of the college experience.' She said, 'The Alpha Psis are good guys. They're the best frat on campus. We don't want to do anything to piss them off, or we won't get paired with them for homecoming, or Greek Week, or anything. Trust me,' Lauren said, 'by the time you're a senior, you'll look back on this and laugh. We all do.'"

"Are you kidding me?" Nora said.

Her mother shook her head and continued: "I took Amy to the dean. She told him she had been raped, and he said that was a serious accusation. He asked if she had made a police report. He asked how many drinks she'd had. What was she wearing? Who entered the room first? Did she say no? He asked if she could identify the two guys. When she said she wasn't sure, all the King Tuts looked the same, he said, 'Well, if you don't know who they are, I can't help you—'"

"Oh my God, Mom," Nora blurted. She had a horrible thought. "What if it was Uncle Aldo? Or Uncle Keefer?"

Her mother shook her head.

"What?" Nora said. She pictured her dad's frat brothers on alumni weekend, filling the house with their cologne and their booming laughs. "It could have been any of them. Right?"

"I don't know," her mom said, shaking her head again. "I have no way of knowing. It was my first college party. It was a blur. All I know is the next day, Amy dropped out of Faber. She told me she needed a fresh start. She told me never to tell anyone what happened. She told me to forget we'd ever met. But I didn't forget." Her mom reached into the chest pocket of her flannel shirt and pulled out a photo. "This was Amy."

Nora looked at the picture. There were two girls standing side by side. One was dark-haired, the other was blond, but they were both wearing jeweled headbands, thick black eyeliner, teeny tiny dresses, and impossibly high, strappy, gold sandals.

"Wait—" Nora squinted at the light-haired girl. "Is that *you*?"

"On the left, yes. And that's Amy on the right."

"Oh my *God*." Nora couldn't believe it. *Her mother* wearing makeup. *Her mother* in a dress so tight and short, it was practically a tank top. She dragged her eyes away from the photo. "Is *that* why you made such a big deal about the skirt?"

"What skirt?" her mom said.

"The one I wanted to get. Before school started,

remember? You wouldn't buy it for me. You said it left nothing to the imagination."

Her mom hesitated. "I remember."

"Was that because of Amy? Did you think if I wore a miniskirt, what happened to her would happen to me?"

"No." Nora's mom frowned. "I mean...on some level, I think, I've always tried to shelter you from...all of that. To keep you from growing up too fast. But it wasn't...What happened to Amy had nothing to do with what she was wearing. Not buying you that skirt—"

"I bought it anyway," Nora blurted. "Julie Golden drove me to the mall and I bought it with my babysitting money, and I hid it in the back of my closet so you wouldn't see. I wear it all the time."

Her mom's eyes widened. *In shock*, Nora thought. Because this wasn't the daughter she knew.

But Nora didn't regret saying it. In a way, she had been waiting her whole life to say it—that she was not, at her core, a perfect little rules follower. She was not her mother.

"I wore it the night of the frat fair," Nora said. "So in a way you were right."

She waited for a reaction.

Diane's face was serious. "Oh, honey. I wasn't *right*. That didn't give them *license*....We should have talked about this....My mother never talked about these things with me, but *I* should have talked about this with you. I should have told you about Amy. *That's* why I was crying the day I met your dad. Not because I was homesick, but because Amy left. Because I'd failed her."

"Mom, no," Nora said. "It wasn't your fault." They were at the top now, standing by the rocks. "It was them. It was those guys. It was their fault, not yours." Nora looked at her mother, and she felt her eyes sting, and suddenly she was sobbing. "It was *their* fault."

"Oh, honey." Her mom was hugging her and smoothing her hair. "Oh, sweet girl."

Nora cried for a while. When she finally stopped, she wiped her face on her mom's flannel shirt. "Sorry about the snot."

Her mom smiled. "I can handle snot. I can handle a lot of things." She reached out and tucked a strand of Nora's hair behind her ear. "Asher told me something, but I'd like to hear it from you. Can you tell me what happened at the fair?"

Could Nora tell her mother what happened at the fair? Up here, by this random rock outcropping covered in graffiti and bird poop? This was possibly the strangest moment of her life. She swallowed. Her throat was thick and sore from crying. She imagined just coming out with it: *They took off my underwear. They branded me like a side of beef.* But she had to know something first. "Are you going to tell Dad?"

Her mom shook her head slowly. "No. But he does need to know. And I will help you tell him. We can do it together. Okay?"

"I don't know," she said.

She looked out over her mom's shoulder, past the rocks. The whole town of Faber was laid out below them like a LEGO village. She could feel her mom's eyes. She could feel the questions floating in the air between them.

They stood in silence for a moment, and then her mom said, "Do you know why I brought you up here?"

Nora shook her head.

"I brought you here so you could climb up on those rocks and scream if you want to. I'll scream with you."

Nora felt her lips twitch. "Are you serious?"

"Absolutely. Screaming is cathartic. When I was in college, I used to come up here and scream all the time."

Nora stared at her mom. "You *did*?"

"Yes. So...we could scream first and then you could tell me what happened. Or you could tell me first and then we could scream. Whichever you prefer."

Nora wanted to laugh, which was crazy. This wasn't funny at all. This was a serious situation. "Let's scream first," she said, "and then I'll tell you what happened."

Her mom held out her hand. Nora took it. Together, they walked to the tallest rock and started looking for a foothold.

ADAM XU

HE KNEW HIS MOTHER WAS DISAPPOINTED IN HIM, BUT he didn't know the extent of her disappointment until he walked up on the porch and she handed him a mop. "You are old enough to do dirty things," she said, "you are old enough to clean."

He tried to explain. "Bu shi ni shuo xiang de," he told her. *It's not what you think.* She was assuming things about him and Camille that weren't true, he said. They were just friends. In fact, they had been helping another girl, which was why Camille had been in his room—because they had been trying to do the right thing.

His mother dismissed Adam's version of events by handing him a bucket. "Come," she said. She strode across the lawn toward the car.

Adam shook his head to clear it. The night before had been so strange. He'd barely slept. *Eighteen holes*, he thought. *Tom Rizzoli. Liam Sullivan. Alec MacInerney.* Camille was on her way to Nora's house, to tell her what they'd discovered.

How would Nora react to this new information? However she felt, he wished he could be there.

"Ba tuoba he shuitong fang dao che li!" His mother was calling out the driver's side window.

Right. He couldn't be with Nora because his mother wanted him to get in the car with his mop and his bucket. This was his punishment. When other kids broke their parents' rules, they got grounded. Adam's mother was bringing him to work with her.

You are old enough to do dirty things, you are old enough to clean.

—⁓—

His mother parked on the street outside Kappa Kappa Nu. The morning was crisp and clear. Adam thought of what she had told him over the years, about the insides of sorority houses, and he longed to stay where he was, breathing in the leafy air. But no. He had to follow his mother up the stone walkway with his mop and bucket.

As soon as Adam's mother rang the bell, a girl in a KKN sweatshirt, dark hair piled on top of her head in a messy clump, leaped out on the porch.

"Jun!" she cried. "Thank God!"

To Adam's surprise, the girl threw her arms around his mother.

"So many pledges got sick last night! There was a graffiti party at Alpha Psi. Who knows what they were drinking. It was impossible to tell. Everything glowed. We opened all the windows, but..."

"Not a problem," his mother said briskly, extracting herself from the embrace. "We clean."

"Oh my God." The sorority girl finally registered Adam Xu's presence. Her brown eyes widened. "Is this your *son*?"

"Is my son. Yes."

"Jun! He's *cute*."

Adam barely had time to be flattered.

"Watch your step," the girl said, flinging the door open wide. She did a giant ballerina leap across the foyer. "It starts here."

A wall of smell hit Adam in the face. He nearly gagged.

After the girl disappeared inside, his mother handed him a trash bag, a face mask, a bottle of bleach, a roll of paper towels, and a pair of rubber gloves. "Stay," she said. "Clean."

She was like an army sergeant, with her short, sharp commands. Adam was used to his mother spouting long streams of Mandarin that he could just let roll right off him. Now, he had no choice but to snap to attention.

"Okay," he said.

His mother nodded, then muttered something he couldn't hear, and he didn't ask her to repeat it. She walked in a wide circle, circumnavigating the mess, then disappeared down the hallway. Adam was left alone in the foyer beside a puddle of vomit that stretched all the way across the tiled floor to a bank of mailboxes. It was disgusting.

228

For years, his mother had done this job. He had never understood it. Why did she clean sorority houses when she felt such disdain for sorority girls? He knew it was a money thing. He wasn't clueless. He knew she sent a check home to her family in Qibao every month, and, even though Adam had never been to China and had never met his mother's relatives, he admired her loyalty and work ethic. But still. With his father teaching at the university, surely his mother could find a better job, even without a degree. She was an amazing cook. Why couldn't she work in the dining hall? Later, he might suggest that to her. But now—Adam made the mistake of inhaling through his nose, and he gagged. Okay, see, he couldn't do that. He had to put on the face mask. He had to use the bleach to overpower the smell. From a chemistry perspective, this was actually pretty interesting. Sodium hypochlorite was an oxidizing agent. When it came into contact with viruses, bacteria, mold—or, in this case, graffiti party puke—it oxidized molecules inside the cells of the germs and destroyed them.

Adam steeled himself for the job.

He looked at the floor again. He would not think about how gross this was; he would think about the chemistry behind it. All these germ molecules to oxidize. It was an impressive number of germ molecules—more than a single human could possibly produce.

So many pledges got sick last night! He replayed the sorority girl's words as he poured and mopped. *Who knows what they were drinking. It was impossible to tell. Everything glowed.*

Adam's brain kept circling back to Nora on the golf course. Lying there, not moving. All she'd had was root beer.

He squatted down to soak up more oxidized puke germs with a wad of paper towels.

Did the brothers of Alpha Psi Beta roofie anyone else last night? Did the girls at the party know they were part of some game? Eighteen holes... Nora was number 9. The girl on Kevin Hamm's phone was number 4. Camille, it was fair to assume, was number 7... Were the numbers assigned at random? Were there fifteen more girls out there, just going about their lives, not knowing they were next?

Adam stood up to toss the wet towel wad into the trash bag, and *crack*. His head hit something hard and sharp. He cried out, rubbing the sore spot behind his ear. *Stupid metal mailboxes!* He gave them a kick.

It came to him then, in that moment. The tiny, wild seed of an idea.

PART
THREE

NORA

ON MONDAY NIGHT, WHEN NORA'S DAD GOT HOME from Massachusetts, she met him at the door. First, she hugged him. Then she said, "When you're finished unpacking...I need to tell you something. No rush, though." Nora knew her dad. After a work trip, he liked to unpack right away. He liked to start a load of laundry.

While he was doing that, Nora's mom gave Asher money so he could take Maeve to the Nautilus for ice cream.

"It's nine o'clock on a school night," Maeve said. "Why are you kicking us out?"

And Asher said, "She's not kicking us out, she's offering us the opportunity of a lifetime. Banana splits in our pajamas." Watching him prod Maeve out the door, Nora felt a twinge of gratitude for her brother. Just a twinge, though. She was still mad at him.

Finally, it was just the three of them in the living room: Nora and her mom on the couch, her dad in the puffy gray armchair, drinking a lemon-lime Powerade. Lemon-lime, Nora knew, was his favorite.

He took a few sips. Then he said, "So, ladybug. What did you want to tell me?"

Nora froze. What did she want to tell her dad? Nothing. She *wanted* to tell him nothing.

Nora could feel her mom's hand, warm on her arm. She swallowed. The last time she had felt this nervous, she was ten years old, climbing the ladder to the high dive at the Faber University pool. Her legs had been shaking. Her heart had been pounding. As soon as she'd reached the top, she'd wanted to climb back down. But there was an actual diving board rule—no backsies—and there was a line of kids at the bottom of the ladder, waiting. Nora remembered standing on the top rung, holding the guardrails and peering down at Cam.

"I can't," she said.

And Cam said, "Yes, you can." Cam, who was afraid of nothing, who had been jumping off the high board since they were six.

"I'm too scared," Nora said.

And Cam—only Cam would have the audacity to do this—cut the line and started climbing the ladder.

The lifeguard blew his whistle. "Hey! One at a time!"

But Cam ignored him. She climbed all the way to the top, and when she reached Nora, she said, "You can do this." Nora remembered how Cam had stood behind her, hands on her waist, as they inched along the diving board like one of those conga trains at a wedding. When they reached the end, Cam said, "Don't look down. Just hold my hand and jump. One...two...three..."

That's what this was. Here, in the living room. It was a hold-hands-and-jump situation. Nora reached for her mom's fingers and squeezed. Her mom squeezed back.

Nora looked at her dad. She opened her mouth: "Something happened, the night of the frat fair. I bought a root beer. Maybe after you saw me at the cotton candy booth. Maybe before. I really don't know. Everything's a blank."

"What do you mean," her dad said slowly, *"everything's a blank?"*

"I mean...I don't remember anything after the root beer. I woke up on the golf course. Well, Cam woke me up on the golf course. She'd gotten a text from this kid Adam Xu, saying I needed help. There were three Faber guys who took off my underwear, and one of them was unzipping his pants, but Adam, he stopped them—" As she said the words aloud, it finally hit her, the magnitude of what Adam Xu had done. "He had a baseball bat, and he chased them away. He saved me from...whatever they were going to do."

He saved me, she thought, *from being Amy Bachman. He saved me from being raped.*

Nora's dad was staring at her. He was completely still, unblinking, like they were playing a game of statues in the living room.

"I'm okay," she said. "I mean, Cam thinks they roofied

me, which makes sense since I can't remember anything, which is bad, I know, but otherwise...I'm okay." She wasn't just saying that; she actually did feel better. She felt relieved. The day before, she had stood on top of the highest rock in Faber and screamed until her ears rang and her throat burned. Then, she'd told her mom what happened. Now, her dad knew what happened, too. The truth was finally out, and her world hadn't imploded. They were all still here, breathing in and out.

Nora's dad shook his head. Slowly at first, then more vigorously. He stood up and started pacing back and forth behind the coffee table.

"Rhett," Nora's mom said.

Nora's dad stopped pacing and rubbed his forehead with his fingers, hard, as if trying to summon a coherent thought. Rubbed and rubbed until Nora's mom said, "Rhett" again.

Finally, Nora's dad looked at Nora. His forehead was pink. His eyes were pink, too. Pink and watery. "Were you...they didn't..."

"No, Dad," she said. She wouldn't mention the underwear on the flagstick, she decided, or the number 9. She had given her dad all the information he could handle right now. "I'm fine," she said.

He heaved out a sigh. "Thank God."

Nora was having a hard time getting past his eyes. Her dad was crying? Really? She wasn't sure what kind of reaction she'd expected from him. Anger, maybe. A call for heads to roll. In a way, this was worse. Nora had never seen her dad cry before—literally, never.

"*Rhett,*" Nora's mom said, even more sharply now. "Three Alpha Psis drugged our daughter, transported her to the golf course, and took off her underwear, with the clear intention of doing something worse. She is not *fine.*" Diane wrapped an arm around Nora's shoulders. "*None of this* is fine."

Rhett frowned. "Alpha Psis?"

Nora nodded. "There's a photo, going around school."

"A photo," he repeated.

"Someone at the frat fair took it, I don't know who. But it shows me and three guys about to get into a car. One of them is wearing an Alpha Psi T-shirt. Also..." She hesitated. She hadn't told her mom this part yet. "There's a video."

"A video," Rhett and Diane said together.

Nora nodded. "It shows what happened on the golf course. You can see the guy's shirt in that, too, Cam said, since Adam Xu enhanced the resolution. And Cam did some research. She thinks she knows their names."

Nora's dad brought his hand to his forehead again, like he was checking himself for a fever. "Jesus H. Christ."

"Rhett," Nora's mom said.

And Nora's dad said, "What?"

"You have to do something."

"Do something?" he repeated.

Nora didn't think he was being deliberately dense. He just couldn't, in his current state of shock, respond clearly.

"You're the AD," her mom said. "Make a formal report. Call for a committee hearing."

Nora's dad began shaking his head again, shaking and shaking, like a wet dog. Nora was afraid he might pull a muscle. "There has to be a mistake," he said finally.

"A *mistake?*" Diane said.

He shook his head again. "There's no way they would do this."

Nora's mom turned her body on the couch. She touched Nora's cheek with the backs of her fingers. "Sweetheart," she said. "Would you give us some time alone, please? Dad and I need to discuss a few things."

"Yeah, okay." Nora's head bobbed. She was the kid; they were the adults. They would take the wheel now. When she rose from the couch, her dad stepped forward, encircling her with his arms, though barely touching her, like she had just been in a car crash and might be gravely injured.

"It's okay, Dad," she said. "I'm okay."

—*z*—

She wasn't trying to eavesdrop. In fact, she was sitting at the breakfast bar, eating a bowl of Rice Krispies and deliberately trying not to listen. She was crunching. She was snap-crackle-popping. But Asher was right: their dad had only one volume. No matter how hard she crunched, words floated in from the living room.

My players . . . the university . . . conflict of interest . . .

Her dad's voice, loud and urgent. Her mom's, low and pleading.

Your daughter...stop and think...Jesus, Rhett.

Nora dumped more Rice Krispies into her bowl. She was starving. Finally, after nine days of barely eating anything, her body wanted food. This was a good thing. A healthy thing. She shoveled cereal into her mouth with abandon. Her parents could have their private conversation about her. She wouldn't intervene. She would sit here and fuel her body.

CAM

CAM WENT TO THE NAUTILUS AT 9:07 ON A MONDAY night because Asher had sent a text asking her to join him and Maeve for ice cream—and because she missed him. It had been days since they'd seen each other. She wasn't mad anymore. Also, she loved ice cream, and the Nautilus, unlike the Blue Bird, had Nutella chip. Cam could eat an entire gallon of Nutella chip.

"Hey there," she said to Asher and Maeve. They were already standing at the counter, surveying the flavors. They were both wearing pajamas. Maeve: maroon and gold stripes. Asher: plaid. Cam had to smile.

"Hey there." Asher smiled back.

"Nice jammies."

"Thank you," Maeve said, with no sense of irony.

They ordered. Cam tried to pay for her own ice cream, but Asher wouldn't let her. "My treat," he said.

"You mean *Mom's* treat," Maeve said. "Because she gave you money."

"Okay, wise guy," Asher said. "*Mom's* treat."

"Mom bribed us to get out of the house," Maeve explained to Cam as they slid into a booth. "So she and Dad could have some *top secret conversation* with Nora."

Cam raised her eyebrows across the table at Asher. He gave her a meaningful look.

"It's probably about that pervy picture," Maeve said, taking a bite of her sundae.

"What pervy picture?" Cam dug her spoon into a cloud of whipped cream.

"Nora and the three frat boys," Maeve said, dribbling hot fudge onto her chin. "People think I don't know things, but I do. I listen. I observe."

"Oh yeah?" Asher said. "What else do you know?"

"This." Maeve waved her spoon between Asher and Cam. "There's something going on here. Between you two."

"Oh, really?" Cam said.

"Yes, really."

Cam wasn't a big fan of kids, generally. But she was a big fan of Maeve. Maeve was her own person. She was a messy-haired, smart-mouthed bookworm who called it like she saw it.

Asher said, "What's going on with us, do you think?"

"I don't know," Maeve said. She shoved another spoonful of sundae into her mouth. "But I have my suspicions."

"You have your suspicions." Asher looked amused. He

nudged Cam's foot under the table. She nudged him back, smiling into her Nutella chip.

They sat in silence for a few minutes, eating. Then Maeve dropped her spoon on the table with a *clang*. "I gotta pee."

Cam slid out of the booth, and Maeve disappeared down the hall to the restroom.

"So," Cam said, sliding back in. "What's going on?"

"With us?" Asher said.

"With Nora. And your parents. Why'd they kick you out?"

"I don't know, but I think she's telling my dad what happened."

"*Really?*" Cam said.

Asher nodded. "She already told my mom. Well, technically, *I* told my mom, which forced Nora's hand, so now she's mad at me..." He frowned. "And I don't exactly blame her."

"You were trying to help," Cam said.

"Yeah, but I shouldn't have gone behind her back."

"You did what you thought was right," Cam said. She took another bite of Nutella chip, considering. Should she tell him? How much should she tell him?

"It's a game," she said finally. "Writing numbers on girls."

"What?" Asher said.

"The Sharpie nine that they wrote on Nora. It's a pledge thing."

"A pledge thing," he repeated.

"The Alpha Psi Betas are playing. They call it eighteen holes."

"How do you know?"

Cam thought about Malik, the two of them on the couch behind the frat house, grinding on each other. She shook her head. She couldn't think about that right now. "It's a long story," she said. "I've been doing some research. I tried to find out more. I googled a bunch of things. 'Eighteen holes.' 'Eighteen holes Faber University.' 'Eighteen holes Alpha Psi Beta.' Nothing came up—"

"Did you try a 'z'?" Maeve said, suddenly materializing at Cam's side.

"What?" Cam said.

"There are these girls in my class. They have this stupid club and they call themselves the Foxes, but they spell it with a 'z' on the end. *F-o-x-e-z*. Every time they take a selfie, they're all, 'hashtag foxez.' 'Foxez foreva.' They think they're so cool. It's really annoying."

"I'll bet," Cam said. *A "z" would be too cutesy for frat boys, wouldn't it?* she thought. Or would it? She'd check later.

"And speaking of *annoying*," Maeve said, sliding back into the booth, "let me tell you about my friend Ella J's mom, who says Harry Potter should be banned from school because it promotes *Wicca*."

Just like that, Maeve was off and running.

Asher nudged Cam's foot under the table. They both grinned.

After the Nautilus closed, Cam walked Asher and Maeve home. When they reached the Melchiondas' front steps, Asher told Maeve to go inside without him; he'd be right behind her.

"Sure you will," Maeve said. From the porch, she waved one maroon-and-gold arm. "Adios, secret lovers!"

"Wow," Cam said.

"Yeah," Asher said.

"How old is she again?"

"Eleven. Going on twenty-five."

Cam shook her head. She remembered Maeve before she was a real person—when she was just a little kindergartener begging Cam to read her a story. Now she said things like "pervy picture" and "secret lovers." How could Nora stand watching her grow up?

"So," Asher said, smiling. "Here we are."

Cam looked at Asher. They were standing on the stone walkway, lit up by the porch light. She wanted to smile back, but they were standing right in front of the house. If Nora came out, how would Cam explain gazing into Asher's eyes with a silly grin on her face? And something else was bothering her, too. It was Malik. Why, oh why had she kissed him? Why hadn't she realized how much she liked Asher until right this very second?

"Come here," she said, pulling Asher away from the light, into the neighbor's yard. "I kissed someone," she blurted. "On Saturday night. But it was for a good cause."

She tried to explain. She had gone undercover to get justice for Nora. She had created not one, but two fake Instagram profiles. She had attended the Alpha Psi Beta graffiti party, armed with Mace and a switchblade comb. She had kissed a fraternity pledge, but only to extract information—okay, in the interest of full disclosure, she had never kissed a college guy before, and she wanted to see if it felt different, but the *point* was, kissing Malik had meant nothing to her. Less than nothing. Because she liked Asher. She really, really liked him.

"You kissed a random frat boy," Asher said.

Cam nodded. "Yes."

"Because you wanted to extract information for your sting operation. And because he was in college."

"It sounds stupid when you say it out loud," Cam said.

"Yes, it does."

"I was an idiot," she said. "I'm sorry."

Asher sighed. He closed his eyes and pinched the bridge of his nose between his thumb and his forefinger. There was something about this gesture that made him look like Mr. M.

"You look exactly like your dad right now," Cam said.

Asher's eyes snapped open. "Don't say that."

"Why not?"

"I don't want to look like him."

"Are you kidding? Your dad's—" She stopped herself. Saying how gorgeous Mr. M was would not help her cause.

"Forget I said that. You look like you. And I like you. And I would like you to forgive me for being an idiot.".

Asher's face looked pained.

"Please," Cam said. Did she need to get down on her knees and beg?

"I have two conditions," he said.

"Shoot," Cam said.

"We get *this*"—Asher waved his hand in the air between them—"out in the open. Which means we tell Nora."

"Fine," Cam said.

"And...you go to the homecoming dance with me."

Cam grimaced. "Are you serious?"

"Yes."

"*Why?*"

"Because I'm a senior, and I have never gone."

"You're not missing anything," Cam said. "Everyone says it's a shit show."

"Well, I'm not everyone, and I want to go with you. So."

Cam sighed. She had painted herself into a corner. "Fine," she said.

"Shake on it," Asher said.

Cam shook on it. "But just so you know," she said, "I will not be wearing a sexy dress. I will probably be wearing sweatpants and flip-flops. And one of my dad's ugly Hawaiian shirts."

"I don't care what you wear," Asher said.

"Really?" Cam said.

"Really."

"So if I showed up in some low-cut, silky number with a slit up the leg, it wouldn't affect you one way or the other?"

Asher smiled. "You have a low-cut silky number?"

"What if I did?" Cam said.

"Then I'd say, don't let it go to waste."

"Well...I don't."

"In that case," he said, "wear whatever you want. Whatever's comfortable to dance in. Wear a trash bag. We can both wear trash bags."

"Kiss me," she said.

And he did.

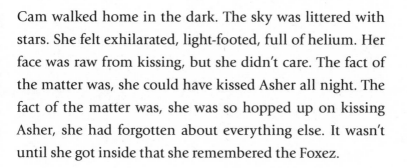

Cam walked home in the dark. The sky was littered with stars. She felt exhilarated, light-footed, full of helium. Her face was raw from kissing, but she didn't care. The fact of the matter was, she could have kissed Asher all night. The fact of the matter was, she was so hopped up on kissing Asher, she had forgotten about everything else. It wasn't until she got inside that she remembered the Foxez.

ADAM XU

HE HAD BEEN SITTING IN THE DARK, PLAYING D&D WITH Tobias Muenker and some of his Cleveland friends—FaceTime wasn't the same as playing in person, but it was better than nothing—when his phone pinged. It was Cam. **You awake?**

He texted back: **Give me a few**

He typed out a message to Tobias: **Gtg. Resume tmrw?** A minute later, his phone rang.

"Hey," he said. He climbed into bed, pulling the comforter over his head to muffle the sound.

"It's with a 'z,' " Camille said.

"What?" he said.

"Eighteen holes with a 'z.' They have a finsta."

A *finsta*. He had to think for a second. "A fake Insta?"

"Yes," she said.

"They let you in?" he said.

"No."

"Then how do you know it's them?"

"I don't," she said. "It's just a hunch. That's why I need you."

"Me?" he said.

"If it's their account, and it's about the game, they'll never grant access to a girl. But they might to Matt R."

"You think they'll grant access to some random high school kid from Michigan?"

"Maybe," Camille said. "It's worth a try. I told you, Nora won't let us report the photo or the video. We have to find another way.... Please, Adam."

He hesitated, wondering if he should tell her. "I did something...earlier today."

"What?" she said.

"I put flyers in all the sorority mailboxes."

"Flyers?"

"Yeah." He told Cam how the idea came to him when he was cleaning puke off the floor in Kappa Kappa Nu and he banged his head on their stupid mailboxes. He told her how he made copies at Staples, and then he swiped his mom's key card so he could get inside the sorority houses, and he put a flyer in every mailbox. "Just giving them a heads-up," he explained. "Saying if they found a number somewhere on their body and they didn't know how it got there, or if they had any information about a pledge game called eighteen holes, they should contact campus police."

There was silence for a second. Then Camille said, "Have I told you lately that I love you?"

"Not lately." He smiled in the dark. "No."

"Seriously, Adam. You're brilliant. You're cute. You bend over backward to help people. How has no girl snagged you yet?"

"Okay," he said. "Now you're just buttering me up."

"Is it working?"

"Possibly."

Camille said, "So you'll do it?"

He said, "I'll try. But don't hold your breath."

"I will literally be holding my breath until you find out what's on that finsta. Call me back."

"Wait—" he said. "You want me to do it *now*?"

"No time like the present."

He started to tell her it was too late—he'd try in the morning—but she had already hung up.

He stared at his phone in the dark.

The problem wasn't logging into Matt R's Instagram account at 11:27 PM and DMing the Alpha Psi who'd invited him to the graffiti party; the problem was not knowing what to say. At school, there were guys who always seemed to know what to say. Like Adam Courtmanche, who had an ease with people that Adam Xu envied. Adam Courtmanche strode through the hallways like he owned them: grinning, fist-bumping, ribbing his friends about something that happened on the football field. That's the kind of guy Matt R needed to be right now: confident and effortless. A guy's guy.

@mattyrtouchdown24
Hey man, sorry I never made it to the
party. I got busted by my mom and
she canceled the trip. Sucks

It took a few minutes. Then a reply appeared:

@danvee99
Troublemaker. What'd you do?

@mattyrtouchdown24
Got caught with a girl in my room

@danvee99
Nice

@mattyrtouchdown24
She was not pleased

@danvee99
The girl or your mom?

@mattyrtouchdown24
Ha! My mom. The girl was plenty
pleased, believe me

Writing those words, Adam felt sleazy. He sounded
like Kevin Hamm in the locker room. But that, he had to
remind himself, was the whole point.

@danvee99
Cocky bastard

@mattyrtouchdown24
Truth. How was the party?

@danvee99
Off the hook

@mattyrtouchdown24
A plethora of hotties?

@danvee99
Sorority girls in white t's as far as the eye could see

@mattyrtouchdown24
Dude seriously?

@danvee99
Let's just say if you play faber football and pledge APB you will be golden

@mattyrtouchdown24
A lot of action?

@danvee99
You have no idea

Adam hesitated. He didn't want to blow it, but he needed to move this thing along. He took a deep breath.

@mattyrtouchdown24
Do you have pics?

When @danvee99 didn't respond right away, Adam tried another tactic.

@mattyrtouchdown24
I'm getting recruited by colgate too. Those guys seem pretty cool. They sent me a bunch of pics

@danvee99

Dude you are not going to fucking colgate

@mattyrtouchdown24

Y not? Gate girls are hot

@danvee99

FU girls are hotter

@mattyrtouchdown24

Prove it

@danvee99

Jesus kid. Balls much?

@mattyrtouchdown24

If you want to be an alpha...

@danvee99

I am just drunk enough to give you 10 min. Send a follow request to @18holez. Get in and get out

CAM

IT WAS AFTER MIDNIGHT WHEN HER PHONE PINGED.

ADAM XU
He gave me 10 min of access. I'm blocked now, but I took as many screen shots as I could. Sending now...

CAM
Omg

ADAM XU
Yeah

CAM
Holy f-ing shit

ADAM XU
I know

CAM
Meet me @ 7-11 before school

NORA

IN THE MORNING, CAM WANTED NORA TO MEET HER AT 7-Eleven. Important, the text said. When Nora got there, Cam was waiting outside on the curb, holding a blueberry muffin and a kid-size carton of milk.

"Sit," Cam said. "Eat."

"I already ate," Nora said, which was true. After all the weekend's drama, this morning had felt surprisingly normal. Her mom had made French toast and turkey bacon. Her dad had kissed her head on his way out the door.

"I don't want you to worry," he'd said. "I will take care of everything."

Everything. The word was both all-encompassing and vague. What did he mean, exactly? Was he planning to make a formal report to the dean? Was he planning to burn down the Alpha Psi Beta house? Nora didn't know—and she didn't ask. She ate a second serving of French toast with an extra drizzle of syrup. She thought, *My dad will take care of everything.* She thought, *This is out of my hands.*

"You don't have to eat," Cam said. "Just sit with

me." She patted the curb beside her. "I have to tell you something."

"You really don't," Nora said.

She already knew what Cam wanted to tell her. She had seen for herself the night before, when she was up in her room, pulling down the window shades. She might not have looked out, but the flood lamp was on, so, naturally, her eyes had been drawn to the circle of light on the grass. At first, she hadn't known quite what to make of what she was seeing in the shadows: two bodies, clenched in an embrace. Was it her parents? Nora squinted into the night. Were her parents *grinding on each other* in the back-yard? Ew. But no. That couldn't be her dad. His arms were too thin. His hair was too long. It was…Asher. Suddenly, Nora remembered his weird announcement at dinner last week: *I think I might have a girlfriend.* She told herself to pull down the shades; this was none of her business. Even though Asher had blabbed to their mom about Nora's personal business, that didn't mean Nora would exact revenge by spying on him and his secret girlfriend. *Look away,* she told herself. *Now.* But something stopped her. It was the sound of laughter rising up from below. Nora knew that laugh. That was *Cam's* laugh. Those were *Cam's* neon yellow running shoes.

Asher and Cam.

She had been stunned—Jesus, she felt like she had been dunked in ice water. Her brother and her best friend. Her *brother* and her *best friend* were hooking up in the backyard.

It was wrong on so many levels, and yet, in a way, it made sense. Asher and Cam were the two bossiest people Nora knew. They were always telling her what to do, how to live her life. They both thought they had all the answers, to everything. They were the perfect match. But that didn't make it any less wrong.

"I saw you and Asher," Nora told Cam, "last night. In the backyard. So...thanks for *that* horror movie."

"Oh," Cam said. She looked surprised. "Shit. It wasn't...I mean, I've been meaning to tell you."

"Oh, really?"

"Yes."

"You've been *meaning to tell me* that you're hooking up with my brother?"

Cam nodded. "Yeah. But that's not why I—" She glanced over Nora's shoulder. "Hey."

"What?" Nora said, twisting around. There was Adam Xu, standing behind her. Khaki pants, green T-shirt, thumbs hooked around the straps of his backpack. He looked taller than she remembered. Cuter, too. Had he gotten a haircut? Was he using *gel*?

"Hey, Nora," he said.

"Hey," she said. It came out less like a greeting and more like a question. *Hey?* Since when did Adam Xu coif his hair and hang out at 7-Eleven?

"I asked Adam to meet us here," Cam said, "because he has been a part of this from the beginning, and what we just found is....well..."

257

"Wait—" Nora said slowly. "This isn't about Asher?"

"No," Cam said.

There was a look on Cam's face, and on Adam Xu's face—although, honestly, when did Adam Xu look anything other than serious? But still. Nora knew something bad was coming.

"Remember how I said the number nine was a pledge thing?" Cam said. "A game? Hang on—" She took out her phone and started tapping.

Nora shook her head. "My dad's already on it. He's taking care of everything. You don't have to—"

"Look."

Cam's phone was in Nora's face. And there...there was her stars-and-stripes underwear, all lit up against the night sky. Under the photo was a caption: **#18Holez #9 #Godblessamerica.**

"Oh my God." Nora felt her stomach lurch. She shouldn't have eaten all that French toast. "Where did you get this?"

"The Alpha Psis have a finsta," Cam said. "They let Adam on it last night. He took screenshots...swipe right."

Nora shook her head. She was thinking about the Sharpie 9 on her crotch, the pile of alcohol-soaked cotton balls she'd used to scrub it off.

"You need to see the others," Cam said.

Nora swiped right. A girl's rear end, red thong underwear, black number 13 scrawled across one butt cheek. **#18Holez #13 #bumstheword.**

"Keep going," Cam said.

Nora swiped again. A new image filled the screen. Lacy bra, cleavage, black four. **#18Holez #4 #doublebubble**.

"Enough." She closed her eyes and shoved the phone in the general direction of Cam. She could feel Adam Xu's hand on her arm. She shook it off.

#18Holez, she thought. Something was glinting at her from the recesses of her brain, like the pennies her dad used to toss into the deep end of the Faber University pool so Nora and Asher could dive down to the bottom and retrieve them.

"It's a *tradition*," she heard Cam say. "Started by some Alpha Psi brother back in the nineties. There's a dedication on their page. They don't say who he is, but they call him the game master."

"What?" Nora's eyes flew open.

"It's a *game* to them. Like they're actually playing *golf*."

Nora's throat felt thick and tight. She could barely get the words out. "I have to go."

"Where?" Cam said.

And Adam Xu said, "School starts in twenty minutes."

Nora ignored them. Her brain was spinning. Was this déjà vu? Or part of a dream she'd had once? It was the kind of thing that— No, it was not the kind of thing that anyone would dream up.

"Nor," Cam said. "Where are you going?"

"Home," she said. Her feet were already moving.

"We're coming with you," Cam said.

Nora didn't care if they came or not. As she ran, her back-pack bumped against her tailbone. The bottoms of her UGGs made a thwacking sound on the sidewalk. *Thwack, thwack, thwack.* UGGs were terrible running shoes—who would run in fleecy cement blocks? They had no arch support.

Nora's feet propelled her all the way home. The front door was unlocked. The front door was always unlocked. Inside the house, down the hall to her dad's office, to the shelf lined with sports books. *Gridiron Genius, Hockey Tough, The Boys of Winter.* This was the first place Nora checked. She scanned the titles, but she didn't see what she was looking for. So she opened the door to the cabinet under her dad's desk, and there it was: *The Mirror.* When Nora was young, she loved seeing the old photos—her mom as a freshman, her dad as a senior, both looking so young. Now, she flipped straight to the senior portraits, arranged in alphabetical order. *Ives, Jameson, Jennings…* Her heart was pounding. She was being paranoid, right? There was no way… *Kurian, Lambeaux, London…* She just had to check… *Marcus, Meehan, Melchionda…*

Rhett Andrew Melchionda.

Nora blinked at her dad's twenty-two-year-old face. She lowered her gaze a centimeter to the italicized writing below. *"Set your goals high, and don't stop till you get there."* —Bo Jackson. Activities: *Rugby 1–4 (Captain 3, 4); Blue Highway (vocals, guitar); Alpha Psi Beta 1–4 (President 4); 18 Holes (Founder, Game Master).*

She felt a wave of nausea roll over her.

"Nor?" Cam said.

"Nora?" Adam Xu said. "What is it?"

Nora wanted to laugh. She wanted to scream. Her life was a dumpster fire!

No. She shook her head. There had to be another explanation. Her dad liked golf. Nora knew this for a fact because he had taken her to the driving range a few times over the years. He had taught her how to swing a 3 wood. And he always played in the alumni weekend charity golf tournament, with his old frat brothers. Had he played golf as a student? She couldn't remember him saying. But he must have. He *must* have. And he'd founded some game, some intramural club for fellow student golfers. He'd been the "master" of *that*. Right?

"Nor," Cam said.

"Nora?" Adam Xu said.

Nora ignored them and stared at her dad's senior portrait. He had a great smile. Everyone said so. How good-looking he was. How charismatic. How amazing he was at his job.

"He is," she murmured.

"What?" Cam said.

"My dad," Nora said. Rhett Melchionda: setter of dislocated shoulders, deliverer of babies, protector of daughters from flying hockey pucks. *That* was her dad. The guy who made pancakes in the shape of *Despicable Me* characters, who cut the crusts off her PB&Js. The guy who taught her to appreciate all the obscure football and hockey rules that no one else knew, who could sing every lyric to every classic rock song ever written. He was the best person she knew. *Rhett Melchionda, athletic director by day, superhero by night.* There was no way. No possible way. So how to explain this feeling, this bubble of panic rising in her chest?

"What about him?" Cam said.

Nora shook her head. She was not, at the moment, able to answer. There was a roaring in her ears, like an airplane taking off. She took hold of the page, felt its slick heft between her fingertips, and yanked.

The paper tore, it ripped.

"What are you doing?" Cam said.

Nora held up the jagged piece of paper. "I think he invented it."

"What?" Cam said.

"Eighteen holes. I think my dad started the game."

Cam shook her head hard, as if trying to shake water from her ears after swimming. "No way."

"Yes," Nora said. "I really think he did."

"No," Cam said firmly. "That doesn't make any sense."

Cam was right: It didn't make any sense. But that didn't mean it wasn't true.

Nora glanced at her phone. It was 7:38. School would be starting in two minutes, but she would not be attending. Nora had entered an alternate universe where the usual rules no longer applied. She folded the ripped-out yearbook page in half, then into fourths.

"Nor," Cam said slowly. "What are you doing?"

Wasn't it obvious? She was folding her father into fourths and stuffing him in her pocket. She was walking out the door.

"Where are we going?" Cam asked, matching her stride for stride.

Nora didn't answer. When he'd said goodbye this morning, he had been wearing his running shoes and hydration belt. She knew where he would be.

"I'll email school," Adam Xu said, tapping on his phone as he jogged alongside her, "let them know we've been delayed."

Delayed? Nora thought. Was that what they were? It was such a civilized word: "delayed." It made her think of Sir Topham Hatt from *Thomas the Tank Engine*. When she and Asher were little, they had been obsessed with that show.

"You have caused *confusion* and *delay*," she said, deeply and Britishly.

"What?" Cam said.

Nora shook her head. She couldn't lose it now. She had to keep it together. There was Crockett Stadium, rising up before them like a castle. She pointed. "He's in there."

"How do you know?" Cam said.

"I just know," she said.

When they got to the entrance, Nora stopped. "You guys should go to school. I've got it from here."

Cam said, "Are you sure?"

Adam Xu said, "We're happy to stay."

Nora shook her head. "I need to do this alone."

"Okay," Cam said. "But before we go, I have to tell you something. I posted this thing on Insta, like an hour ago . . . well, Katie J posted this thing on Insta—"

Nora looked at her sharply. "What *kind* of thing?"

"Hang on." Cam fiddled with her phone.

When she handed it to Nora, there was a photo of the Alpha Psi house. And this:

> @katiegategrrrl
>
> @supfaber
>
> @fabergazette
>
> The alpha psi beta pledges are playing a game.
> These photos are from their finsta account @18Holez.
> #faberuniversity #faberNY #thisisourtown
>
> #standup #getoutraged #wearenotagame

Nora dragged her eyes away from the screen.

"I know," Cam said. "I should have asked you first. But I had to do something. When I saw all those girls, those hashtags, I was so mad, I just—"

"I made a flyer," Adam Xu blurted.

Nora turned to look at him.

"Warning the Faber sororities about the game. Telling them to go to campus police if they had any information. I put copies in all their mailboxes."

Instagram posts to the *Gazette*? Flyers in mailboxes? The words floated into Nora's ears like a foreign language, phrases she couldn't translate.

264

"We were trying to help," Cam said.

Nora shook her head slowly. "I have to go in."

"Nor," Cam said. "You could be wrong."

"I'm not," she said.

"Just give him a chance to explain."

"I have to go in," she repeated. Her voice sounded buzzy in her ears. Her whole body was thrumming.

She said goodbye.

She swung open the gate.

She walked out onto the track. Her dad was just below the press boxes, sprinting up the stadium stairs. Fast feet, high knees. He had textbook form.

Her breath felt thick and tight in her chest. Was this a mistake? Maybe she should call her mom first. Diane was at a PTO meeting, but she wouldn't mind being interrupted, not for—

"Hey there!"

Too late. He was on his way down. He was waving.

"Shit," Nora murmured. What was she doing? She should be in homeroom. She should be standing at her desk, hand to heart, reciting the Pledge of Allegiance.

Shit, shit, shit.

He was walking over. Sweat dripping. Eyebrows raised. He was about to ask any number of questions: *What are you doing here? Is everything okay? Shouldn't you be in school?*

Nora's heart hammered, as if her body was trying to stop her from talking. "What's eighteen holes?"

Her dad gave her a quizzical look. "Well, hello to you, too."

"Dad," Nora said. She dreaded the answer, but she needed to know. "What's eighteen holes?"

He raised his eyebrows at her. She saw the thin, pink scar on the right side, just barely visible, and she had a flashback to sitting beside him in the stands at Tayte Rink on her tenth birthday.

"It's a complete round of golf," he said.

She shook her head. "No."

"No?"

She reached into her pocket and pulled out the piece of paper. She shoved it at him. "I mean this."

He unfolded the paper. Then he looked at Nora with surprise. "Is this a page from my Faber yearbook?"

"Yes," she said.

"You ripped it out?"

"Yes."

"Why?" He sounded confused, maybe even hurt.

"Because I need to know the truth."

"The truth about what?"

"*Dad.*" She was getting frustrated now. Was he being deliberately dense? "Just tell me. What's eighteen holes? I know it's not golf."

He unsnapped one of the bottles from his hydration belt, took a sip of water, snapped it back on. "Ladybug—" He frowned at his watch. "Shouldn't you be at school?"

She shook her head. He still hadn't answered the question. She asked, for the fourth time: "What's eighteen holes?"

His expression was inscrutable. "It was a fraternity thing," he said. "Back in the day."

"What kind of fraternity thing?"

"I can't tell you that."

"What do you mean you *can't tell me that*? You were the *founder.*" She pointed to the yearbook page clutched in his hand. "It says so right there."

He shook his head. "I took an oath."

"You took an *oath*?"

"When I pledged Alpha Psi Beta, I took an oath of loyalty. I know that may sound strange to you, but..."

No, Nora thought. It did not sound "strange" to her. It sounded ridiculous. Her dad was a grown man, a *father.*

"The Greek system can be hard to explain," he continued, "to someone on the outside. Traditions and rituals are an integral part of any fraternity...."

He kept going, but Nora was no longer listening. He took an *oath*? He pledged his *loyalty* to a bunch of frat boys, twenty-plus years ago, and now he was using that as an excuse for not answering her question? Nora felt a surge of white-hot anger. "You know they're still playing it, right?" she said.

"What?" her dad said.

"The Alpha Psis. They're still playing eighteen holes. It wasn't just *back in the day.* They wrote on me, the night of the frat fair. On the golf course, when I was passed out. They wrote a number nine, right here—" She pointed between her legs. "With a Sharpie. They hung my underwear on a flagstick, and they took a picture. They posted it on their secret Instagram page. Hashtag eighteen holes. Hashtag nine. Hashtag God bless America."

Nora's dad went silent. She wasn't sure what she'd expected, but he was giving her nothing. She allowed herself a moment to really look at him. At the impossibly bright blue of his eyes.

"Dad," she whispered. "Why do your old frat brothers call you 'master of the universe'?"

He shook his head. All the color had leached out of his face.

"I need to hear you say it."

He started to pace, the way he always did. *Really?* Nora thought. He was just going to walk back and forth, raking his fingers through his hair? He wasn't going to answer her?

He can't admit the truth, she thought. *He wants to keep it a secret.* Just like Asher and Cam wanted to keep their relationship a secret. Just like Nora's mom wanted to keep Amy Bachman a secret. Just like Nora wanted to keep everything those frat boys did to her a secret.

She was *so done* with secrets.

"Dad," Nora said. Her voice came out strangled. She was thinking about the girls in the other pictures, the other numbers, the other hashtags: #bumstheword. #double bubble. She was thinking about Peyton Mallory and Jason Mann. Were they Alpha Psis, too? Had her dad really thought that the girls who accused them of sexual assault were *lying*? Was her dad's loyalty so blind that he actually ignored the truth? Did he *cover* for his players when he knew they were guilty? Of course he covered for his players when he knew they were guilty. God, it was suddenly so obvious that she wanted to throw up. Did her mom know? And if her mom knew, how could she stay married to someone like that? Nora couldn't think straight. Her brain was spinning too fast. It was slipping off the rails.

I don't want you to worry, her dad had said to her at breakfast. *I will take care of everything.* He'd said that, and yet he was the one who had started the game. He was the reason Nora's underwear was posted on Instagram. He was complicit in all of this.

Nora felt a hot gush of anger rising in her chest. An animal roar came out of her, and this made her dad stop pacing.

"Are you okay?" he said.

She stared at him, gaping in disbelief. "No, I am not okay!" She let loose another roar. "They drugged me and took off my clothes and wrote on me because of *you! You* started this! I blame *you!*"

Her dad looked stunned. Nora couldn't believe she'd said those things. It was like a plug inside of her had suddenly come loose and every true and furious thought in her head was erupting out of her mouth.

"You don't mean that," her dad said.

"I *do* mean that," Nora said. She could feel her legs shake. She could feel her hands clenched painfully at her sides, but she kept going. "I have spent all this time being scared that you would find out what happened, that you would think less of me. But I'm not the one who should feel ashamed. *You* should feel ashamed."

"Ladybug—" Her dad reached out his hand, but Nora swatted it away.

"Stop calling me that!"

Her dad blinked.

"I am not a bug!"

"I can see that you're upset," he said evenly. "And I'm going to give you some space to calm down."

He turned and started walking away.

He was actually *walking away from her.*

The hot lava inside of Nora rose again. She considered chasing after him—he was only ten feet from where she was standing—but she was too angry to move.

"No!" she yelled. "I'm going to give *you* some space! To fix this!"

—z—

Nora wasn't going to school. She had already decided. She was going to tell her mom about her dad. He was her husband; she deserved to know the truth about the man she'd married. But when Diane learned about eighteen holes, what would she do? Would she crumple up in a ball? Would she kick Nora's dad out of the house? Nora had felt, in the two days since she and her mom had screamed side by side on top of Mount Aggie, that they had forged a connection.

Her mom had been open about her past; she had revealed a whole new side of herself—a side that wore micro dresses and eyeliner and howled at the sky. Nora found it hard to admit, but she may have been wrong about her mother. She had thought that Diane was flawless and untouchable, like one of those Teflon pans that nothing adhered to, and was therefore clueless to the messiness of life. But she wasn't.

Nora assumed that her mom would be home from the PTO meeting by now. And she was right. Diane was in the kitchen, sitting at the breakfast bar, drinking a cup of tea.

"Mom?"

When Diane looked up, her mouth formed an O of surprise. "What's wrong? Are you sick?"

"I have to tell you something," Nora said. She wasn't sure she could do this. She didn't want to see the look on her mom's face when she learned the truth. Diane loved Rhett; she had loved him since she was eighteen years old.

"Tell me," she said.

Nora lowered herself to a stool. The cushion was covered in yellow fabric with tiny white flowers. Her mom had sewed it herself; she had sewed all the cushion covers in the kitchen, and the curtains for the windows, too. Her mom could sew anything. She had every life skill necessary to survive.

Nora said, "It's about Dad." And it all came pouring out, like water from a pitcher.

Cam crashing the Alpha Psi Beta party. *I met this frat*

boy . . . and he wrote a number seven on me. . . . He said it was for a game, some pledge thing.

The finsta photos. *#18Holez #9 #Godblessamerica.*

The yearbook. *18 Holes (Founder, Game Master).*

Nora confronting her dad in the middle of Crockett Stadium and him trying to explain his actions. *I took an oath of loyalty.*

And then, even though she wasn't proud to admit this, Nora said, "I told him it was his fault what happened to me. I yelled at him, and he walked away. He said I needed some space to calm down."

Nora's mom covered her eyes with her fingers the way Nora used to cover her eyes with her fingers whenever she and Cam watched *The Exorcist.* The story of her dad was like *The Exorcist.* It was her family's own private horror movie, and God, Nora just wished she could clap her hands as the credits rolled and walk out the theater doors into the sunshine. For a few seconds, her mom didn't speak at all. She might have been in shock, or she might have been trying to process this information, Nora wasn't sure. Either way, the truth was out, filling the air molecules between them.

"Mom?" she said.

When Diane opened her eyes, she wore an expression Nora had never seen on her before. She was wearing her usual peasant blouse/gold cross combo, but she didn't look like herself. She looked grim—no, she looked *pissed.*

"I'm going to drop you off at school," she said.

School? Nora thought. *Now?*

"And then I am going to find your father."

Right, Nora thought. She was going to confront him. She was going to demand action.

Diane stood up, and Nora stood up, too, thinking, *You got this, Mom! Stay strong!* Would she make her dad confess to the dean?

Her mom headed out the door.

Nora followed. Until that moment, she had never imagined her mom confronting her dad about anything. But her dad's terrible life decisions couldn't be undone, any more than that night on the golf course could be undone, any more than Cam's Instagram post or Adam Xu's flyers could be undone.

Everything was out there.

CAM

SHE WAS STILL IN A STATE OF SHOCK. MR. M HAD CRE-
ated a game, the goal of which was to sexually assault
girls? *Mr. M?* The thought was inconceivable to Cam. It
was—how else could she say it?—soul crushing.

"This is going to blow up," Adam Xu said, as the they
walked into school together. "Because of us."

"Probably," Cam said. "Yeah."

Adam was right. By the time they picked up their late
passes and headed to second period, Katie J's @supfaber
post had already traveled around the high school like
a virus. Everyone was talking about it. Everywhere Cam
went—the science lab, the girls' room, the gym—she heard
people murmuring the same two words: "Eighteen holes."

"Did you see this?" Chelsea and Anna and Becca asked
in the hall between classes. All three of them shoved their
phones in Cam's face to show her Katie J's post.

"I saw it," Cam said.

I wrote it.

At lunch, Chelsea and Anna and Becca scrolled through

photo after photo. Number 4. Number 13. Number 2. "Is one of these girls Nora?" Chelsea asked.

Cam shook her head mutely. The truth rested on her tongue like a communion wafer. She wanted to spit it out, but she couldn't; she had to choke it down. This whole time, Cam had been telling herself that she was being a good friend—making decisions for Nora because Nora wasn't thinking straight. But Cam was the one who had set all this in motion. *Cam* had blown off the frat fair and sent Nora there alone. *Cam* had created fake Instas and gone undercover and flirted to convince a drunken pledge to reveal his secrets. It was all so fun and exciting! Making out in closets, making out on couches, pretending to be Michelle, pretending to be Katie J. Novelty! That's what Cam had been after, right, if she was brutally honest? She had convinced herself that she was being a good friend, when really, she was the opposite. Cam hadn't helped Nora. She'd blown up Nora's life.

I think my dad started the game.

No. Cam couldn't stand to think about Mr. M right now. Could not stand it! She picked up her Hoodsie ice cream cup and held it to her hot forehead.

Better.

"What are you *doing*?" Anna said, looking vaguely disgusted.

"Trying to reset my brain," Cam said.

ADAM XU

IN THE HOT-LUNCH LINE, HE DEBATED. BURGER OR PIZZA? He had just put a burger on his tray when he heard a voice.

"Adam?"

He turned around, even though whoever had spoken was probably talking to Adam Courtmanche. But no— it was Nora, looking right at him, which was a surprise. When they'd said goodbye on the Faber campus, he hadn't expected to see her at school.

"Hey," he said.

"Hey," she said. Then: "Can I eat with you? I don't feel like dealing with anyone right now."

Adam nodded. "Yeah. Of course."

He waited for Nora to load her tray: turkey sandwich, chips, apple. They flashed their lunch cards at the cashier and walked through the cafeteria to an empty table by the window. He could feel eyes watching them. *Adam Xu and Nora Melchionda eating lunch together?* This was highly unusual. Adam was used to sitting on the perimeter. When Tobias still lived in Faber the two of them would sit at one of the corner tables, where they could hear each other talk. Now, he usually sat alone, reading a book, while Nora invariably sat at one of the large, loud, center tables, surrounded by friends. A month ago, eating lunch with Nora Melchionda would have been his dream come true. He would have been falling over himself, stuttering with nerves. But his feelings for Nora were...How to explain? He still liked her; of course he did. And he was happy to sit with her at lunch. But he didn't feel nervous. When they'd said goodbye earlier, outside the stadium, it had suddenly occurred to him: Nora wasn't a fantasy anymore. She was a serious and complicated person—more serious and complicated, perhaps, than he had given her credit for. She wasn't just a database of observations that he had collected over the years. She was a real human being in an unfathomable situation, and she needed a friend.

"I really appreciate this," she said as they sat down.

"It's no problem," he said.

"I was right," she said. "My dad didn't deny it."

"Oh." Adam nodded slowly. "Wow...Are you okay?"

"I think I'm in shock," she said.

"Do you...want me to walk you to the nurse?"

Nora shook her head. "I need to eat something." She unwrapped the plastic wrap from her sandwich. "I told my mom. She went to see him. To confront him. I've never seen her so mad." Nora took a bite of sandwich and a blob of mustard oozed out onto her chin.

Adam handed her a napkin.

"Thanks," she said, swiping at the mustard.

Adam took a bite of burger.

They ate in silence for a little while. Then Nora said, "So I have to ask you something."

"Okay," he said.

"Why did you make that flyer?"

Adam reached for his lemonade and took a sip. He set the bottle on the tray. "I didn't want anyone else to get hurt. After seeing you..."

She cocked her head at him.

He took a deep breath. "Seeing you on the golf course like that, just lying there? I thought you were dead. It was awful. "

Nora frowned.

"I didn't mean—" He scrambled to explain. "It was awful for *you*. Way more awful for you. I'm sorry."

"Don't apologize," she said, her frown deepening. "What you did for me that night...I owe you, Adam."

"You don't owe me."

"Yes," Nora said. "I do. You saved me."

"Anyone would have—"

"No." She shook her head. "Do you realize what my life would be like right now if you hadn't stopped them? If they had actually raped me? I would be so messed up. For a long time. Maybe for the rest of my life. Okay? So just let me say what I need to say."

Adam nodded. His cheeks were hot. "Okay."

"*Thank you*," she said.

"You're welcome," he said.

Nora reached for her bag of chips and ate several in rapid succession. Then she looked at her tray as if searching for the drink she'd forgotten to buy. Wordlessly, Adam handed her his lemonade.

"Thanks," she said. She took a few gulps, then set the bottle down. "So..."

"So," he said.

"You play baseball, right?"

It was an awkward subject change, but he understood. She was done talking about that night. "Yeah," he said. "Third base."

"The hot corner."

He looked at her, surprised.

"When your dad's the AD," she said, "you learn a lot about sports. What got you into baseball?"

What *got him into baseball*? He could answer this question any number of ways, depending on how painfully honest he wanted to be. He hesitated, then said, "It's kind of a funny story, actually." And he told her about fourth-grade gym, the first time he picked up a bat. He told her about his weak dribbler up the third-base line. Kevin Hamm yelling, "He didn't touch first! He missed the bag!" Running to first base, squatting down, and touching the bag with his hand. How everyone laughed. The Chinese kid touched the bag! *Touched* the bag! *Literally!* Hahahahahahahaha!

"Oh my God," Nora said. "What a-holes."

"Yeah, well." Adam shrugged. "That's what made me

decide to learn how to play. To prove them wrong. And I guess I did, because I started JV as a freshman, so..."

"How does it feel?" Nora said.

He looked at her.

"Being one of them?"

He thought about the baseball team GroupMe. **Dudes, u have to see this.** The picture of Nora and the three frat boys that someone had posted to the chat. He thought about the comments that followed. **Damn. Nice ass. I'd hit that.** How sick those words had made him. How he'd wanted to call out his teammates. They had *no idea* what really happened. He was *there* that night; he chased those guys away. But Adam hadn't called out his teammates, because calling them out—reminding them that Nora was a *person*, not just a body—would have been awkward. It would have been complicated. So he'd stayed silent. He wasn't proud of that. If he were very honest with himself, he wasn't proud to be on the team at all.

"I'm not one of them," he said.

Nora raised her eyebrows.

He wanted to explain, how, if you were a guy in Faber, if you didn't fit a certain mold, you didn't fit. Yeah, he liked baseball, but he wasn't just a jock. He wasn't just a brainiac, either. He was a lot of different things. "What I mean is—" he started to say, but Camille suddenly appeared at their table, cutting him off.

"Since when do you sit over here?"

Nora looked at her blankly. "I'm sitting with Adam."

Camille's head swiveled. "Hey, Adam."

"Hey," he said.

"Because *Adam*," Nora said, "is my *friend*."

Ouch, Adam thought, not for himself—he was beyond thinking that he and Nora would ever be more than friends—but for Camille, who was wincing.

"Okay, I deserved that. Look...I'm sorry I didn't tell you about Asher or ask you about that post. I screwed up. And you can be mad at me later, I promise. But right now I need to know what happened."

Nora hesitated.

"*Please*," Camille said. "I've known your dad my whole life."

"No, you haven't," Nora said flatly.

"Yes, I have—"

"He started the game."

Camille shook her head. "No."

"He invented it."

"I refuse to believe that."

"I didn't want to believe it, either," Nora said. "But he did."

"*How?*" Camille said, collapsing on the chair next to Adam. "I don't understand. Why would he *do* something like that?"

Nora shook her head. "I don't know."

"I mean, I *know* there are guys who do things like that. Sick, twisted guys. Woman haters. But *your dad*? Even if he was in college...I can't imagine...shit," Camille said.

Nora nodded mutely. Adam was amazed at how calm she was, how well she was holding herself together. Was this what shock looked like?

"I am *so* sorry, Nor," Camille said.

"Yeah," Nora said. "Me too."

"Do you hate him?"

Nora shook her head. "I don't know. I can't feel anything."

The three of them sat in silence for a minute. Then Camille grimaced. "I know this is the last thing you want to hear right now, but eighteen holes has pretty much gone viral. Everyone's talking about it."

"Shocker," Nora said.

"And I realize that's my fault," Camille said, "but I don't want you to panic because it's all going to be okay."

Nora looked at Camille like she was completely and hopelessly insane. "It's all going to be *okay*?"

"Yes," Camille insisted. "Because you've got us. Me and Adam. Right, Adam?"

Adam nodded. "Absolutely."

"And Asher." Camille reached for Nora's hand. "I know you don't want to think about him right now, but that's too bad, because he loves you and there's nothing you can do about it. And Chelsea and Anna and Becca. We all have your back and *we* are going to get you through this."

The bell rang for sixth period. Adam picked up both trays, and Cam wrapped her arm around Nora's shoulders, and the three of them walked out of the cafeteria.

NORA

SHE SPENT THE REST OF THE DAY ON AUTOPILOT. SHE went through the motions of school and field hockey, a facsimile of herself, nodding and taking notes and shooting goals. She may have fooled everyone into thinking she was fine, but she wasn't. Her dad's words kept churning in her head. *I'm going to give you some space to calm down.*

Calm down? she thought. *Calm down?*

How could she *calm down* when she no longer trusted a word he said? How could she *calm down* when she still had so many unanswered questions? She thought about showing up at his office and refusing to leave until he answered them. *How could you start this thing, Dad? How could you let it continue? How can you live with yourself?* She thought about chaining herself to his desk like one of those environmentalists who chain themselves to trees. How far would she have to go for him to tell her the truth?

When Nora got home, her dad's truck was in the driveway. When she walked inside—drenched because the sky had opened up as soon as she left practice—there he was, sitting at the kitchen counter, scrolling through his phone.

"You're home," she said stupidly.

"Hi," he said. "Do you need a towel?"

Did she need a *towel*?

"You look a little wet...here." He grabbed a dishrag from the hook by the sink and handed it to her. "How was your day?"

How was her *day*? Nora stared at her father. He was acting like nothing had happened, like everything was normal. He smiled, and suddenly all the questions she wanted to ask him—all those pointed, probing questions—congealed in the back of her throat like a glob of peanut butter. Because a part of her wanted to pretend, too. A part of her wanted to leap into his arms the way she used to when she was little. She wanted to bury her face in his sweatshirt and smell his aftershave. She wanted him to tell her everything would be okay. But she couldn't pretend, because nothing was normal anymore. Her dad's smile was fake. There was a soggy bucket of KFC and a liter of 7UP on the counter. When Nora saw this, she did a double take. Her mom prided herself on serving healthy, home-cooked meals to her family every night. She never bought soda. She always used real dishes and silverware and cloth napkins. Yet here she was, tossing paper goods onto the counter.

"Mom," Nora said slowly. "What's happening?"

Diane shook her head. Instead of answering the question, she said, "Dig in."

"This looks great," Nora's dad said with forced cheer. He looked at Asher and Maeve, who had just walked into the kitchen. "Doesn't this look great, guys?"

Nora's mom muttered something under her breath.

Maeve looked from one parent to the other and back again. "What's going on?"

Asher said, "It appears that Mom has handed the onerous task of cooking over to Colonel Sanders."

Nora's dad laughed, like Asher was a comedian.

Nora's mom said nothing.

The tension between them hung in the air like a low-lying cloud. Was this it, then? They really weren't going to talk about her dad being the game master? They were just going to sit at the table, listening to the rain, stabbing fried chicken parts with plastic forks? Nora pictured a lifetime of tense family dinners. One by one, they would leave for college. First Asher, then Nora, then Maeve, until only their parents remained, stooped over this same table, silent and bitter, stabbing away at their Extra Crispy meal for two with their plastic forks. The thought of this made Nora panic. What if they never talked about it? They *had* to talk about it.

"*Mom*," she said.

Diane looked up from the drumstick she was gnawing.

Nora widened her eyes, giving her mother a pointed look, an invitation to say something—*anything*—to address what was really going on here. But no. All her mom did was shake her head, toss a package of Double Stuf Oreos onto the table, and announce, "Dessert."

"Double Stufs?" Maeve looked at Diane in amazement.

When the Melchiondas wanted cookies, they baked their own, minus the lard and the high-fructose corn syrup. Nora reached for an Oreo in spite of herself. She unscrewed one chocolate wafer and licked the vanilla filling in a circular motion. This was her dad's pet peeve: children playing with their food. Normally, Nora would avoid provoking him after a long day of work. Now, she didn't care if she provoked him. She *wanted* to provoke him. *I can see that you're upset. I'm going to give you some space to calm down.* She licked harder, in his direction. It tasted so good. She hated how good it tasted. The goodness was distracting Nora from her complicated feelings; it was making her grab another Oreo, pop the whole thing in her mouth.

Suddenly, there was a noise from above. A loud cracking sound, followed by a *whoosh*. Nora bit her tongue in surprise.

Maeve shrieked.

"What the—?" Nora's dad said. He looked up at the ceiling.

"Did we just get struck by lightning?" Asher said.

"Tell me that wasn't the roof," her mom said.

"I think it was," her dad said.

"I told you we needed to get that leak patched," her mom said.

"I thought you called the roofing guy," her dad said.

"No," her mom said. "*You* said—"

Another loud crack from above. Out of instinct, Nora wrapped her arms around her head. She thought, ridiculously, of Chicken Little. *The sky is falling! The sky is falling!* Water began to drip steadily onto the stove. *Plink, plink, plink.*

Nora's dad pushed back his chair. "I'm going up."

"I'll come with you," Asher said.

Nora's mom ran over to the stove, moving a soup pot under the leak. "Girls," she said, "grab all the towels from the mudroom and the sheets from the linen closet."

"You get the towels," Nora told Maeve. "I'll get the sheets."

"Aye, aye, captain," Maeve said. Her teeth were blacked out with Oreos. Maeve's teeth reminded Nora of the time her dad asked one of his players on the Faber hockey team to remove his dental bridge and show Nora why she should always wear a mouth guard when she played sports, to protect her beautiful teeth. For fifteen years, he had been spouting the same line. *I'm your dad, ladybug. It's my job to protect you.*

The irony was almost laughable.

"Someone grab Dad's toolbox!" she heard Asher yell

from upstairs. "And a tarp!" Then: "Scratch that! We need plywood and roofing tar!"

Plywood and roofing tar? What was this, Ray's Hardware?

"I'm getting sheets!" Nora yelled back.

Her dad and Asher came sprinting down the stairs, past Nora, and through the door to the basement. They returned with a roll of clear plastic, a rectangle of wood, her dad's green metal toolbox, a rusty can, and a device that Nora recognized as a putty knife. Her mom had showed her how to use it once, to scrape off old wallpaper in the spare room. As Nora watched her dad and brother pass by—they were both soaked and grunting from exertion—she realized that Cam would be disgusted with her. The menfolk were doing the heavy lifting while Nora was just standing there, holding an armful of pretty, floral linens.

"Come on," she said to Maeve and her stack of towels. "We're going up."

ASHER

IT WOULD BECOME A STORY THEY WOULD TELL OVER and over again, the night their mom served KFC and Oreos and the roof caved in. It was prophetic, really. How everything collapsed from the top down.

Asher regarded the patch job—a hodgepodge of plastic sheeting and plywood and nails and roofing tar—and wondered if it would hold. The rain was still pelting down outside. There were shingles floating in the bathtub, chunks of dirt, wood. Every bedsheet and towel in the house was on the floor, drenched.

"Well," Asher's father said, wiping his hands on his pants. "Mission accomplished."

"*Mission accomplished?*" Asher's mom said.

Rhett lowered his voice. "Come on, Di. I'm trying here."

"No. You're not *trying*. You're putting a Band-Aid on a gushing wound and calling yourself a surgeon. It's what you *do*, Rhett. You say whatever you need to say to justify your position."

Asher looked at his parents and thought, *There's no way this is going to hold.*

NORA

"WHAT DO YOU WANT FROM ME, DIANE?" NORA'S DAD
said. His face was streaked with dirt. His hair was dripping. All their hair was dripping. They were a family of drowned rats.

"What do I *want* from you?" her mom said. "I want the same thing I asked you for earlier and you refused to give me. I want the truth."

Her dad said, "The truth is complicated."

"No." Her mom shook her head. "The truth is simple. *Lying* is complicated."

Nora's dad glanced up at the ceiling.

Nora's mom gave him an exasperated look. She thought...what? That he was looking to *God* for answers? That he was hoping his patch job would collapse so he could escape out the roof?

"The truth about what?" Maeve said. "What are you even talking about?"

Nora's dad looked at Maeve, and he looked at Nora and

Asher, and then he cleared his throat. "One mistake. One stupid mistake I made when I was a boneheaded kid."

"You were hardly a kid," Nora's mom said. "You were twenty-two."

"What kind of a mistake?" Asher said.

Nora held her breath. She hadn't realized she was holding it until she started to feel light-headed and she had to let it out.

"When I was a senior at Faber," her dad said, "as you know, I was voted president of my fraternity."

True.

"I was in charge of the new pledge class."

True.

"As president, I was required to invent a challenge for the pledges to complete. So I made up a game. Which, in retrospect, I never should have done. But I was young and foolish, and I didn't think it through."

"What kind of game?" Asher said.

Nora's dad hesitated. He glanced at Maeve, who was looking at him with rapt attention.

"Answer the question, Rhett," Nora's mom said. "I want your children to hear you say it."

"Yeah, Dad," Maeve said. "Your children want to hear."

Rhett exhaled a long stream of air, to let everyone in the bathroom know that he was answering against his will. "It was a hookup game."

"What's a hookup game?" Maeve said.

Nora had been waiting for this moment—for her father to have no choice but to admit what he'd done—but looking at Maeve, she wavered. Maeve was just a kid. She still believed in magic. Once Nora told her, Maeve's innocence would shatter like a pane of glass. But if Nora *didn't* tell her, what would stop Maeve from going to the frat fair herself someday, drinking from a red cup, and waking up on the golf course?

"It's where boys try to get girls to have sex with them," Nora said. "Whether they're conscious or not. And they write numbers on the girls' bodies, and then they take pictures to prove that it happened. Just like they did to me."

Maeve's mouth fell open.

"Jesus Christ," Asher murmured.

Rain pelted onto the roof. The crazy patch on the ceiling made a creaking sound. Everyone looked up. Nora held her breath, waiting. It was like watching the tipping bucket at Shipwreck Island, all the kids huddled together in their bathing suits, sharing the deliciously terrifying anticipation of freezing-cold water crashing down on their heads. Any second now... any second now...

But nothing happened. The patch held. Nora felt oddly disappointed.

"It was a different time," Nora's dad said to the ceiling.

"What?" Nora said.

Nora's dad lowered his gaze. "It was a different time, when your mom and I went to college. We didn't know about these things."

"What *things*?" Nora said.

"The Me Too movement," he said. "It wasn't in the zeit-geist yet."

"It wasn't *in the zeitgeist yet*?" Nora's mom said.

"What's the zeitgeist?" Maeve said.

"The spirit of the time," Asher said.

"That," Nora's mom said, poking a finger in the air at her dad, "is complete *bullshit*, and you know it."

"It's not bullshit. It's true."

Nora's mom shook her head in disbelief. "I don't know what to say to you right now. I don't even know who you are."

"I'm the same person I've always been, Diane."

Nora found herself thinking, *Really?* She opened her mouth to speak. She had so many questions. "What about Peyton Mallory?" she blurted. "And Jason Mann?"

"What about them?" her dad said.

"Were they Alpha Psis?" she said.

"They may have been," her dad said.

"Were they playing eighteen holes when they assaulted those girls? Was that why you covered for them?"

Her dad frowned. "I didn't *cover* for them. I advised them in their disciplinary hearings, at their request."

"Because they knew you would get them off. Because you're the *master of the universe*." She scratched quote marks in the air with her fingers. "You can do anything."

"That's not true. There's a disciplinary committee. I was only their adviser."

"Advising them to lie?" Nora said.

"I *never* advised them to lie." He was getting angry now, but curiously, Nora didn't care.

"They know you're the master, though," she said. "They know you started the game. Just like all your frat brothers know you started the game. Did Uncle Aldo and Uncle Keefer drug girls at parties?"

"What?" Her dad looked stunned. *"No."*

"Is drugging girls part of the game? Did you tell your pledges to put roofies in girls' drinks?"

"No!" His face contorted. "It wasn't like that!"

"What's a roofie?" Maeve said.

"It's a drug that makes someone pass out," Nora said. She looked at her dad. "You knew your players were doing it. You knew, and you looked the other way."

He shook his head. "No. *No.*"

"I don't believe you," Nora said. Her voice was shaking now. Her whole body was shaking. "I don't believe anything you say anymore."

She felt an arm wrap around her shoulders. Asher. Nora couldn't remember the last time her brother had wrapped an arm around her.

"Dad," Asher said. "You need to go."

"I need to *go*?" Rhett said.

"Yes. You need to leave the house."

The strength of Asher's words and the arm around her shoulders made Nora feel strong by association.

"Leave," she said.

Her dad pointed to himself. "*My* house. You want me to leave my own house, after I just fixed the roof."

"We all helped, Dad," Maeve said.

"Rhett." Diane's face looked pained. "Don't make this any harder than it already is."

"*You* want me to leave, too?" he said.

"I do."

"You're kicking me out," he said.

"I am, yes."

Nora could hear the conviction in her mom's voice. She meant it.

Nora expected her dad to argue, to defend his position, but instead he nodded. "I'll pack a bag," he said.

ASHER

THERE WAS AN ATMOSPHERIC SHIFT AFTER HIS FATHER left, a rearrangement of the air molecules in the house. It was palpable. Asher could literally feel the tension leaching from his body. After a few days, he asked Nora if she could feel it, too. They were making dinner together in the kitchen, giving their mom a break. Nothing fancy— just English muffin pizzas, salad, fruit. Asher's prevailing thought was that since his mom was the only parent in the house now, they needed to pitch in more.

He said to Nora, "Can you feel the difference?"

Nora looked up from the pile of cheese she had grated. "Using fresh mozzarella?"

"No," Asher said. "Him being gone."

She nodded, scooping up cheese shreds and spooning them onto an English muffin. "Yeah."

Asher said, "He took up so much space."

"Takes up," she said.

"What?"

"He's not *dead*, Ash. He's taking up space *somewhere*."

"Right," Asher said. Their father still existed; he just hadn't come home yet. Probably he was staying with one of his coaches, keeping it on the down low. If he stayed at the Super 8 or the Faber Inn, it would become Faber gossip-mill fodder. People would say he was having an affair. He was too smart to subject himself to that.

"I know you hate him," Nora said. "You've always hated him."

"I haven't *always hated* him," Asher said. "I just didn't think he was perfect, like you did."

"Perfect?" She snorted.

Asher looked at his sister and saw the layers of emotion on her face. Anger. Disgust. Grief. It had to be hard, to worship someone your whole life only to discover that your hero had no moral compass. At least Asher wasn't disillusioned. He had known, for a long time, that Rhett Melchionda wasn't the great guy everyone thought he was. The eighteen-holes thing only confirmed it. But now, what was Asher supposed to do? How could he possibly make this okay for his mom and his sisters?

"You're not perfect, either, you know," Nora said.

Yes. Asher did know that. He cringed thinking about the comment he'd made to her, about guys seeing a short skirt as an invitation. Asher wanted to think that he was blameless, that he was nothing like his father. That he had never wanted to tell his sister to cover herself up. That he had never overheard one of those phone conversations—*It's her word against yours, kid*—and let his father convince him it was nothing. That it hadn't crossed his mind that girls were being hurt, that the truth was being buried. That he had believed his father's denials.

But Asher would be lying to himself.

Was he perfect? Not even close.

"You're right," he said. "I'm not perfect. The difference is, I'm man enough to admit it."

Nora put down the grater. "What does that even mean?"

"I take responsibility for my mistakes."

"No," she said. "*Man enough*. It's such a stupid expression. It's not a *man* thing to admit you're wrong."

"You're right," Asher said.

"It's a human-decency thing."

"Point taken," he said.

Nora sounded a lot like Cam, calling him out on his word choice. Of all the girls Asher had known in his life, Camille Dodd was the first to hold him accountable for the things he said. *Words matter, Ash.* Unlike Asher's father, Cam wasn't a hypocrite. Her moral compass was intact. Even admitting she'd kissed that frat boy—a fact Asher would like to forget—spoke to Cam's principles. A lot of people would have chosen to hide that information, but Cam had been willing to risk losing Asher's respect by divulging what she'd done, which, paradoxically, had made him respect her more.

"Do you think there's any way Dad's telling the truth?" Nora asked. "That he didn't know what was going on?"

Asher looked at Nora. He thought about giving her false hope by saying anything was possible. He thought about it, but he couldn't bring himself to do it. "Not a chance," he said.

NORA

IN THE DAYS AFTER HER DAD LEFT, NORA TRIED NOT TO think about him. She woke up in the morning and got dressed. She ate breakfast with Asher and Maeve while her mom slept in. She went to school and field hockey. She did her homework. She played cards with Maeve—spit and hearts and crazy eights—games she hadn't played in years. There was one afternoon where Cam showed up on the front porch with a tube of cookie dough.

"I know everything sucks right now," she said to Nora, "and I'm here for you. But I'm also here for Asher. And I need to make sure you're okay with that."

Was she okay with that? Nora didn't know. She listened to Cam try to explain, how kissing Asher just happened, they didn't plan for it, they got caught up in the moment. How Cam had *wanted* to tell Nora, but that was the night of the frat fair and she already felt like a bad friend. If she hadn't gone to Kyle's party, Nora wouldn't have ended up on the golf course, and telling Nora about Asher while she was dealing with the aftermath of getting roofied would have added insult to injury. And *yes*, Cam knew they'd made a vow in sixth grade to tell each other everything boy-related, but come on, that was *sixth grade*, and did Nora *really* want to hear the details about Cam hooking up with her brother? Not that Cam was trying to make excuses. She realized that hooking up with Asher wasn't her worst transgression; sneaking around behind Nora's back was her worst transgression. Because they were best friends. And best friends didn't sneak around behind each other's backs. They told the brutal truth.

"Are you done now?" Nora said, when Cam finally came up for air.

"Do you forgive me?" Cam said. "Because if you don't forgive me, I will keep going. I can go all day. I'm sorry for being a crappy friend. I'm sorry for going behind your back. Not just with Asher, but with that post. I should have asked you first. I should have let you decide. Because you were right. What happened to you happened to *you*, and I shouldn't have taken away your power. And I'm sorry. I'm sorry. I'm sorry—"

"Oh my God," Nora said. "Stop."

"You're my best friend," Cam said, and she swiped her eyes roughly with the sleeve of her sweatshirt. "And I'm sorry I like your brother. I really am. If I could stop liking him, I would. But I can't."

"*Why?*" Nora said.

Cam shrugged. "It's biological. I like the way he smells."

"Ew," Nora said.

"What? Pheromones are legit."

"Please don't talk about how my brother smells. Ever."

"He's also a really good guy," Cam said. "A *really* good guy. Now can I please come in and make you both some comfort cookies?"

"Fine," Nora said. And she opened the door.

Was she okay with it? Was she okay with anything? She could barely wrap her mind around Cam and Asher, let alone her father. Adam Xu kept asking her, every day, how she was doing, and it was so hard to explain. How, now that her dad was gone, her feelings had nowhere to touch down. Her emotions were in a holding pattern, hovering somewhere outside her body, waiting for a place to land.

"Compartmentalizing," Cam had called it. She said Nora's brain was trying to protect her.

Nora wondered if her dad's brain was doing the same thing for him. For a second, she started to feel guilty. If she hadn't gone to the frat fair alone, if she hadn't drunk that root beer, none of this would be happening. Her dad would still be here. He wouldn't have been banished from his own home. But then Asher's words came back to her—the ones he had spoken after she'd asked if their dad could be telling the truth—those three words: *Not a chance.*

Those three words lit a tiny fire inside her.

⟋

"Where is Dad staying?" Maeve asked at dinner.

"With Coach Delorme," Nora's mom said.

Nora nearly choked on a bite of mini carrot. Coach *Delorme*? She babysat for the Delormes. Those kids were holy terrors. Also, their house was the size of a garden shed. "Where is he *sleeping*?" she said.

"On the couch," her mom said.

The *couch*? The Delormes had only one couch, and it was disgusting. It was stained and covered in Cheerios and Goldfish cracker dust. If anyone else were sleeping on that couch, Nora would feel sorry for them. But her dad? No. *No*. This was karma. He had made his bed. Now he literally had to lie in it.

"When is he coming home?" Maeve asked.

Nora's mom picked up her water glass, took a sip, set it back down. "Well," she said. "That depends on him."

"How does it *depend on him*?" Maeve said.

"If your father wants to come home," Nora's mom said, "he needs to own what he's done."

Maeve said, "How?"

"By taking responsibility for his actions."

"*How?*"

"That is for your father to figure out."

"Is that what you've been talking about on the phone?"

Nora's mom looked surprised. "How do you know we've been talking on the phone?"

Maeve said, "Because I can hear you, right outside your bedroom. You've been talking to Dad every night."

"Maeve," Nora said. "That's rude."

"What's rude?"

"Eavesdropping on a private conversation."

"It's not private if I can hear it." Maeve looked at Diane. "If you're so mad, why are you talking to him?"

"Because—" Nora's mom hesitated. "We are all affected by this, and I need to know what's going on with your father so we're not blindsided by anything else."

"If he doesn't own his behavior, will you get a divorce?"

"Jesus, Maeve," Asher said.

"What?" Maeve said.

"It's been three days."

"So? I was just asking."

"Give Mom time to get her bearings."

Nora looked at her mother, lifting her glass again, taking another sip of water. She didn't look shocked by Maeve's question. She had already thought about it; Nora could tell.

"I have a lot to consider," Diane said. "Let's just take this one step at a time."

They sat in silence for a while, but Nora kept turning the word over and over in her head: "divorce." She tried to picture it, her dad moving into one of those seedy apartments on the edge of town. Having to see him every Wednesday—going out for the meat loaf special at the Blue Bird, or, worse, him cooking dinner for Nora and Asher and Maeve in his sad bachelor pad, which would smell like cat pee even though he didn't have a cat. Soon, Rhett and Diane would join Match.com. They would start going on dates. No—Nora wouldn't think about that—she couldn't. When she thought about how her parents *were* as a couple— always kissing, and mamboing around the kitchen, and reminiscing about the day they met—she couldn't imagine anything else. How could they get *divorced*? How could *Rhett and Diane* be with anyone but each other?

And then Nora's anger returned full force. The day her parents met was a lie, too. The day her parents met was the day her mom's roommate left college. *That's* why Diane had been crying, not because she was homesick, but because Amy Bachman was raped, by an Alpha Psi pledge.

"Did Dad plan that King Tut party?" Nora blurted.

Her mom looked at her, frowning slightly.

"What's a King Tut party?" Maeve said.

Nora's mom shook her head. "He was in the health center. He was too sick to go."

"King Tut was an Egyptian pharaoh," Asher explained.

"He still could have planned it," Nora said. "Even if he didn't go. The game could have started that night. Mom, they all would have listened to him. Uncle Aldo. Uncle Keefer. Joey D. They would have done whatever he said—"

Diane shook her head again. "I can't think about that right now."

"We *have* to think about it," Nora said.

"Think about what?" Maeve said.

"Who your father *is*," Diane said, "and what he may have done are two separate things."

"*May have done?*" Asher said.

"He did this," Nora said.

"Yes, but it is up to *me*," her mom said, "to decide how I am going to respond. And right now, I am asking all of you to give me some time to process."

CAM

IT WAS ERICA SWISHER, A REPORTER FROM THE *FABER Gazette,* who reached out to Katie J on Instagram, requesting more information. What was Katie J's connection to @18Holez? Did she know any of the girls in the photos personally? What about the perpetrators? Was Katie J willing to go on record?

Cam stared at Erica Swisher's message. This was actually happening. Katie J had *made* this happen.

Cam's fingers itched to respond. But she knew that she couldn't answer any of Erica Swisher's questions—not in good conscience—without talking to Nora first. So she made the call.

"Nor?" she said. "I have to ask you something."

After that, she made another call.

"Adam? You're not going to believe this."

―――

Three days later, the *Faber Gazette* ran a front-page story. The headline read: FRATERNITY PLEDGE GAME LINKED TO RAMPANT SEXUAL ASSAULT ON CAMPUS.

The article stated that seven female Faber University students, seven "Jane Does," had come forward to file formal complaints against ten male Faber University athletes, all members of the Alpha Psi Beta fraternity, known for recruiting heavily from the football and ice hockey teams. The article chronicled the history of complaints lodged against Faber fraternities over the years, including reports filed against Peyton Mallory, Hobey Baker Award winner and former goalie for the Faber University hockey team, and Jason Mann, Walter Camp Player of the Year and former Faber University quarterback. The dean of students, Barton Hodge, was quoted as saying that the accused students had been "cleared of all charges due to disciplinary process"—which of course made Cam wonder how fair this "disciplinary process" actually was. Were the accusers present during the hearings? And who at the university supported them? If Mr. M spoke up for Peyton Mallory and Jason Mann because they were his athletes, who spoke up for the assaulted women? And what if *they* were athletes, too? Cam had so many questions.

The article went on to describe the Alpha Psi Beta pledging game, 18 Holes, and the content of the photos from the fraternity's now-defunct Instagram page @18Holez. It recounted the stories of two students from Faber Central School who had felt it their duty to investigate the pledging game after finding a female friend unconscious and disrobed in the presence of three male college students on the Faber University golf course. The *Gazette* declined to publish the minors' names but did offer a quote from nineteen-year-old Alpha Psi Beta pledge Malik Jones: "I thought joining a fraternity at Faber would be a good thing. As a recruit you're taken to these frats.... Every football recruit is brought to Alpha Psi. The coaches are aware. They want it to happen; it's a recruiting tool for the teams, promoting 'brotherhood' and all that. But I didn't come here to play a game like eighteen holes. Preying on girls when they're drunk, as some way to prove myself? I wasn't raised like that. I just came here to play football."

When asked about the culture of indifference and denial by the Faber University Athletic Department in response to sexual assault allegations, athletic director Rhett Melchionda, himself a Faber University alumnus, said: "I care deeply about this institution and its students. I regret any lapses of judgment I may have exhibited or pain I may have caused in my role as athletic director. In light of recent reports, the athletic department is currently reevaluating its programs and practices. I am committed to being part of the solution." When asked about his own membership in the Alpha Psi Beta fraternity, Melchionda said, "Greek life is a staple of the Faber University experience. When I was a student, the fraternity system provided me with a sense of community and an opportunity for service, just as it continues to do for current students. However, the pledge period—namely the excessive drinking and hazing activities associated with initiation—does warrant a closer look. The university's educational purposes and its responsibilities compel a stronger response now than it has given in the past."

In response to Melchionda's pledge for change, Faber University president Harrison Leahey issued the following statement: "Let us not conflate Faber University athletics with the Greek system. Fraternities at Faber University are private associations. They are governed by an interfraternity council that is associated with but independent from the university. We regret that the actions of a few bad apples would malign the good name of the Faber University Athletic Department and the outstanding programs and athletes it serves."

Cam balked at President Leahey's statement. *Let us not conflate Faber University athletics with the Greek system? The actions of* a few bad apples? *That's all the president had to say?* Cam herself had several comments:

1) Malik was a rock star. He had pulled through in the clinch just like she'd hoped he would when she floated his name to Erica Swisher as a potential source, confirming for Cam what she had secretly suspected to be true: not all frat boys were asshats. A lot of them were, but not all.

2) Mr. M sounded like he was reading from a script. At least until the end, when he sounded like he was passing the buck to the university, which was either cowardly or ballsy—she couldn't decide which.

3) Hello? *Two students from Faber Central School who had felt it their duty to investigate?*

"Dodd and Xu," Cam said to Adam the next morning.

"What?" he said. He was distracted by Brittany Carr, who was walking by his locker as he was pulling out books.

"Hey, Adam," she said.

"Hey, Brittany."

"You read the article, right?" Cam said. "I sent you the link last night."

"Yeah," he said.

"Famous crime-fighting duos always go by their last names. Holmes and Watson. Mulder and Scully. Bones and Booth." She handed him a hard copy of the *Gazette* that she'd picked up at 7-Eleven. "For your files."

"Thanks," Adam said. "But technically, 'Bones' isn't her last name. It's Brennan. Temperance Brennan."

"Oh my God," Cam said, smiling at him. "You totally binge-watched *Bones*, didn't you?"

He shrugged and smiled back. "I may have watched a few episodes. Based on your recommendation."

"You know what this means, right?"

"What?" he said.

"You're coming for Thanksgiving," Cam said. "My uncles are going to have a field day with you."

NORA

WHEN NORA WOKE UP ON FRIDAY MORNING, THERE WAS a text from Cam. She'd sent it at 10:37 PM, but Nora was just seeing it now.

Article dropped

Nora clicked on the link. She read every word, sitting cross-legged on the floor in her pajamas.

After she finished reading, she knocked on her brother's door.

"You have to see this," she said, holding out her phone.

Asher glanced at the screen. "I already did," he said. "Sup Faber is blowing up."

Of course it was.

Nora tapped on Instagram: @supfaber had posted the front page of the *Gazette*. Nora scrolled through the comments. They went on and on.

How do they know those girls r telling the truth?

Why would anyone lie about being assaulted, a-hole?

Idk 2 get attention

Spoken like a true guy

That game is sick, no way those girls knew what
was happening to them

This town has a problem, and the frats are only
a symptom

"Oh my God," Nora murmured.

"I know," Asher said.

"Do you think Dad meant what he said? About being
part of the solution?"

Asher shook his head. "He's just covering his ass. He's
saying what the university wants him to say."

"We need to show Mom," Nora said.

"She's probably already seen it," Asher said.

"Come with me," Nora said. "Please."

When Nora and Asher walked into the kitchen, they found
their mother standing at the counter in her bathrobe.

"Mom," Nora said. "Have you seen the *Gazette* article?"

"I have." She picked up a bunch of bananas, ripped one
from the bunch, and handed it to Nora.

"What do you think?" Asher said.

Diane raised her eyebrows. She ripped another banana
from the bunch, handed it to Asher. "I think that article
should have come out twenty years ago, that's what I think."

"What article?" Maeve said, appearing in the doorway.

"In the *Gazette*," Nora said. "About all the girls who've come forward, accusing the Alpha Psis of sexual assault."

"How many?" Maeve said.

"Seven," Nora said.

Diane handed Maeve a banana. "Your father called me last night. He's been asked to take a temporary leave of absence. For two weeks."

Nora and Asher and Maeve stood in silence for a moment, holding their bananas.

"Because he confessed?" Nora said.

"Not directly," her mom said. "He did tell the administration about his role, but according to Dean Hodge, creating a pledge game isn't a criminal offense, and it happened long before your father worked for the university. There's a statute of limitations—"

"What's that?" Maeve said.

"It means too much time has gone by," Asher explained. "They're not going to blame Dad because it happened so long go."

"But they're still *playing*," Nora said. "They're playing *because of him*."

"I know," her mom said. "I'm not saying I agree with the university, I'm just telling you how they're responding. They didn't suspend your father because of the game. They suspended him because he didn't toe the party line in the article."

Asher looked surprised. "President Leahey didn't feed him that script?"

Diane shook her head. "Not the part about the university needing to take a stronger stance against the fraternities."

"What's wrong with that?" Maeve said.

"The university doesn't want to admit guilt or responsibility."

Maeve frowned. "But you said Dad needed to take responsibility for his actions."

"Yes."

"Did he do that in the article?"

"I think he tried to, yes."

"If he's trying to do the right thing, why is he being punished?"

Nora's mom sighed. "It's complicated, Maeve. This is bigger than any one person…there are a lot of moving parts…look—" She glanced from Maeve to Nora and Asher. "People may be talking at school today, about what's happening on campus, about your dad."

People may *be talking?* Nora thought. *Ha!*

"Don't let them get to you," her mom said. "Hold your heads high."

"I always hold my head high," Maeve said. "If I look down, I see how gross the floor is in the cafeteria."

"She means figuratively, Maeve," Asher said.

Maeve rolled her eyes. "I *know.* It's called *levity*, sheesh. Humor as a coping mechanism?"

Nora looked at her little sister. High ponytail. Scorn on her face. When had she grown up? Overnight, it seemed.

Nora walked to school alone. Her mom had offered to drive her, but she said no. Cam had asked her to meet at 7-Eleven, but she said no to that, too. She needed time to prepare herself.

Outside the school, Nora saw kids clustered together on the grass, talking, laughing. As she approached the entrance, she heard the voices fade, become whispers, then stop altogether as she passed by. She clutched her backpack straps, lifted her chin. She kept her eyes straight ahead, all the way to sophomore hall.

When she got to her locker, someone was waiting.

Adam Courtmanche.

He was scrolling through his phone.

Nora felt the urge to keep walking, right past him. Her books were in her locker, but so what? Anything was better than having this conversation.

But it was too late. He was looking at her.

"Hey," he said.

"Hey," she said.

He held up his phone. "I've read this article three times, and I can't stop thinking about it. Is it you? The girl on the golf course?"

She thought, *Shit, shit, shit.*

"Is it?"

She took a deep breath, reached past him to fiddle with her lock.

"Nor," he said softly. "Come on."

She turned her head and looked at him. The green eyes fringed with dark lashes that had won him Best Looking Boy in their middle school yearbook. The lips she had kissed for the first time in front of the flagpole—and another twenty times after that. She and Adam had known each other their whole lives. They had been in every class together, from kindergarten to eighth grade. Literally, every class. This town was so freaking small.

"Yes," Nora said.

"Did those guys..."

"No." She shook her head. "It could have been a lot worse."

His forehead crinkled. "Why didn't you tell me?"

She said, "You never gave me the chance."

He said, "I didn't know."

She said, "You didn't ask."

He said, "Were you drunk?"

Nora flared up with anger. She was so sick of that question. What difference did it make if she was drunk, or high, or roofied, or sober, or wearing a prairie dress, or a thong, or if she knew the guys, or if she'd never seen them before in her life?

"No," she said, looking Adam squarely in the eyes. "I was not drunk."

"I believe you," he said.

She almost said *Thank you*, but she stopped herself. Why should she thank him for believing her? She was telling the truth.

"Trey won't talk about it," Adam said. "I asked if he knew about the game, or about the guys being accused, but he wouldn't tell me anything. Even though he texted me one of those photos."

Nora looked at him sharply. "What?"

"The girls, with the numbers. It was a few weeks ago. I didn't know what it was when he sent it to me. I swear to God. It was just some boob shot with a number four written on it. I wanted to delete it, but Hamm grabbed my phone and sent it to himself. Then he showed a bunch of guys in the locker room. No one knew what it was."

"Oh my God." Nora stared at Adam. "Trey was playing eighteen holes."

"I don't know. I told you, he won't talk about it."

"In your gut, though."

Adam shook his head. He couldn't imagine it, his own brother doing something like that. "If he did..." Adam hesitated. "If he gets caught...your dad would help him, right? Trey could get kicked off the team. He could lose his scholarship."

Nora shook her head slowly. "My dad wouldn't be able to help." That was the hard, awful nugget of truth. There was nothing more she could say, really.

Adam frowned. This wasn't what he wanted to hear.

Not my problem, Nora thought. *Trey Courtmanche is not my problem.* She wouldn't take it on.

"But you *know* Trey," Adam said. "You know he's a good guy. You wouldn't put in a word for him, to your dad?"

"Are you serious?" she said.

"What?"

"You say you believe me. You say you feel bad about what happened to me. But you want me to ask my dad to put in a good word for Trey so he doesn't get caught doing *exactly what those guys did to me*?"

Adam shook his head in disbelief. "He's my brother. He could lose his scholarship."

"That's not my problem," she said.

"Wow." Adam narrowed his eyes. "I never thought I would say this, but you're being a coldhearted bitch."

Jesus. Nora felt awful. Her heart wasn't made to withstand other people's disappointment. She wanted to apologize. She wanted to prove she wasn't a bitch, to make sure he wasn't mad at her. But no. *No.*

She turned to her locker, grabbing books indiscriminately off the top shelf and shoving them into her bag. The bell rang—thank God—and she flung the strap over her shoulder.

"Just so you know," Adam said, "I was going to ask you to homecoming. I had this whole plan of how to ask you. It was really fucking creative, but now . . . I don't think I want to go with you."

Her eyebrows shot up. *Really?* She laughed.

Adam looked offended. "What's so funny?"

"I don't know," Nora said, throwing her hands in the air. "Nothing. Everything. My life is ridiculous!"

And she walked away.

Mrs. Bell was writing conversation points on the board. They were supposed to be working in small groups to discuss the theme of justice in *The Crucible*, but Nora couldn't focus on Reverend Hale or Elizabeth Proctor or anyone else. Her brain was spinning.

"I want to file a complaint," she said.

Cam said, "Me too. *The Crucible* is the worst."

"No," Nora said. "A formal complaint, with the university."

"Against the three guys?" Adam Xu said.

"Yes," Nora said. "And I don't want either of you to tell me that the hearing will be a shit show because I'm a minor and that changes everything, or that the whole town will be talking about me, or that I probably won't win, because I already know those things and I want to do it anyway. And I want to submit the photo and a copy of the video for evidence, so—" She looked at Adam Xu. "I'm going to need your help with that."

His head bobbed. "Yeah. Of course."

"Also." She turned to Cam. "I need proof I was roofied." She reached behind her ear, wiggled some hairs loose from her ponytail, wrapped them around her finger, and yanked. She handed the hairs to Cam. "Ask your uncles to test these, please."

"Oh my *God*!" Cam said.

"Camille, Nora, and Adam."

Adam Xu nudged Nora's arm.

"Are you *serious*?" Cam stared at the tangle of blond in her hand. "This is so—"

"*Camille, Nora, and Adam,*" Mrs. Bell said again. "If you are not discussing the theme of justice—"

"We are." Nora sat up straight in her chair. "We're..." Her brain scrambled. "Making personal connections to the characters."

"Books as mirrors," Adam Xu said.

"And if you don't mind, Mrs. Bell," Cam said, "we need an envelope or a Ziploc bag."

ADAM XU

THIRTY-SEVEN MINUTES: THAT'S HOW LONG IT TOOK HIM to download the digital file from his computer to the flash drive he'd bought at P. M. Jones. It should have taken him five, but he had never done it before and he had to teach himself how.

CAM

FIFTY YEARS: THAT'S HOW LONG THE CAR RIDE TO THE
Wallie Howard Jr. Center for Forensic Sciences took,
because her mom wouldn't stop peppering her with questions. Had Cam read this article in the *Gazette*? How
were she and her friends responding? What was the high
school doing to address the issue of sexual assault? The
questions went on and on.

NORA

SINCE HER DAD HAD LEFT, HE'D SENT NORA FOUR TEXTS and left her six voice mails. She had ignored every one. But now, she found herself standing on the Delormes' front porch, ringing the doorbell. She was jangling with nerves. The walk over had taken her twice as long as it normally did because she kept stopping to convince herself that she had to do this.

The door opened.

There he was, clutching the youngest Delorme, Opal, under one arm, like a football.

"Nora," he said.

"Noa," Opal said. Opal was only three. She couldn't say the letter "r" yet.

"Hi, Opal," Nora said.

"Hi Noa. Whett is here."

"Yes," Nora said. "I can see that Rhett is here."

"You know Whett?"

"Yes," Nora said. "I know Rhett."

Did she know Rhett? Nora hadn't seen her father since

the night the roof caved in, so she was totally unprepared for what she saw now. There were bags under his eyes. His hair was a nest. He hadn't shaved. Rhett Melchionda with a beard? He literally looked like a different person. A person she had never met. His cheeks were pink. His eyelids were blue.

Nora squinted. "Are you wearing *makeup*?"

"We were playing beauty shop." He turned around slowly. The back of his head was full of plastic barrettes. Turtles. Bunnies. Ducks.

When, in his entire life as a father, had he ever played *beauty shop*? Nora willed herself not to ask if he was having a mental breakdown.

"Want to come in?" he said. He gestured behind him. Nora could see the boys, Chad and PJ, running around, shooting each other with Nerf guns. "I'm watching the kids while their mom is at the store."

Nora shook her head. "I just came to tell you that I'm going to file a sexual assault complaint, as soon as I get the tox screen back."

Her dad lowered Opal to the ground. "Go play with your brothers, Ope, okay?"

"'Kay," Opal said. She took off down the hall.

Nora's dad stepped onto the porch. He reached out his hand. "Nor—"

"Don't." She took a step back. "I gave Cam a hair sample, and she's giving it to her uncle at the forensics lab in Syracuse, to test it. I'll have the results by Thursday. Where do I make my report?"

Her dad blinked at her. "What?"

"Where," she said, slowly and deliberately, "do I file my sexual assault complaint? Faber PD or campus security?"

He was quiet. Nora thought he might try to talk her out of it, but he didn't. He cleared his throat. "Either. They work together....Nora—"

He reached out his hand again, but she swatted it away. "How long will it take from there? From the time I file until the disciplinary hearing. How long will I have to wait?"

"Three weeks. Maybe a month."

Nora stared at him. "A *month*?"

"After a formal report is filed, there's a fact-finding period. It's a process."

A month sounded like a lifetime. She wanted to do it *now*. She wanted to walk into that hearing room, tell her story to a bunch of strangers, and walk out, leaving it all behind her. She wanted her life to go back to normal. But that wasn't going to happen; she knew it wasn't. Nothing would be the same, ever. Her dad had given her this weight to carry around. Nora would always be the girl in that photo, with a frat boy's hand on her ass. Those other girls would be weighed down by their photos, too—by whatever had been done to their bodies. The men who assaulted them would be treated like boys, their behavior excused as "locker room banter" and "blowing off steam," and the girls they assaulted would be accused of drinking too much, of dressing like sluts, of not reporting it sooner, of lying, of wanting attention, of ruining lives, of starting a male witch hunt. And for all that, Nora's dad was getting what? A two-week suspension. A slap on the wrist. Did he feel better admitting his "lapses of judgment"? She hoped so. She really effing hoped so.

"Are you sure you want to do this?" her dad said.

"Yes," she said.

"It could get messy."

"I *know* that." Nora felt a rush of anger at her dad, standing there with his stupid beard and those pink circles of blush on his cheeks, like some kind of clown. "I wouldn't have to *do* this if it weren't for you."

"I know you're mad at me," he said. "And I get it, but I didn't invent the wheel."

"You didn't *invent the wheel*?"

"Faber fraternities have existed for two hundred years. *Pledging* has existed for two hundred years."

"Oh my God." Nora snorted in disbelief. "Are you seriously blaming the system right now? You're saying you were *forced* to create that game? That you were just a…just a *cog* in this *wheel* you didn't invent?"

"No." His expression was pained. "I'm trying to give you some context."

"I don't care about context. You knew girls were being roofied!"

"I did *not* know about that," her dad said sharply. "I would *never* defend that."

"Oh, so you'll just defend a guy who rapes a girl he *hasn't* roofied?"

He closed his eyes.

"Dad," Nora said.

He took a deep breath in through his nose, then released it in a long, slow stream. "I didn't mean for anyone to get hurt."

He *didn't mean for anyone to get hurt*? Was he serious right now?

"I'm sorry," he said.

"*Are* you?" she said.

"Of course I am."

"See, I don't think you are. I think you're just sorry I found out you're the game master."

"That's not true," he said.

"You're *not* sorry I found out you're the game master? You wish it was still a secret?"

He shook his head. "You're twisting my words."

"Oh, I'm twisting your words? *I'm* sorry. Oh, wait. I'm *not*."

She couldn't believe she was still talking. She couldn't believe she wasn't walking away.

"It breaks my heart what happened to you!" her dad said, his voice rising and cracking. "Don't you know that? It breaks my heart!" He pounded his chest with his fist.

For a moment, Nora was caught off guard. But then she recovered. "What about *my* heart?" She pounded her own chest. "You said it was your job to protect me! And I *believed* you! My whole life!" Nora lifted her chin and screamed at the wide open sky. "I BELIEVED YOU!"

Her dad opened his mouth to speak, but she cut him off.

"What about all those other girls, Dad? Did you think about *their* hearts? Or Mom's? Or Asher's? Or Maeve's? Do you have any idea how many people you've hurt?"

"I didn't assault anyone," he said.

"No. You just paved the path."

He pressed both his palms together, like a prayer. "Tell me what to say, Nora. Just tell me what to say, and I'll say it."

Nora stared at her father. "You're the *adult*," she said. "It's not my job to fix this for you."

When she got home, she was still reeling.

"I told him I'm getting a tox screen. I told him I'm filing a report. And now . . . *now* he says he's sorry."

"I think he *is* sorry," her mom said.

Nora snorted. "Yeah. Because his job is at stake. Because he's been kicked out of his own house."

"I'm angry, too," her mom said. "For you. For Amy. I'm angry for all the girls in that article and all the girls and women who have yet to come forward. Believe me, I'm angry. But your dad did say the university needs to take a harder stance against the fraternities, and I think he means it. I think he *is* trying to make amends."

"Amends," Nora said.

"Yes."

"How is he going to make amends to all those girls?"

Her mom shook her head. "I don't know."

"He can't, Mom."

This was the crux of the problem; her dad couldn't erase the last twenty years. He couldn't erase a single night.

The days dragged by. On Thursday, in the middle of lunch, Cam got a text. After she read it, she grabbed Nora's arm and pulled her out of the cafeteria.

"What?" Nora said.

And Cam said, "You weren't roofied."

"I wasn't?"

Cam shook her head. "My uncle Brody says it wasn't Rohypnol. It was...hang on—" She looked down at her phone. "GHA. Gamma hydroxybutyric acid, otherwise known as liquid ecstasy."

Nora blinked at Cam. "Oh my God."

"I know."

"Holy shit, Camille."

"I *know*," Cam said. "Brody said he'd fax the report to the Faber PD or campus security, whichever you—"

"Campus security," Nora said.

"Straight through the belly of the beast?" Cam said.

"Yes."

"Okay, so whenever you're ready. Should I tell him to send it this afternoon?"

"This afternoon," Nora repeated.

"After school. Adam said he has the photo and the video on a flash drive. We can stop by his house first."

"Okay." Nora's head bobbed. "Yes."

—✐—

Both Cam and Adam Xu went with her to the campus safety building. Nora had spent her entire life on the Faber campus—she had walked up and down University Avenue a thousand times—but she had never walked up the stairs to the campus safety building. She had never opened the red door. She had never said, "Excuse me. Hi. I'd like to file a sexual assault complaint."

"Are you a student?" the woman behind the desk asked. She was wearing a blue collared shirt, a red Faber University safety badge, and a walkie-talkie clipped to her shoulder.

"Not here," Nora said. "No."

Cam piped up, "She's in high school. We already know the report procedure. We just need the form."

The woman nodded. She reached into a drawer and pulled out a clipboard with a piece of paper and a pen already attached. She handed it to Nora. "My name is Officer Quain," she said. "That's *q-u-a-i-n*. You'll need that for the form, hon."

"Thank you," Nora said.

"You're welcome."

The three of them sat on a bench against the wall. Nora looked down at the clipboard. *Faber University Sexual Assault Report Form. Assault reported to . . . sex offense classification . . .*

date of incident... location of incident... She could feel her heart pound. She could feel that strange, floaty sensation taking over her body.

"Nor," Cam said.

"Are you okay?" Adam said.

"Yeah." Nora shook her head to clear it.

"Do you want me to write for you?" Cam said.

"No." Nora uncapped the pen. "I've got it." Once she started writing, it didn't take long to answer the questions.

"Is this all you need?" she asked, holding out the clipboard to Officer Quain.

Officer Quain looked down at the form. She looked up at Nora. "Melchionda?"

Nora nodded.

"You're not Rhett Melchionda's daughter, are you?"

Nora froze. *Rhett Melchionda's daughter.* She didn't know how to respond.

"Yes, she is," Cam said smoothly. "And yes, he knows. And you should be getting a fax from my uncle, Officer Brody Dodd from the Syracuse PD, any minute now, with results from the tox screen."

"Also." Adam Xu reached into his backpack and pulled something out. "We have a photo and video of the incident to submit for evidence." He placed a black lanyard on the counter. "They're both on this flash drive."

Office Quain's eyes widened. She looked at Nora. "You have some good friends here, hon."

"Yes," Nora said. "I do."

Gamma hydroxybutyric acid. Nora practiced saying it on her way home. Gamma hydroxybutyric acid. Gamma hydroxybutyric acid.

"The tox screen came back," she told her mom. "It wasn't Rohypnol. It was something else. Gamma hydroxybutyric acid. That's what they put in my root beer."

Her mom's hug was fast and fierce.

"I just filed the report," Nora said into her mom's shoulder. They were both crying a little.

The hug went on for so long, Nora thought her mom might never let go. But she finally did. She stepped back and placed her hands on either side of Nora's face. "You are not alone in this," she said. "You are *not alone*."

Nora nodded. "I know."

At school, she felt like she was walking through the halls inside one of those hurricane simulators. The 18 Holes drama was whipping all around her—every day, it seemed, there was a new piece in the *Gazette*, a new rash of comments on @supfaber, even a report on ABC7NY—but Nora kept her feet planted. She kept her eyes on the horizon.

Then, two surprising things happened. First, Brittany Carr came up to her in the hall, crying. Nora hadn't spoken to Brittany since she'd hooked Nora's ankle with her field hockey stick and sent Nora face planting into the mud in that Mount Markham game. Suddenly, Britt was bawling and saying she had a confession to make. Nora almost said, *Do I look like a priest?* That's what she wanted to say, but she swallowed her snark because Brittany looked so bad. Her eyes were two red puffballs.

Nora said, "What is it?"

Brittany took a deep, quivery breath. Then, in one long stream, she said, "I'm the one who took that picture of you and those guys at the frat fair. I'm the one who posted it on Sup Faber. I had no idea what they did to you until last period, when Jenna said that Kevin said you're the girl they were talking about in the *Gazette* article. The girl from the golf course. I swear to God, Nora, I didn't know. When I saw you with those guys I just thought you were with them, like, by choice. And I guess I was jealous. Because, you know, *college guys.* Which, I wasn't surprised because guys love you. *Everyone* loves you. Because you're so pretty and perfect and smart and—God!" Brittany threw up her hands. "You're so good at field hockey! Why do you have to be *so* good at field hockey? Why does everything come so easily for you? And you don't even seem to try. Or care! We used to be friends, remember? Back when we were young? We were actually *friends.* But then you started hanging out with Chelsea and Anna, and you guys are all so pretty, and you have your perfect foursome with Cam, well, and sometimes Becca, and you always get so much attention, your little group, but especially you, and I guess I just kind of, I don't know, wanted to take you down a notch. And I'm sorry. I am so, so sorry I took that picture and posted it. And I'm sorry I tripped you in the Mount Markham game. I *did* do it on purpose. I don't even know why. I just knew you were about to score, and I wanted to stop you. And I'm sorry. Because you're probably the nicest person I know, which makes it even worse because you're literally impossible to hate."

Nora accepted this apology with gaping, wide-eyed astonishment. What could she say? It made a certain kind of sense.

"Do you want to kill me?" Brittany said.

Nora shook her head. "No." It was true that if Brittany hadn't posted that picture, Cam and Adam Xu might never have gone to the Alpha Psi party to try to ID the three guys, and then Cam wouldn't have met Malik and found out about 18 Holes, and Nora wouldn't have discovered her dad's involvement. But what happened wasn't Britt's fault. Not really. "I don't want to kill you," Nora said.

"Are you sure?"

"Yes," Nora said.

"Okay," Brittany said. "Then can I ask you a totally unrelated question?"

"Sure," Nora said.

"Are you and Adam together? I mean, I know he's not the only guy who likes you, obviously, but are you two, you know..."

Nora almost laughed. She and Adam hadn't spoken since he'd invited and disinvited her to the homecoming dance in the same sentence and she'd yelled, *My life is ridiculous!* down the hall. "No," she said. "We are *not* together."

The second surprising thing happened the next day, at the water fountain. Nora had been bending down for a drink when she felt a tap on her shoulder. Startled, she turned around, dribbling water down her chin.

It was Jonah Hesse. Jonah Hesse of the "Nice to meet you, Dirty." Jonah Hesse of the "consolation cookie."

"Hi," he said.

She took a step back, wiping her wet chin with the back of her sleeve. Her mind began to race. This was sophomore hall. Seniors didn't come to sophomore hall unless they took wood shop or metal shop. Did Jonah Hesse take wood shop or metal shop? Or maybe this was a setup. *You da man, Hesse! Close the deal!* Nora scanned the hallway for his posse of boneheads. But all she saw was sophomores, scurrying to seventh period.

"I wanted to ask you something," he said.

Nora took another step back. She could see where this was going. "Yes," she said flatly. "I'm the girl from the article. You can tell all your friends."

"What?" Jonah looked confused.

"The *Gazette* article?" she said. "Those accusations against the frat boys? I'm the girl who was passed out on the golf course."

"Oh." His eyebrows shot up. "Wow. Hey. Are you okay?"

"Yes," Nora said. Now *she* was confused. "I'm fine."

"Are you sure?"

"Is that what you wanted to ask me? If I was okay?"

"No." Jonah shook his head. "I mean, I *do*. Want to know if you're okay. But that wasn't my question."

He took a deep breath, puffed out his cheeks. There was a white smudge in the corner of his mouth. *Toothpaste*, Nora thought. She was tempted to reach out her thumb and rub it off, which was a strange thing to want to do to a guy she'd literally talked to twice. A stupid thing to do.

Jonah unpuffed his cheeks. Something was happening here. What was happening?

"I know this sounds weird," he said, "but...at the beginning of the school year, I saw you sitting outside on the stone wall. You were watching this bird. Everyone around you was staring down at their phones, tapping away, but you were watching this little brown bird, hopping around in a circle, and you were smiling. And I thought...I want to talk to that girl. And anyway, it's taken me a while to get up the nerve, but..." He pulled a flower out from behind his back. A daisy.

Nora stared at it.

"I wanted to ask you to the homecoming dance."

"Oh," she said. She had *not* seen this coming.

"I know we got off on the wrong foot the other day," he said, "but I was hoping"—his eyes locked on Nora's, brown eyes, little green flecks—"you'd give me another chance. I mean, if you don't have a date already."

Nora shook her head slowly. "I don't have a date."

"You don't?"

"No."

"So…" Jonah raised his eyebrows. Nice eyebrows. Dark and straight.

Nora said, "Can I get back to you?"

He opened his mouth to speak, but she shook her head. "I'm not saying no. I just need to do something first."

The bell rang. She looked at the daisy, still in Jonah's hand. "Is that…"

"Oh…yeah," he said. "It's for you."

Their fingers touched as she took the flower. It was a little awkward, but not awful. "Thanks," she said. "I'll find you later, okay?"

"Yeah." He nodded. "Okay."

~

Nora knew that Adam Xu had a crush on her. Of course she knew. How could she not know? She'd known for years. And she had never really taken the time to get to know him. She was ashamed to admit this now, but it was true. She had taken his crush for granted. But over the past three weeks, through everything that happened, Nora had realized something: Adam was an amazing person. He was kind and funny and loyal. In another universe—a universe where he hadn't found her half-naked on a golf course—she might have had a crush on him, too. But in this universe, they were friends. Real friends. And the last thing she wanted to do—the very last thing—was to hurt him.

Nora found Adam at his locker after the dismissal bell, loading up his backpack.

"Hey," she said.

He looked up, surprised. "Hey."

"How was your day?" she said.

"It was pretty good," he said. "How was yours?"

"Pretty strange, actually."

He cocked his head at her.

"That guy Jonah, the senior, from the soccer team, asked me to the homecoming dance. I just wanted to tell you. I haven't said yes yet, because...well...I was hoping we could all go together. You and me and Cam and"—Nora tried not to make a face—"my brother. And I don't want it to be weird for you. I don't want you to feel like...I mean, I don't *have* to go with Jonah. You and I could go together as friends if you—"

"It's okay," Adam said. "I actually have a date."

"You do?"

He ducked his head, smiling. "I'm going with Brittany."

"*Carr?*"

"Do you know another Brittany?"

Nora shook her head.

"She asked me last period, in chemistry. She spelled out clues for homecoming using the periodic table. Hydrogen. Oxygen. Manganese."

"Oh." Nora nodded. Her brain was struggling to catch up. "Ohhh." Britt hadn't been asking her about Adam *Courtmanche*; she had been asking about Adam *Xu*. "Wow," she said. "Adam, that's great."

"Yeah." His smile widened. "I think so, too."

ASHER

THEY WERE OUT IN THE DRIVEWAY, PLAYING BASKET-
ball. It was a ritual they had developed, just over the past
few nights. The four of them would go outside after dinner and play two-on-two, Asher and Maeve versus Nora
and their mom. These were not high-octane games, but
Asher was surprised at how good it felt to be dribbling a
ball again, to be eyeing those little red hooks on the rim.
Toes to fingertips, one fluid motion, *swish*. The past few
nights, Asher had experienced the particular looseness
in his limbs that he normally felt only while painting, as
though he were coming into his body again.

"Ash!" Maeve called from under the basket. "I'm open!"

He passed the ball to Maeve and she caught it—a victory in itself. When Nora went in for the steal, Maeve spun
around in dramatic fashion, flinging the ball through the
air like a discus. It disappeared, out of the floodlight and
into the dark.

"Sorry," Maeve said cheerfully. "I stink at this."

"It's okay," Asher told her. "I'll get it."

He turned on his phone light and headed toward the edge of the yard. Finding the ball didn't take long—it had lodged itself between two bushes—but as he was heading back, something else caught his eye: a familiar truck, pulling into the driveway.

Asher froze. He squinted, hoping he was wrong. There were a lot of Ford F-150s in Faber. Maybe the truck would back up, turn around, drive off.

But no. It was parking. The driver was getting out.

"Hey, Ash."

Asher had a visceral urge to hurl the basketball through the air at his father. It might hit him in the face, it might draw blood, but so what? That would be nothing compared to the pain he'd caused. Asher had regrets; of course he did. When he'd first realized his father was covering for his players, he should have told someone. His mom. The president of the university. Anyone. But he hadn't. Asher had turned a blind eye to his dad, just like Rhett had turned a blind eye to his athletes, and look what happened to Nora. Look what happened to all those girls. Now, anger surged through Asher's veins. If his father took one more step, Asher would nail him with the basketball. But Rhett swung himself into the flatbed.

Asher thought, *Jesus, what is he doing?*

Maeve said, "What's going on?"

Nora said, "Is that *Dad*?"

"Rhett?" Diane said. "What are you doing here?"

Asher stood there, mutely, flanked by his mom and his sisters. He cocked his chin, gripped the basketball in both hands. He wasn't a fighter by nature, but so help him, if his father did anything—*anything* to upset his mom or Nora or Maeve, he wouldn't be afraid to act.

NORA

"RHETT?" HER MOM SAID. "WHAT ARE YOU DOING HERE?"

It took Nora a second to realize what, exactly, was happening. Her dad's truck was in the driveway; he was walking around the flatbed, doing—what? There was a blaze of light in the dark...then another...it looked like...was he lighting *tiki torches*? Why was her dad lighting *tiki torches* in the back of his truck?

"What the hell?" Nora murmured to Asher.

The four of them were just standing there, in the circle of floodlight. No one was moving. It was like that time the cashiers from Price Chopper had gone on strike for higher wages, and Nora's mom told them, "Never cross a picket line."

"Not even for a pack of gum?" Maeve asked.

And Diane said, "Not even for a pack of gum."

The crackling of a speaker. Music, soft and twangy. A *country song*? Rhett hated country music. He was a classic-rock guy. Nora's mom was the one who liked country. She'd grown up listening to it in Montana. George Strait. Reba McEntire. Travis Tritt.

Baby, close that suitcase you been packin'.

"Jesus H. Christ," Asher muttered.

"*Dad*," Maeve said. "What are you *doing*?"

Finally, Rhett swung himself out of the flatbed. "Hi, kids. I'm here to take your mother on a date."

"Oh, for Pete's sake," Nora's mom said.

"Diane." He reached out a hand. "Please join me for a picnic in the back of my truck."

Maeve said, "We already ate, Dad."

Asher said, "We're doing fine without you. Better than fine. We're doing *great*."

"I'm sure you are," Nora's dad said.

He stepped completely into the light. He was wearing a plaid shirt that Nora had never seen before. His beard was even thicker now. He looked like a lumberjack. Like Paul Bunyan. A part of Nora was fascinated. She stared at her father, the way she used to stare at the silverback gorilla in the Utica Zoo, trying to understand how—and why—he did what he did. Nora wasn't sure she trusted what she was seeing. The tiki torches, the music, the outstretched hand. This wasn't innate behavior. This was *learned* behavior. This was how her father operated: using charm to get what he wanted. He was a fraud and a hypocrite. Right? But another part of Nora—she wasn't proud of it, but she couldn't help it, really—thought this was terribly romantic. She loved him for doing it. She hated him, too. God, the pain of having all these contradictory feelings, of not knowing what to believe.

Nora turned to look at her mom and saw that Diane's hand was over her mouth. Her eyes were shining in the light. Was she *crying*? Nora's unflappable mother?

"Don't fall for it, Mom," Asher said. "Please."

"We don't have to eat, Di," Nora's dad said. "Just come talk to me."

Her mom was silent for so long, Nora thought that she might not have heard him.

"I know I screwed up," Nora's dad said. "*Screwed up* doesn't even begin to cover it. I know that. But please, give me a chance to redeem myself. To *try* to redeem myself."

Nora's mom shook her head.

"I made chocolate mousse..."

He made *chocolate mousse*?

Nora's mom turned to Nora and Asher and Maeve.

"Don't, Mom," Asher said. "He's a snake."

"Mom," Maeve said. "It's *chocolate mousse*. If you don't get in the truck, I will."

Diane looked at Nora, the tiebreaker. "How," she said quietly, "am I supposed to separate who he is from what he's done?"

Nora didn't know how to advise her mom; she really didn't. So she hugged her instead. She smelled her apple shampoo. "Just hear him out, I guess," Nora whispered.

"Okay," her mom whispered back.

CAM

SHE WAITED A WEEK. SHE TOLD HERSELF THAT NORA'S hearing wasn't until November; she could take a beat, let the dust settle. But the stories kept coming. Every day, it seemed, Erica Swisher at the *Gazette* reported another incident. In response to each Jane Doe coming forward, the university gave the same statement: "No comment."

By the twelfth accusation, Cam couldn't take it anymore. She called a lunch meeting with Nora and Chelsea and Anna and Becca and Brittany—because Nora had insisted that Brittany be there, too.

"You guys," Cam said. "We have to do something."

"What kind of something?" Anna said.

"I don't know," Cam said. "But all these girls, including Nora, have been brave enough to come forward and file reports, and now they have to sit around and *wait*? While the guys who assaulted them try to find ways to discredit their stories, and the university does damage control? It's bullshit."

Chelsea turned to Nora. "How are you holding up?"

Nora chewed, swallowed, set down her sandwich. "Depends on the day," she said.

"What helps?"

"I don't know," Nora said. "You guys. Knowing you have my back."

"Yes." Cam snapped her fingers and pointed at Nora. "Sisterhood. We need a showing of female support."

Becca said, "What about ribbons? Like the pink ones for breast cancer awareness. We could all wear them."

"That's a good idea," Brittany said.

"We need something bigger," Cam said.

"T-shirts?" Anna said. "Julie was in town yesterday, and she said she saw a bunch of guys outside the Blue Bird wearing 'Save the Alphas' T-shirts."

"Save the *Alphas*?" Chelsea snorted. "Like 'Save the Whales'? Do they think they're going extinct?"

"They *should* go extinct," Anna said.

"What would our T-shirts say?" Becca said.

"I don't know." Anna chewed her bottom lip. " 'We believe you'? 'Strength in Sisterhood'?"

" 'Our bodies, our choices,' " Chelsea said.

"Isn't that about reproductive rights?" Brittany said.

"No," Chelsea said, "it's about our *choices*. We should get to *choose* to have sex if we want to. Or not. These are *our* bodies. Either way, we shouldn't be called sluts."

"Amen, sister," Anna said.

"I feel like we're getting off message," Becca said. " 'Alpha Psis Tell Lies'?"

"Oooo," Brittany said. "I like that."

"We'll come back to T-shirts." Cam tapped on her phone. "I'm putting it in Notes. What else?"

They all sat around the lunch table, thinking. Slowly, more ideas came.

A petition.

A rally.

Posters.

A social media blitz.

A vigil.

Cam squinted. "A vigil," she repeated. "Yes. On the town green."

"With candles," Becca said.

"Tons of candles," Cam said. "We'll light up the night."

Brittany said, "I like that."

"Me too," Anna said. "But I still like the T-shirt idea."

"'Extinguish the Alphas,'" Chelsea said.

"A little frat boy dinosaur on the front," Anna said.

"Getting hit by an asteroid," Chelsea said.

"You guys," Nora said.

"I thought the dinosaurs died from starvation," Becca said.

"It was the volcanoes," Brittany said. "All those gases and dust."

Chelsea looked at Anna. "When did we study dinosaurs, third grade?"

"I think it was second," Cam said. "Mrs. Plourde. She had that stegosaurus headband."

"Oh my God." Anna snorted. "The stegosaurus head-band."

Nora stood up. "You *guys*," she said. "Stop talking about *dinosaurs!*"

They all stopped.

Nora said, "I have an idea."

NORA

SHE DIDN'T WEAR A MINISKIRT. SHE DIDN'T WEAR THE prairie dress, either. She wore a simple, emerald-colored sheath unearthed from a trunk in the attic.

"I haven't worn this since college," her mom said. "I think it will be perfect."

Was it perfect? The dress was comfortable. She liked the color. So...yeah.

She twisted her hair into a messy bun. She put on lip gloss, mascara, the tiniest hint of blush. She grabbed her bag and walked out into the backyard where everyone was waiting. Cam in her flip-flops and cutoff shorts. Asher in his tuxedo T-shirt and jeans. Adam, pink-cheeked and nervous in his navy suit and fuchsia tie, attempting to pin a corsage on Brittany, who looked even more pink-cheeked and nervous in her fuchsia dress. He was bucking the system—a sophomore boy going to the homecoming dance—and Nora was glad. He and Britt were so stinking cute, she could barely stand it.

"Wow," Jonah said when he saw her. Nora took one

slow, awkward step after another down the patio steps. She never wore heels. She felt equal parts sophisticated and ridiculous.

"Wow yourself," she said.

"You look...incredible."

"So do you." Unlike Asher in his tuxedo T-shirt, Jonah was wearing an actual tuxedo, with the bow tie and the tails and the shiny shoes.

"Here," he said. He handed her a box. "It's a wrist corsage."

"Thank you," she said.

"You wear it like a watch," Maeve said, popping up out of nowhere. She had been popping up out of nowhere all day.

"Yes," Nora said, ruffling Maeve's hair. "I get it."

"How about a group shot?" Nora's dad said. He was holding the big honking camera with the telephoto lens.

Nora looked at his freshly shaved face and felt—what? A jumble of feelings. A confusing mishmash of anger and sadness and annoyance and sympathy and disgust and love and regret. Her dad hadn't moved back home, but her mom had let him come for dinner a few times. On Monday, he'd gone back to work. He'd told Nora that he was "in her corner." He'd said that he was "trying to make changes to current policies and procedures." *Current policies and procedures.* What did that even mean? It sounded like something a shady politician would say to his constituents.

"He *is* a shady politician," Asher told Nora. Asher was still mad; he was barely civil when their dad was in the house. But Nora really wanted to believe that her dad wasn't just a shady politician—that he was trying to make something good come out of this.

"Everyone get together," Nora's mom said. "In front of the willow tree."

Nora stood between Jonah and Cam. Cam wrapped an arm around Nora's waist and said, "You ready for this?"

Nora nodded. "I think so. Are you?"

"I was born ready."

"Smile!" Nora's dad said.

Nora smiled. It was only seven fifteen, and already her stomach was abuzz with nerves. She was never going to make it.

"'Homecoming' on three," her dad said, "One, two, three..."

"Homecoming!" everyone said.

The six of them piled into Nora's mom's minivan. Asher and Cam in front, like the parents; Britt and Adam in the middle; Nora and Jonah jammed into the back row with two econo-size jugs of apple juice and five multipacks of paper towels.

"Sorry," Nora said. "My mom must have just done a Costco run."

And Jonah said, "I don't mind." As Asher pulled out of the driveway, honking and waving, Jonah moved some of the Brawny out of the way and took Nora's hand. "Thanks for coming with me," he said.

And she said, "Thanks for asking."

The gym had been transformed. There were metallic balloons and paper lanterns and fairy lights and glittery streamers everywhere. The whole place glowed. But it still smelled like feet; Cam pointed this out as soon as they walked in.

"Suspend your disbelief, m'lady," Asher said. "We have entered a magical kingdom."

"Have we?" Cam said. "Because I'm pretty sure they didn't have breakaway rims in the middle ages."

"Don't be a party pooper," Nora said.

"A *party pooper?*"

"Yes," Nora said. "Just because you're dressed like a beach bum doesn't mean you can't have fun."

"*Fun?* Oh, I'll show you fun."

They followed Cam onto the dance floor. The bass was pounding. How could she not dance? At first, they all just stood around in a loose circle, watching Cam make a spectacle of herself. But soon, as the gym started filling up, all six of them were dancing, even the guys. Asher was doing the sprinkler, Jonah was doing the shopping cart, and Adam—Adam Xu, not Courtmanche—actually started to floss, circa fifth grade, while Britt laughed and snapped pictures of him on her phone.

Chelsea and Anna and Becca arrived late, in a flurry of hugs and glittery eyeshadow. The football team arrived even later, en masse. All blazers and hair gel, cockiness wafting off them like fumes. They'd beaten Sherburne-Earlville, 20–19, Chelsea said, and had been partying all day. The game had been epic, Anna said. Nora should have been there. Adam Courtmanche had scored the winning touchdown with three seconds left on the clock. Hearing this, Nora felt a twinge of regret. She scanned the wall of blazers until she found Adam. Kevin Hamm had him in a headlock and was knuckling the top of his head. They were bucking the system, too, coming tonight. Nora smiled. She couldn't help it. They looked like two third graders out on the playground, giving each other noogies. Two third graders in ties.

"Hey," Jonah said, holding out a paper cup. "I got you some warm punch."

"How warm?" Nora said.

"Bathwater."

She took a sip. "That is disgusting."

"Yet oddly addictive."

A slow jam came on.

Jonah cocked his head at the dance floor. "Want to be cheesy with me?"

"Um," Nora said.

"We don't have to," he said quickly.

"No," she said. "I want to."

She took his hand. They joined the swaying couples. The music was soft and sweet. *Here with you, just waking up.*

It was weird how, when she thought about it, that night still seemed like a dream—riding the Yo-Yo, drinking the root beer, waking up on the golf course to Cam and her raccoon eyes. Some of her memories were laser sharp, but others spun and twisted like snowflakes, melting before they hit the ground. Had any of it been real? She knew that it had been; she knew when Jonah placed his hands on her hips and her heart began to race. Her breath came fast and shallow.

"Are you okay?" he said. "We can go sit down if you want."

And then her chest loosened. Her body remembered how to breathe. "I'm okay," she said. She rested her head on his shoulder.

When the song ended, there was Lady Gaga. Then NF. More dancing. More sweating. More warm-punch drinking. And then a light went on—a single spotlight, over the makeshift stage.

Nora's stomach clenched.

She watched Principal Hicks tap his finger on the microphone. "Hi, gang. How's everyone doing tonight? Everyone having fun?"

Cheers from the crowd.

"Can I get a round of applause for our amazing volunteers? The decorating committee?...The chaperones?..."

"Listen." Nora grabbed Jonah's hands. "I'm about to do something crazy."

"You are?" he said.

"Yes. And you're not going to understand why. But I promise I'll explain everything tomorrow." She leaned in, kissed his cheek. "I had a really good time tonight."

"Wait—" he said.

She let go of his hands. Before she could lose her nerve, she headed for the stage.

Afterward, people would say that they couldn't believe she'd done it. Nora Melchionda, stepping out in front of Mr. Hicks just as he was about to announce the homecoming court? Nora Melchionda, removing her black, patent leather sling-backs, holding them high in the air, releasing them to the stage like a mic drop? It was inconceivable.

Even in that moment, Nora couldn't believe she was doing it. And she couldn't believe—she *really* couldn't believe—how many girls in the gym were taking off their heels, raising them in the air, dropping them to the floor. There were even a few seniors.

"How do I know they'll follow me?" Nora had asked Cam earlier, when she was suddenly plagued with jitters.

"Because you explained how important it was." Cam had said. "Why wouldn't they follow you?"

"I don't know. I'm just one girl."

"So's Greta Thunberg."

"Greta Thunberg has a mission," Nora said. "She actually knows what she's doing."

"You know what you're doing."

"Remind me. Please."

Cam had taken Nora by the shoulders and said, "Greta Thunberg is taking on world leaders who refuse to address the climate crisis. You are taking on systemic patriarchy. And even if no one else follows you, I will."

Cam was true to her word. She followed Nora out of the gym and into the girls' locker room. They opened their PE bags and put on their sneakers. Some other girls put on sneakers, too. Some put on flip-flops or UGGs. A few laced up combat boots. The strangest thing—the coolest thing—was how quiet everyone was. Inside the gym, the bass continued to thump. When they walked out of the locker room and into the hall, Mr. Hicks sputtered in confusion.

Mr. Kavanaugh barked that if they left the dance, they wouldn't be allowed back in. "Do you hear me, girls?" he said.

They heard him.

Outside, the only sound was their feet—dozens of feet, crunching down the sidewalk. And their dresses—or, in the case of Cam, cutoffs—swishing against their legs. The air was cool and crisp.

When they got to the green, Nora's breath caught in her throat. Her mom and Maeve had pulled through. The path from the Faber Public Library to the fountain was lined with LED tea lights. Nora and Cam had bought those at the last minute—an impulse purchase—six for a buck at Dollar General. The path was all lit up like a birthday cake.

There weren't as many college students as Nora had hoped for. Sorority girls didn't exactly pour in from Greek Row; it was more like a trickle. But Maeve's friends came on their scooters and bikes, headlamps clamped to their helmets. And Ms. Sauce was there. Coach Schepps. Mar from Mar's Hairy Business, who gave Nora a trim every eight weeks. Lucy Howe, the YA librarian. A handful of moms. Erica Swisher from the *Faber Gazette* (Cam was exceedingly proud of this) and one of the *Gazette* photographers, a woman named Randy. Adam Xu (yes, Nora knew he was a guy, and yes, he was the only guy on the green, but there was no way she was doing this without him).

Chelsea and Anna handed out the Sharpies. Becca and Britt handed out the flagsticks. (Okay, they weren't really flagsticks. Nora had checked three golf supply websites and found that real ones were too expensive, so she had gone with the cheapest imitation she could find—a bulk order of fiberglass reflector sticks that Ray from Ray's Hardware had told her would glow in the dark.) Nora and Cam had cut out the "flags" themselves, using yellow construction paper, and stuck them on with packing tape.

Now, Nora stood on the edge of the fountain, holding up the sign Asher had made for her—bold, neon colors, outlined in black—WE ARE NOT A GAME. She reached her arms as high as they would go and watched as her friends wove their way through the crowd.

"Here," Chelsea and Anna said. "Write a name on the flag."

"Here you go," Becca and Cam and Brittany said. "Write a name on the flag."

Watching her friends handing out Sharpies, Nora suddenly realized something. They had all been branded. They hadn't been allowed to choose who they were; the town of Faber had marked them in the simplest terms, by the most limiting definitions: *Party girl. Gossip. Goody-goody. Jock. Snob.* They were all of these things, and they were none of these things. They were only beginning to find out who they were.

It wasn't choreographed. No one blew a whistle or shouted into a megaphone to tell them what to do. They just did it. One by one, and in their own time, they plunged their sticks into the ground, until all those girls and women—in homecoming dresses and combat boots, hoodies and cardigans, knitted caps, peasant blouses, and Gryffindor quidditch jerseys—were standing in a field of flag sticks. A field of names.

"Look at that," Cam said, appearing at Nora's side.

"Yeah," she said.

"You did that."

"It was a team effort," she said.

Cam shook her head. "It was your letter."

Nora's letter. Part of her couldn't believe she'd written it. The other part couldn't believe it had taken her so long to find the words. *It's time for a reckoning.* Nora had asked "Katie J" to post the letter on social media, not because Nora was afraid to use her own name, but because tonight wasn't about her. It was about every girl and woman in this town.

"You," Cam said, "convinced all those people to drop what they were doing on a Saturday night, write a name on a piece of construction paper, and stick it in the ground in the name of solidarity."

Nora smiled in spite of herself. "You know there's nothing better to do in Faber on a Saturday night."

"True," Cam said.

"So," Nora said. "Let's light this town up."

"Light it up."

Nora grabbed Cam's hand. Cam grabbed Chelsea's. Chelsea grabbed Anna's. Anna grabbed Becca's. Becca grabbed Maeve's and Brittany's. Hand after hand, they reached for one another, until they were all connected— all these girls and women of Faber, New York. They may have been just a tiny speck in the universe, but they were enough to be heard. Enough to lift their voices to the sky, to unleash their rebel yell.

EPILOGUE

THE TOM RIZZOLI HEARING TOOK PLACE ON A WEDNES-day in mid-November. The night before, three inches of snow had fallen, blanketing Faber in white. Nora and her mom could see their breath as they walked. Their boots left footprints on the quad.

It was 8:17 AM on a school day, but already a small crowd was forming outside Rand Hall: girls in puffer coats and fleece beanies, scrolling through their phones; moms with takeout coffees from the Blue Bird, warming their hands. And the Alpha Psis, of course—out in full force, lining the stone walkway in their hoodies and flat-brimmed hats. Their signs read TEAM RIZ.

To Nora, it seemed like more people had shown up for her, for her first hearing, than they had for any of the other girls. And she knew why. Of course she did. It wasn't just the chance to be on TV—the FOX 40 news truck had been parked on University Avenue for days. It was because Nora's story was different. The AD's fifteen-year-old daughter was accusing three of her dad's players of sexual misconduct.

She was a minor. They were Division I athletes. This was Netflix-worthy drama.

To the adults of Faber who had known Nora her whole life—who remembered her as a pudgy-faced toddler riding through town on her father's shoulders—she still looked impossibly young. Those two French braids. Those pink cheeks. A victim of sexual misconduct? Really? It was hard for them to wrap their minds around, even harder to imagine how Rhett and Diane must be feeling.

As they approached Rand Hall, Nora turned to her mom and said, "Thank you. For being here." Six weeks ago, she never would have said that. Not in a million years. But now, when Nora's mom reached for her hand and squeezed, Nora felt a surge of gratitude that nearly knocked her over with its strength.

―✐―

At 8:17 on Wednesday morning, Cam was standing on the top step of Rand Hall, holding the same sign Nora had held on the green that night: WE ARE NOT A GAME. Cam was so proud of Nora, she might combust. If Cam could have seen her best friend an hour earlier, loading up her pockets with all the good luck charms of their youth—the purple rabbit's foot from the arcade at Sangertown Mall, the shamrock charm from their trip to the New York State Fair, the horseshoe from their riding days—Cam would have rolled her eyes. She would have said, "You don't need *luck*, Nor. You have evidence."

From her own pocket, Cam's cell phone pinged. It was a text from Asher. **You look good up there.** She scanned the crowd until she found him, standing on a bench, waving. He was holding up a piece of paint-splattered poster board that read, in black lettering, GUYS, REEXAMINE YOUR BEHAVIOR.

Cam smiled, thinking, *That is so Asher.* She hoped those Alpha Psi asshats could read his sign. She texted back, **You look good down there too.**

───── ✐ ─────

At 8:17 AM on Wednesday, Adam Xu was knocking on Brittany Carr's front door so the two of them could walk to the quad together, to show their support for Nora. It still boggled his mind that Britt had pursued him, and that, a month after homecoming, they were still together. She was teaching him how to Rollerblade. For so long, Adam had been hung up on Nora; he hadn't even considered that someone might be hung up on him.

"Are you kidding me?" Britt said when he told her how surprised he was that she'd asked him to the dance. "I've liked you since seventh grade."

Since seventh grade—before he even made the baseball team. Britt was the one who'd convinced Adam's mother that not all American girls were "hen suibian de," who'd showed her Nora's letter and explained why Adam needed to go to the quad today. Now, Britt was opening the front door, stepping out onto the porch, smiling.

"Hi, Adam."

"Hi, Britt," he said, wrapping his arms around her.
"Ready to watch Nora kick some ass?"

He said, "Absolutely."

At 8:17 on Wednesday morning, when they should have been learning about improper fractions, Maeve and the Foxez were playing hooky. Seriously? The *Foxez*? But yes. The Foxez had a new obsession, and it wasn't taking pictures of themselves. It was taking pictures of the scene outside Rand Hall: **#faberuniversity #faberNY #thisisourtown #standup #getoutraged #wearenotagame**. Their new obsession was Nora. Ever since that night on the green—when all the girls and women of Faber had held hands and unleashed their battle cry for the whole town to hear—the Foxez had declared Maeve's sister the coolest human being on earth.

"Other girls aren't your enemies," Nora had told them that night. "I wish I'd known that when I was your age. You're stronger together." Now, the Foxez didn't just want to support Nora; they wanted to *be* her. And, just by association, they had decided that Maeve was cool, too. Maeve wasn't sure how she felt about this yet. She was still trying the Foxez on for size. But in the meanwhile, she was on Team Nora, ready to fight—like Neville Longbottom, the least likely wizard of all, standing outside Hogwarts with his wand in the air, yelling, "It's not over!"

On the top step of Rand Hall, Nora paused and looked out. She scanned the faces. She knew Jonah wouldn't be here. He had a physics test third period. He would come the next morning, though, for the Alec MacInerney hearing. But there was Chelsea and Anna...and Imani...Becca... Adam and Britt...Asher, standing alone on a bench, holding up his funny sign...Maeve. Was her dad out there somewhere, watching from a safe distance? Incognito in a baseball cap? For a moment, time froze on the top step, the cold air making Nora's eyes sting. She thought of all the things she wanted to say to him, wondering if she could ever distill it down to a single statement. She didn't think she'd be able to. Her disappointment in him—in *who he turned out to be*—cut too deep. He had promised to be a part of the solution, and she wanted to believe him. She really did. But he still hadn't publicly admitted his role in the game. He still hadn't disowned Alpha Psi Beta. He just kept saying the same thing: *Systems need to change.* Some days, Nora could almost understand how this had happened—how her dad had been a part of something bigger than himself, how the power structure of the fraternity had ingrained in him a series of faulty beliefs and assumptions that he now needed to unlearn. Other days, Nora thought that was bullshit. Right was right and wrong was wrong, and her dad was too smart not to have known the difference. It was time for him to *do something* about it. The night before, he'd stopped by the house to wish Nora luck in the hearing.

"It takes a lot of courage to do what you're doing," he'd told her. "A *lot* of courage."

Nora had accepted his hug. Despite everything—all of his blind spots and shortcomings and horrible choices— she chose to believe that her dad was proud of her.

"Nor?" Cam said. She and Nora's mom were standing by the double doors, waiting. "Ready?"

"Yes," she said. The truth.

Maybe her dad was out there, leaning against a pillar in front of the student union or watching from a window in one of the academic buildings. Maybe he wasn't.

Either way, this was happening.

In a second, Nora would turn around. She would walk through those doors. She would look Tom Rizzoli in the eye, and she would tell her story. She would own every word of it, and she would set herself free.

Acknowledgments

Huge, Taylor Swift–level thanks to my editor, Liz Kossnar, for taking this leap of faith, and to everyone at Little, Brown Books for Young Readers for working their magic: Lucia Picerno, Megan Tingley, Jackie Engel, Alvina Ling, Andy Ball, Jen Graham, Erica Ferguson, Sasha Illingworth, Marisa Russell, Savannah Kennelly, Stefanie Hoffman, Shanese Mullins, Christie Michel, Shawn Foster, Danielle Cantarella, and Claire Gamble.

Thank you to my agent, Rebecca Sherman, for making me dig deeper than I thought possible, and to everyone at Writers House for helping to put *Wolves* out into the world: Allie Levick, Laura Gruszka, Cecilia de la Campa, Jessica Berger, Aless Birch, and Jenissa Graham.

Thank you to Tom Scarice and John Smith for sharing the inner workings of high school administration and counseling.

Thank you to Gwen Lexow for her expertise in Title IX regulations and the disciplinary process. Thank you to

Kevin and Carah Cahill for their insight into the culture of D-I athletics, the Greek system, and the collegiate response to sexual misconduct.

Thank you to Officer Steve Manware, guru of toxicology reports and reporting procedures.

Thank you to Benji Ooi, Maggie Yin, and Mia Pope for their extraordinary authenticity and sensitivity notes.

Thank you to Gabby Pildner for the Insta/finsta lesson. I am so much cooler now.

To Camp Laurel, Summer '92, for "smack the rat" and those stars-and-stripes shorts.

To Lyle Micheli, MD, who probably doesn't remember me, but whose story of resetting his own broken arm to go back in the rugby match lives large in my memory.

To my dad, George Friend, who, like Rhett Melchionda, once took a sacrificial puck to the face in a college hockey game.

To Hamilton, New York—the town that raised me—and to the Seven Oaks golf course, keeper of many secrets.

Boundless thanks to my tribe—Mieka, Steph, Toby, Heather, Dori, Julie, Katina, Liz, and the indomitable meditation mamas—for keeping my head above water.

Thank you to the great and powerful Beebs, for her wise counsel, and to Jack, Ben, and Emma, my fierce and funny trio, for being exactly who they are.

Finally, thank you to Chanel Miller, Christine Blasey Ford, Alyssa Milano, Tarana Burke, and all the brave women and girls of the #MeToo movement, for paving the way.

NATASHA FRIEND

NATASHA FRIEND

is the author of nine young-adult and middle-grade novels that tackle the truth about teens and tweens. She lives on the Connecticut shoreline with her family and invites you to visit her online at natashafriend.com.